The Adventures of Byomkesh Bakshi

Volume 2

Sharadindu Bandyopadhyay

Translated by Mishul Das

Copyright © 2023 Mishul Das

All rights reserved.

An Introduction

Sharadindu Bandyopadhyay was born in March 1899 to Tara Bhushan and Bijaliprabha Bandyopadhyay at his maternal grandparents' home in Jaunpur, United Provinces of Agra and Oudh, British India (now in Uttar Pradesh, India). The Bandyopadhyay family's residence was at Purnia, Bihar, India, his father Tara Bhushan's workplace, but the family originally hailed from Baranagar, North Kolkata, West Bengal, India. He completed his matriculation in 1915 at a school in Munger. He wrote his first story, "Pretpuri," a Boroda story, when he was only 15 years old. After matriculation, he joined Vidyasagar College, Kolkata. Sisir Bhaduri, the doyen of Bengali stages, was his English professor there. After completing graduation, he went on to study law in Patna. He was only thirty years old when he gave up his practice and started working as a writer. He received a call from the Mumbai film industry as a scriptwriter. He left Mumbai in 1941 and settled permanently in Pune, where he breathed his last in the early 70s. The 1960s and 1970s saw enormous popularity for his writings. He has written numerous historical novels, long stories, short stories, dramas, and last but not least, the iconic Byomkesh Bakshi. Byomkesh Bakshi is a detective who calls himself Satyanweshi, or the Truth-Seeker. He is known for his proficiency with observation, logical reasoning, and forensic science, which he uses to solve complicated cases, usually murders.

These stories were written from 1932 to 1970, a remarkably long period. More than 35 Byomkesh thrillers were written in the form of long short stories and novels.

Sharadindu Bandyopadhyay's most well-known fictional character, Byomkesh Bakshi, first appeared as a character in the story Satyanweshi (The Inquisitor). The story is set in 1932 in the China bazar area of Kolkata. The majority of the Byomkesh Bakshi tales are recounted from the viewpoint of Ajit Kumar Banerjee, who first encounters Byomkesh in the China bazar mess. Later, Ajit is invited to live with Byomkesh as his assistant and chronicler in his three-story rented home on Harrison Road. The only other person in his household is his attendant, Puntiram.

Byomkesh Bakshi is introduced as a man of twenty-three or twenty-four years of age who seems well educated. Byomkesh is a Hindu and often wears a white shirt or kurta with a white dhoti, with the exception of when he drapes a shawl. He doesn't have a fancy life, but he has a lot of books. He frequently travels, doesn't have a gun, and doesn't see himself as an expensive helper. He often smokes and drinks tea with milk. He speaks Bengali, Hindi, and English with ease. Byomkesh does not like being called a detective and finds the word "investigator" even worse. Thus he fashions a new name for himself, which he inscribes on a brass plate in front of his house. The plaque read "Byomkesh Bakshi: Satyanweshi" (The Inquisitor).

CONTENTS

	Acknowledgments	i
1	**Satyanweshi**	Pg 1
2	**Adwitiya**	Pg 28
3	**Dustu Chakra**	Pg 46
4	**Heyalir Chonde**	Pg 67
5	**Khuji Khuji Nari**	Pg 90
6	**Lohar Biscuit**	Pg 106
7	**Monimandan**	Pg 119
8	**Adrishya Trikon**	Pg 141
9	**Chitrachor**	Pg 161

Satyanweshi

(The Inquisitor)

I first had the pleasure of meeting Byomkesh Bakshi in the year 1924. I had just finished writing my final exams at the university. There was no monetary strain on me, the interest of the money that father had kept in the bank is sufficient for the expenses of my single life which would have been quite modestly spent in a Calcutta hostel. So, I decided to take a vow of virginity and lead a literary life. In the enthusiasm of my early youth, I thought that by worshiping Vagdevi alone, I would soon bring about a revolution in Bengali literature. During this period, the Bengali youth dreams a lot, although it does not take much time for these dreams to get shattered.

But let's keep that talk aside. Now let me tell you how I met first met Byomkesh. Those who are intimately familiar with the city of Calcutta may not know that in the center of the city there is a unique area, it is unique because one side of this area is populated by the poor Bhatia Marwari community, one side is a slum, and the third side is populated by the slant eyed yellow Chinese community. The delta which is formed in the midst of this tri confluence, does not seem to have any unusual feature in the hustle bustle of the day, but after evening, a strange change starts to happen in this area. By eight in the evening all the shops are shut down and the place has an eerie feeling to it. Only one or two Pan shops are open far and wide. At this time, those who transverse in this area, mostly walk silently like shadows, and if any ignorant passerby happens to come in this way, he too does hurriedly pass through this area.

How did I come to this neighborhood and become a resident of a hostel? If I write about this, then it would become a huge novel. It would just suffice to say, that I saw the neighborhood during the day and did not suspect anything, and I got a very large airy room on the second floor of the hostel very cheaply and I took possession of it without wasting time. Later, I got to know that in this neighborhood, at least two or three dead bodies with severe injuries are seen lying on the street every month and the police conducts raids in this area at least once a week for various reasons. But by this time, I had a heartfelt connection with this room that I never thought of packing my belongings and shifting to a new abode. Especially in the evenings I was engrossed with my writing, there was no reason to leave the room hence I was never in the way of any personal danger.

There were five rooms on the upper floor of our building, each occupied by a gentleman. They are all employed and elderly; they used to go home on Saturday, return on Monday and start commuting to office. They have been living in this hostel for along time. Recently a gentleman retired from work and vacated his room, and I took over the empty room. In the evenings the residents used to sit for a game of cards or dice, this time the silent hostel used to get lively due to the excited voices of the inhabitants of the hostel. Ashwini Babu was a very good player, and his permanent rival was Ghanshyam Babu. Ghanshyam babu used to create a ruckus on losing to Ashwini Babu. Then exactly at nine o'clock, the cook would come to announce that dinner was ready to be served. Then everyone would get up calmly and finish their meal and retire to their respective rooms. In such undisturbed peace the days passed by; I also got habituated and accepted this peaceful way of life.

The landlord used to live in the lower floor rooms of the building. The landlord Anukul babu is a homeopath and a good-natured person. It seems that he was not married, because there was no wife and family in his rooms. He managed the hostel and looked after the comfort of the tenants. He used to do all the work in such a neat manner that no one would complain about it. At the start of every month, we would pay twenty-five rupees for lodging and fooding in his hands and be rest assured of everything.

The doctor was quite popular among the poor community of the neighborhood. Every morning and afternoon his living room was crowded with patients. He used to distribute medicines for a very low price sitting at home. He did not go to the patient's room much, but if he did, he never charged them for the visit. For this reason, residents of the neighborhood respected him very much. In a short time, I too became his ardent follower. By ten o'clock everyone else in the hostel would leave for office, only we two would remain. We used to have breakfast together, then the afternoons were spent discussing the newspaper articles and gossips. The doctor was of a very innocent nature, but he was a good speaker. He was under forty years of age. He did not have a university degree but had acquired immense knowledge of so many diverse subjects sitting at home, that it was amazing to listen to him. When I would express my surprise at his immense pool of knowledge, he would just shy away and say, "I don't have any work, I just sit at home and read books. Everything I collect is from the books."

After spending two months in this room, one day at around 10 o'clock, I was sitting in Doctor Babu's room and flipping through the newspapers. Ashwini babu went to the office while chewing a pan. Then Ghanshyam Babu came there and asked for medicine from Doctor Babu for toothache, then he too left for office. The other two residents also left for office one by one. The room was empty for the whole day.

Doctor Babu still had one or two patients, after they took medicine and left one by one, he raised his glasses to his forehead and asked,"Is there any news in the papers?"

"There was a police raid in our neighborhood yesterday evening."
The doctor smiled and said - "This is a daily affair. Where did the raid happen?"
"Nearby, at number thirty-six. In Sheikh Abdul Ghafoor's room."
The doctor said, "I know the guy, he often comes to me for medicine. What was his room searched for?
Have they written something about it?"
"Cocaine. Here have a look." Saying, I forwarded the Dainik Kalketu newspaper to him.
The doctor pulled down his spectacles again and started to read.

"Yesterday the police have raided room number thirty-six in this area. The room belongs to a leather merchant named Sheikh Abdul Ghafoor, but no illegal goods were found. The police suspect that there is a secret cache of cocaine somewhere in the area, from where cocaine is being supplied everywhere. Some gang is running this illegal business from this area and have been avoiding the vigilant eyes of the police for a long time. But unfortunately, who is the leader of these criminals and where is their secret hideout is yet to be determined, even after many investigations."

The doctor thought for a while and said, "That's right. I also suspect there's a big cocaine cache somewhere in this area. A couple of times I got this hint, you know different people come to me to take medicine. No matter what, a cocaine addict can never hide the symptoms from the doctor. But this Abdul Ghafoor man does not seem like a cocaine addict to me. Rather, I can strongly say that he is a seasoned opium addict. He too does not deny this fact himself."

I asked, "Well, then what is the reason that there are so many murders in this neighbourhood?"
The doctor said, "It has a very simple reason. Those who break the law and run a huge illegal business always fear getting caught. If by chance someone learns their secret, there is no other option but to kill him. Think about it, if I deal in cocaine and you find out about it, would it be safe for me to let you live? If you leak the matter to the police, then I will go to jail, and immediately such a big business will collapse. Goods worth lakhs of rupees will be confiscated. Can I let that happen?"
The Doctor started laughing after saying this.

I said, "I see you have studied the mentality of criminals!"
"Yes. I have an inclination towards such topics!" After saying so he rose from his seat.

I was also getting ready to leave, when a man entered the room. His age would be around twenty or three-twenty-four, he looked like an educated gentleman. His complexion was fair, he was a handsome well-built guy and there was an impression of intelligence on his face. But it seemed that recently he has fallen into some trouble; because his hair was unkempt, his shirt dirty, even his shoes were rough due to lack of polishing. His face had an expression of request. He turned his face from my direction to Anukul babu and asked, "I hear it's a hostel. Is there any vacant room?

Both of us were looking at him with surprise, Anukul babu shook his head and said, "No. What do you do?"

The man slumped wearily on the patient's bench and said, "Currently I am applying for the available jobs and seeking a shelter in this city. But in this wretched city there is not even a hostel to be found, every corner is filled to the brim."
In a sympathetic tone, Anukul babu said, "It is very difficult to find a place in a hostel in the middle of the season. What is your name?"

"Atul Chandra Mitra. After coming to Calcutta, I have been wandering around in search of a job. The little money that I brought from home after selling off everything is also almost finished. I am left with around twenty-five-thirty rupees. But how long will it last if I have to eat two square meals a day in a hotel? Hence I'm looking for a good hostel--not long, in a month I shall land a job, but till that time I need a place to stay and just two square meals a day to suffice myself."

Anukul babu said, "I am very sorry, Atul Babu, but all my rooms here are full."
Atul took a deep breath and said, what else to be done, I will have to go again in search of accommodation. Let me check if I can get some space in the hostel of the Oriya's. It's nothing else, I'm just afraid, maybe they will steal my money when I am asleep at night. May I have a glass of water?"

The doctor went to fetch water. Seeing the helpless condition of the man, I felt great compassion. I hesitated a little and said, "My room is quite big there will be no problem if there are two people staying there. If you don't have any issues, we can share."

Atul jumped up and said, "What do you say, issues? You are my saviour; I just need a safe place to stay." He quickly took some money from his pockets and said, "how much do I need to pay you? Wouldn't it have been better if you took some money in advance."

I simply laughed at his antics and said, "Hold on, pay the money later, there is no rush." Doctor Babu came back with water, I said to him, "He is in trouble so let him stay in my room for now, I will not have any trouble."

Atul said in a grateful tone, "You have been very kind to me! But I promise, I will not trouble you. I will keep search for accommodations and as soon as I get one, I will vacate your room." Saying this he put the glass of water down on the table.

The doctor turned to me in a bit of surprise and said, "In your room? That's fine with me. When you have no problems, then what do I say? You will also benefit as the rent will be shared."
I said hastily, "That is not the issue, I am doing so cause this gentleman is in trouble."
The doctor smiled and said, "yes indeed." "Then bring your things, Atul Babu and stay here for now."
"Yes Sure. I just have few belongings, a bedding, and a bag. I have kept the same at the custody of a guard of a hotel, I will bring it right away.
I said, "Yes go and bring it, we will have lunch here together."
"Well, that will be great," said Atul and left the hostel with a grateful look in his eyes.

After he left, we were silent for a while and Anukul babu began to clean the glass of his spectacles.
I asked, "What are you thinking, Doctor babu?"
The doctor was startled and said, "Nothing. The endangered should be sheltered, you have done well. But you never know what kind of a person he is. Let us hope, no problems will arise."

Atul Mitra came to live in my room. Anukul babu had an extra bed which he sent upstairs for Atul to use.

Atul didn't stay in the room during the day. He used to leave early morning in search of job opportunities and return around ten - eleven in the afternoon, after having lunch he used to venture out again in search of work. But for the little time he stayed in the room, he got along well with everyone in the hostel. He used to be invited by everyone to play cards and dice but as he did not know how to play cards and dice, he used to sit there for a while and then walk downstairs to have a chat with the doctor. We had become good friends too as we two were of the same age and lived in the same room. Hence it didn't take long to shed the formalities between us.

After Atul's arrival, a week passed quite uneventfully. Then various strange things began to happen in the hostel.

In the evening, Atul and I used to sit and talk in the room of Anukul babu. The number of patients had dwindled, every now or then some patient would come, describe their symptoms and take medicine for the same. Anukul babu was chatting with us while diagnosing the patients and keeping the money received in the hand-box. Last night there was a murder almost in front of our hostel, this morning the body was discovered on the road which caused a bit of commotion. We were discussing about this incident. The reason for the commotion was that the dead body was of a poor labourer and in his waistbelt was found ten-hundred-rupee notes. The doctor said, "This is nothing but cocaine money. Think about it, if he had been killed for money, then a thousand rupees wouldn't have been found on his waist. I think the man was a cocaine buyer; he had come to buy cocaine when he learnt some deadly secrets about the cocaine-dealers. Maybe he tried to scare them or even blackmail them saying that he will report to the police, After that, it's all over for him."

Atul said, "Only God knows the reason for this murder, I am very scared now, if I had known that this neighborhood is not safe, then I would not have taken rooms here."
The doctor said with a smile, "Then you would have gone and stayed along with the Oriya's. But we are not afraid. I have been staying in this neighborhood for the last 10-12 years, but I have never been in trouble because I don't engage or meddle in other people's affairs.
Atul whispered, "Doctor Babu, you surely know something. Don't you?"

I heard a Tap sound and turned my back to see Ashwini Babu of our hostel was listening to us with his face peeking through the gap of the door. Seeing the unusual look on his face I asked, "What happened Ashwini Babu, what brings you here at this time?"
Ashwini Babu stammered and said, "No, nothing. Nothing important. I was thinking of going to buy bidis." He said these words and instead of going out went up the stairs to his room.

We looked at each other. We all used to respect the senior, serious natured Ashwini babu, but why did he come down quietly and snoop on our conversation?

At the dinner table, I came to know that Ashwini Babu had already finished his dinner and had retired to his rooms. After finishing dinner, I lighted a cigar, which was my regular routine and entered my room. I saw Atul was lying on the floor with just a pillow. I was a little surprised, because it was not so hot that it might be necessary to lie on the floor. The room was dark, Atul did not respond, so I thought he had fallen asleep. I didn't have a habit of sleeping early, but if I sat down to read or write with the light on, Atul might wakeup, so I started walking around the room barefoot. After walking around for a while, I suddenly thought that I should ask Ashwini Babu whether he had any illness or not.

Ashwini Babu's room is after two rooms to mine; I went and saw that his door was open, and there was no response when I called from outside. Then I got curious and entered the room; The switch was next to the door, I switched on the lights. I looked around and saw that there was no one in the room. I went to the road facing window and looked outside but could see no one.

I thought, Its strange, where did the gentleman go at night? Suddenly it seemed to me that he might have gone to take medicine from the doctor. I quickly went down the stairs and found that the doctor's door was locked from the inside. The doctor might have been asleep by now. After stood there in front of the closed door and lighted a cigarette, when I heard voices from inside the room. Ashwini Babu spoke in a very excited but low voice.

I felt greedy for once, I thought to listen to what was being said. But immediately I suppressed that desire, maybe Ashwini babu is talking about his illness, I should not listen, I stepped back and walked silently up the stairs.

When I came back to my room, I saw Atul lying on the floor as before, he looked at me and said, "What, Ashwini Babu is not in the room?"
I was surprised and said, "No. were you awake?"
"Yes. Ashwini Babu is downstairs in the doctor's room."

"How do you know?"
"How did I know? If you want the answer, lay down on the floor with your head on this pillow."
"Hey, are you in your senses?"
"My head is perfectly fine. Just lay down and listen."

Out of curiosity, I lay down with my head next to Atul's head. Nothing was audible for a while, then a sound of a vague conversation started coming to my ears. Then I could clearly hear, Anukul babu saying, "You are very excited. It is nothing but your illusion. Sometimes it happens while sleeping. I am giving you medicine, eat and sleep. Get up tomorrow morning if you still have this belief, then do whatever it seems suitable to you."
What Ashwini Babu said in reply, could not be heard. I understood by the sound of pulling the chair, that both of them got up to leave.
I left the floor, sat up and said, "I didn't remember that the doctor's room is right underneath our room. But tell me what happened to Ashwini Babu?"
Atul yawned and said, "God knows. It's very late now, come let's go to bed and sleep.

I asked curiously, "Why were you sleeping on the ground?"
Atul said, "I was tired from walking around all day, the floor felt quite cold, so I lay down. I was almost asleep, but their conversation awoke me.
I could hear the footsteps of Ashwini Babu on the stairs, he entered his room and closed the door.
I looked at the clock, it was almost eleven o'clock at night. Atul was sleeping, the hostel was completely silent. I lay on the bed and fell asleep while thinking about Ashwini Babu.

I was awoken in the morning by a hard push. I saw Atul was pushing me. It was already seven o'clock. Atul said, "Hey, get up quick."
"Why? What happened?"
"Ashwini Babu is not opening the door of the room. There is no response to our calls."
"What happened to him?"
"That cannot be said. You come" said he and quickly left the room.
I followed him and saw that all residents were present there making anxious speculations and slamming on the door. Anukul babu has also

come from below. Worry and anxiety were increasing gradually, because Ashwini babu never sleeps till this time. In addition, if he was sleeping, why was he not waking to our calls?

Atul went to Anukul babu and said, "Listen, let's break the door. I am not getting a good vibe."
Anukul babu said "Yes, yes, sure indeed. The gentleman may have been knocked out, otherwise is he not responding? Let's not wait further Atul babu, break down the door."

Not an easy task, a wooden door one and a half inches thick, with a yale lock on it. But when Atul and two or three others pushed hard together, the imported lock broke, and the door opened with a clang. Then, seeing the object that appeared in the open doorway, no one spoke in amazement and fear. We all were amazed and saw that Ashwini Babu was lying face down with a large gaping cut across his throat. Under his head and neck, lay a pool of thick blood, as if a red velvet carpet had been laid. And, in his outstretched right hand, lay a blood-smeared razor still drenched in blood.

We stood motionless in fear for a while, then Atul and the doctor entered the room together. The doctor looked at Ashwini babu's horrible corpse and said in a trembling voice, "So scary, Ashwini babu finally committed suicide!"

But Atul's gaze was not fixed on the dead body. His eyes were wandering around the room like blades of a sword. He scrutinized the bed, looked out of the open window on the side of the road then said in a low tone, "It's not suicide, Anukul babu, it's murder, brutal murder." I am going to call the police, please none of you touch anything."

"What did you say, Atul Babu, murder? But the door was locked from the inside! Apart from that look there" he said pointing his finger and showing the bloody razor in the dead man's hand. Atul shook his head and said, "So be it, but this is murder!" You guys stay here, I'm calling the police right now." Saying do he exited the room hurriedly.
Doctor Babu sat there with his hand on his forehead and said in disgust, " such a terrible incident had to happen in my building."
The police arrived in sometime. They started taking the statement of every resident of the building. I said whatever I knew. But nothing was

revealed in anyone's statement which could suggest the cause of Ashwini Babu's death. Ashwini Babu was a man of clean character; it was not known if he had any friends except in this hostel and his office. He used to go home every Saturday. Since the last ten-twelve years it has been going on like this, never been an exception. He was suffering from polycystic kidney disease for some time; these were the few facts which were revealed during the interrogation.

Dr. Anukul babu also gave a statement. With what he said, the mystery of Ashwini babu's death became more complicated. His statement is quoted below –

"For the last twelve years, Ashwini Babu was residing in my hostel. His hometown is Hariharpur village in Burdwan district. He worked in a trading office, earning approximately one hundred and twenty rupees a month. With such a paltry salary he was not able to reside in Calcutta with his family, hence he stayed in my hostel. Almost everyone in this hostel does that."

"As far as I know Ashwini Babu, was a simple and dutiful man. He never left any dues unpaid, nor he owed anyone a single penny. I am not aware if he had any substance abuse or addiction; Everyone else in the hostel can testify to this."

"I have not noticed anything unusual or suspicious about him during these twelve years. He was suffering from diabetes since last month and was under my treatment. But no symptoms of his mental illness were seen earlier. Yesterday I suddenly noticed that he seemed a bit disturbed."

"Yesterday morning at about a quarter to ten, I was sitting in my clinic when Suddenly Ashwini Babu came and said, "Doctor Babu, I need to have a secret word with you." "I looked at his face with a little surprise; He seemed very disturbed. I asked, what is the matter? He looked around and said in a strained voice "Not now, another time. After saying so he left hurriedly for office."

"Yesterday evening, I, Ajit babu and Atul babu were sitting in my room gossiping, when suddenly Ajit babu saw Ashwini babu standing by the door and snooping on our conversation. When asked what he was doing there, he quickly left with a weird excuse. We all were surprised at his actions and were thinking, what has happened to Ashwini Babu."

"Then at ten o'clock at night he came to me surreptitiously like a thief. I understood by looking at his face, his mental state was not normal. After closing the door, he began to blabber about various things. He said that he had a terrible dream while sleeping then he said he had come to know of a deep secret. He kept blabbering away about different things. Finally, I gave him a full sleeping pill and said, "Go sleep tonight, I will listen to you tomorrow morning."He went upstairs with the medicine."

That was my last meeting with him, then this morning this incident happened. Yesterday after evaluating his actions, I thought there was something wrong with him, I did not think that he had lost his mental sanity, but I had never imagined in my wildest dreams that he would commit suicide in this momentary excitement."

When Anukul Babu became silent, the daroga asked, "Do you think this is suicide?"
"What else can it be? But Atul Babu was saying that this is not suicide but something else. He might know more about it, so he alone can comment."
The daroga turned to Atul and said, "you are Atul babu, right? Is there any reason to think that it is not suicide?"

"There is. People cannot slice their own throats like this with their own hands. You have seen the dead body, don't you think, it's impossible?"

The daroga thought for a while and said, "Who is the murderer, do you suspect anyone?"
"No."
"Are you aware about the motive of murder."
Atul pointed at the road facing window and said, "this window is the reason for the murder."
The policeman was shocked and said, "The window is the reason for the murder! You mean, the killer entered the room through this window?"
"No. The killer entered the room through the door."

The daroga said with a soft smile, "You probably don't remember that the door was locked from the inside."

"I very well remember."
The daroga said in a sarcastic tone, "Did Ashwini Babu close the door after his throat was slashed?
"No, the killer closed the door from outside after killing Ashwini Babu."
"How could he?
"Atul said with a smile on his face. "Very easily, if you think about it, you will understand."

Till now Anukul babu was staring at the door for long, he said, " that's right! that's right! The door can be easily closed from the outside, it never occurred to us until now. Don't you see the door is fitted with a yale lock?
"Atul said, "The door closes when you pull it from outside, then there is no way to open it except from the inside.
The senior policeman put his hand on his cheek and said, "He's right, but I have a small doubt. Is there any evidence that last night Ashwini Babu slept with the door open?"

Atul said, "No, on the contrary, there is evidence that he had closed the door. I know, he slept with the door closed."
I said "I know too. I had heard him close the door."
Daroga said, "Then? Ashwini babu got up in the night and opened the door to the killer, this assumption does not seem plausible."
"Atul said, "No. But you probably don't remember that Ashwini Babu was suffering from an illness for the last few days."

"He was suffering from an illness! you are right, you are right, Atul Babu! I did not remember that."
The daroga said a little morosely, "You seem quite intelligent, why don't join the police! You can have a great career as a policeman. But this case is getting very murky. If it really is a murder, there is no doubt that the killer is very intelligent and daring. Don't you people suspect anyone?"
Saying this, he looked at the faces of everyone present there.

Everyone nodded their heads in silence. Anukul babu said, "Look, there are often one or two murders in this neighborhood, this news is not new to you. Just day before there was a murder right in front of our house. Seeing all this, it seems to me that all the murders are linked to each other. If one of the murder cases are solved all cases will be solved. Of course, if Ashwini babu's death is accepted as murder!"

The daroga said "That may be. But if we sit hoping to the other murders to be solved then we might have to wait for an eternity."

Atul said, "Darogababu, if you want to solve this murder, then think carefully about this window there."

The daroga said, "we have to think everything through, Atul Babu. Now I want to search each and every one of your rooms.

Then all the rooms were frantically searched up and down, but nowhere was found anything that could throw any light on the mystery of the death. Ashwini Babu's room was also searched as usual, but nothing was found except a couple of very ordinary personal letters. The empty sheath of the razor was lying on the bed. We all knew that Ashwini Babu used to shave himself hence we had no difficulty in recognising that the razor and its sheath belonged to Ashwini Babu. Ashwini Babu's dead body had been moved and after searching his room it was locked and the door sealed. At about a half past one the daroga left our premises after concluding the search.

A telegram was sent to Ashwini Babu's family asking them to come immediately. In the evening his sons and other relatives arrived at the hostel. Everyone was astonished and bewildered after hearing his demise. Although we were not related by blood still, we were deeply hurt by this sad death. We all consoled his family for the loss they had to bear. We were also fearful for our own lives cause when a murder can happen in the adjoining room then how can we sleep peacefully? The next two days passed in such anxiety and fear.

Before going to bed at night, I went to the doctor's room and saw him sitting with a bewildered face. Today's incident has left dark lines on his calm face. I sat next to him and said, "The residents of the hostel are pondering about whether to move out or not."

With a faint smile, the good man said, "They can't be blamed, Ajit babu! such things happen. Who wants to live in a hostel where a murder happens in the next room! But one thing I do not understand at all, how can it be called murder? If it is indeed a murder, then it cannot be committed by someone from the outside. First, how did the killer reach upstairs? You all know that the staircase door is bolted from within during the night. If it can be assumed that the man climbed up using some trick, but how did he kill Ashwini babu with Ashwini babu's razor?

Is this even possible? So, it is certain that no outsider is involved in his death. If so, who is left? Those who reside in the hostel! Is there anyone among us who can kill Ashwini babu? Of course, Atul Babu has only come recently, and we don't know anything about him.
I was surprised and said, Atul?

Doctor babu lowered his voice and said, " Yes Atul babu, what do you think of the man?"
I said, "Atul?" No no, this is never possible. Why will Atul kill Ashwini Babu."
The doctor said, "Look, your words are proving that no one in the hostel can do this. So, what remains is that he committed suicide, isn't this the only plausible cause of death."

I said, "but he should have a reason to commit suicide?"

"I thought about that too. You remember a few days ago I said there is a secret cocaine gang which operates here in this neighborhood. No one knows who the gang leader is."
"Yes, I remember."
The doctor slowly said, "Now imagine if Ashwini Babu is the leader of this illegal business?"
Stunned, I said, "How can this even be possible?"
The doctor said, "Ajit Babu, nothing is impossible in the world. Rather, this suspicion is intensified by what Ashwini babu told me last night very likely he was very scared. Too much fear can make people behave unnaturally. Who can say, maybe he committed suicide because of this unnatural inclination! Think about it, doesn't this hypothesis seem reasonable?"

My head was totally blown away after hearing this novel theory, I said "I am not sure,Doctor babu, I can't imagine anything like this. If you have your suspicions, why not tell it to the police."
The doctor stood up and said, "I will tell them tomorrow. I will not be at peace till this problem is resolved.

Two or three days passed after the murder, and we were scared for our lives. Our mental state was not great and different policemen from the CID department questioned us regarding the murders for two days straight. We had mentally become exhausted. Everyone in the hostel was trying to leave this hostel for a new abode but were scared to so, cause if they did, they might as well be suspected as the prime accused in the murder.

I got a hint from the police investigation that they suspect someone from our hostel to be the murderer and the police were closing on that person. But I could not guess who that person was. Sometimes my chest pounded with unknown fear thinking that the police don't suspect me, do they?

One morning Atul and I were sitting in the doctor's room reading the newspaper. The doctor had received a package containing medicine. It was a medium sized packing case; he opened the box and carefully took the medicine out and arranged them in the cupboard. The packing case had an American imprint on it. Doctor babu did not use local medicines, if necessary, he used to bring medicines from America or Germany. Almost every month he would receive a box of medicine.

Atul put down the half-folded newspaper and said, "Doctor, why do you bring medicines from abroad? Is the local medicine not good?
Atul took a big sugar-of-milk vial and had a look at it, then he read out the manufacturers name, "Eric and Havel. Do they make the best medicine?"
"yes"
Well, does homeopathy really cure diseases? I don't believe it. Will a disease cure from drinking a drop of water?"
The doctor said with a soft smile, "So many people who come to take medicine, are they deluded?
Atul said, "Maybe the disease gets cured by itself and people think it was cured by the medicine." Belief sometimes works wonders, maybe homeopathy acts as a placebo."

The doctor just smiled and said nothing. After some time, he asked,"Is there any news about our hostel in the newspaper?"
"There is," saying so I started reading out the news aloud. "The Unfortunate Ashwini Kumar Choudhury's murder mystery is yet to be solved. The CID division of police have taken the reigns of this case. Some critical information has also been unearthed and it is hoped that the accused will be arrested soon."

"The police cannot solve this case; it is out of their league." Doctor Babu turned his face and saw Darogababu was standing at the door. What is it Daroga babu? he said.

The Daroga entered the room, accompanied by two constables. Without wasting any time, he went in front of Atul and said, "There is a warrant in your name. You have to come to the police station with us. Don't try to resist the arrest, it won't work. He said "Ramdhani Singh, please handcuff this man." A constable quickly came and handcuffed him.

We stood up in unison. Atul said, "What is this!"
The Daroga said, "Here is the warrant. Atul Chandra Mitra shall be arrested for being a prime suspect in the killing Ashwini Kumar Chowdhury. Both of you identify this man as Atul Chandra Mitra?
We shook our heads silently and said yes.
Atul said with a soft smile, "So the police is making me a scapegoat for the murder. Well, let's go to the police station. Ajit, don't worry, I am innocent.

A police van had already stopped in front of the building, Atul was pushed in the police van and then the van drove away. The doctor said with a smile, "Atul babu is the culprit then! So terrible! So terrible! There is no way to understand a man's character nowadays. Atul babu never looked like a murderer.

I was speechless. Atul is the killer? After living together with him for these few days, I had started a loving friendship towards him. His nature is so sweet that he won my heart in such a short time. This very guy is a killer! I was unable to fathom this fact that he is the prime accused in this murder case. My heart could not accept what had just occurred.

The doctor said, "This is why it is forbidden in the scriptures to shelter an unknown person."But then who would have thought that the man was such a big criminal."

I didn't feel well, I got up went to my room, closed the door and lay down. I was not in a mood to eat lunch. I looked towards the other side of the room; Atul's belongings are spread out in his bed. I almost cried thinking about the incident and realized how much I loved Atul.

Atul said when he was leaving, that he is innocent. Did the police made a mistake! I sat up on the bed and tried to remember all the sequence of events that happened the night when Ashwini Babu was murdered. Atul was listening to the conversation between Dr. Anukul and Ashwini babu with his ear on the pillow on the floor. Why was he listening to their conversation? For what purpose? Then at eleven o'clock at night I fell asleep and woke up in the morning. In the meanwhile, did Atul-?

But Atul has been saying from the beginning, that this is a murder is not suicide. If he is the murderer himself, will he say such words and try to incriminate himself? Or, it could also be that Atul is saying this to throw off any doubts on himself, so that the police think that when Atul insists on murder, he is never the killer. With such a troubled mind, I lay on the bed and began to toss and turn, sometimes I got up and started walking around the room. The morning passed like this.

It was three o'clock. I suddenly thought to consult a lawyer. I didn't know what to do in such a situation, I didn't know any lawyer. In any case, finding a lawyer would not be very hard so I got dressed up and was ready to leave when there was a knock at the door. I opened the door and saw Atul.

"Ah Atul?" Saying so, I almost hugged him with joy. The thought of him being innocent or not was completely wiped of my mind.

With a disheveled head and dry mouth, Atul laughed and said, "Yes brother, I am back." I had a very distressing day! With great difficulty I found someone to secure a bail for me, hence I am back otherwise I would have spent the night in prison. Where are you headed to?"
I said a little awkwardly, "To find a Lawyer."
Atul held my hand with affection and said, "I don't need him anymore, brother!" The police will not harass me again.

We both came into the room. Atul said while changing the dirty clothes, "My head is aching a lot. Could not eat or drink the entire day. It seems that you too did not eat! Poor thing! Come on, let's have a quick wash and have something to eat because I am really starved."

I was still in dismay and hesitantly said, Atul, did you? Did you?

Did you what?" Did I kill Ashwini babu or not?" Atul said softly, "That will be discussed later. I need something to eat now. I have a terrible headache, anyway, a cold bath may cure it."

The doctor entered our room. Atul looked at Anukul babu and said, look I am back. You must have heard the idiom "a bad penny always turns up" my condition is almost the same, the police also returned me.

The doctor said a little seriously, "Atul babu you have come back, it is a matter of immense happiness. Hopefully, the police acquitted you because you are not guilty of any crime. But you cannot stay here at my hostel anymore. You can understand, as a warrant was issued in your name hence people may be opposed to you residing in this hostel and also your stay here will bring a bad name to the hostel. Everyone is already planning to shift away from here. I don't have any grudge against you, but I too need to run this hostel as it is my bread and butter. Hope you understand."

Atul said, "No, no, what are you talking about! I am now a tainted accused, why would you be in danger by sheltering me? Who knows tomorrow if the police don't find any way out, they may again arrest me and even arrest you for aiding and abetting me. Do you ask me to leave today itself?

Doctor remained silent for a while and reluctantly said "No, stay tonight; but tomorrow morning you should leave."
Atul said sure, I will not embarrass you again tomorrow. I'll find a place to stay anywhere, at least there's the Oriya hostel" he said and laughed.

The doctor then asked what happened at the police station. Atul gave a cursory reply and went to take a bath. The doctor said to me, "I understand that Atul Babu is upset but tell me what can be done? The murder has already given the hostel a bad name. If I shelter an accused arrested by the police, will it be safe, you tell me?"

Realistically no one can be blamed for showcasing such caution and selfishness. I shook my head in disgust and said "That's it, it's your hostel, do what you think is best." I threw the towel over my shoulder and left for the bathroom.

As we returned to our room after having bath and lunch, we saw Ghanshyam babu returning from office. Seeing Atul in front of him, he was startled as if he saw a ghost, and said with a smile "Atul babu you, you?

Atul smiled softly and said, "It's me Ghanshyam babu. Don't you believe your eyes?
"Ghanshyam babu said "But the police had arrested you. After saying this he hurriedly entered his room. Atul's said in amusement, "Once arrested by the police the society treats you as a criminal even when you are acquitted. I seems that Ghanshyam Babu is very scared of me."
That evening, Atul said "Oh, look, the door lock is not working."

I tried to figure out what was wrong with the lock, after few futile attempts I called Anukul babu, he came and inspected the lock and said " This is a problem with these locks; when they are good all is fine, when there is an issue, you have to call an engineer. Our desi tower bolts are way better than these. Anyway, I'll fix it tomorrow." He said and went down.

Before going to bed at night, Atul said "Ajit, the headache is increasing gradually, what should I do?
I said, "why don't you take some medicine from the doctor."
Atul said: "Homeopathy medicine? Will it work? Well, let's check the efficacy of Homeopathy medicine.
I said, "Come let's go to the doctor, my body is not doing well either."

The doctor was about to close his room's door when we appeared in front of him. He inquisitively looked at us. Atul said, "we came to check the efficacy of your medicine. I have a severe headache since morning. Can you give us some medicine?"

The doctor happily said, "Obviously! I will give you medicine to cure your headache. You hadn't eaten anything in the morning hence the headache due to acidity. Please sit down, I am giving you the medicine." He said and brought the new medicine from the cupboard. "Go, eat and then off to sleep. There will no headache left tomorrow morning. Ajit babu, your health is not looking good either, you are feeling tired due to the excitement this morning? You too have skipped meals today hence your body is aching? Right? Got it, you too take this medicine and by morning you will be re-energized.

Going out from his room, Atul asked, "Doctor Babu do you know someone by the name Byomkesh Bakshi?"
The doctor was shocked and said, "No who is he?"
Atul said, "I don't know. I heard his name today at the police station. Heard that he is investigating this murder?
The doctor shook his head and said, "No, I don't know him."

Coming back to our own room upstairs, I said, "Atul, now tell me everything. Tell me what happened today?"
"What happened?"
"You are hiding something from me. But that won't work, you have to explain everything to me."

Atul remained silent for a while, then looked at the door once and said, "Well, I'm telling you. Come, sit here next to me. I realised before itself that I would not be able to hide things from you."

I went and sat next to him on his bed, he closed the door and sat next to me. I had the packet of medicine in my hand, I thought, after taking it I will listen to the story with all attention. As I was about to open the packet and have the medicine, Atul held my hand and said, "Stay now, listen to my story and then decide if you want to take it."

Atul switched off the lights and sat close to me and whispered his story in my ears. I listened to him in amazement. His story made my hairs stand on end due to fear and anxiety.

Fifteen minutes later, Atul finished the story in brief and said, "Till here today, I will tell you everything tomorrow in detail." He looked at his Radium watch and said, "There is still time left. Nothing's happening before two o'clock, you better get some sleep already, I'll wake you up in time."
I think it would be half past one. I was lying in the bed staring away at complete darkness. My sense of hearing had become so sharp that I could clearly hear the rise and fall of the body on the bed while breathing. The thing that Atul had given me, I was holding the same with a firm fist in my right hand.

Suddenly in the dark, I heard no sound, but Atul slightly touched me. The gesture was pre decided upon, I began to breathe heavily like a person in deep sleep. I understood, the time had come.

Then when the door opened, I did not hear; Suddenly there was a thump sound on Atul's bed and immediately the light came on. I got up with the iron rod in hand in a flash and jumped out of bed.

I saw Atul holding the light switch in one hand and a revolver in the other hand and sitting on his knees beside his bed. Anukul babu was staring at Atul like a wounded tiger looks back at the hunter.

Atul said, "It is very sad if a seasoned person like you kills a pillow in the end! Don't move! Drop the knife. Yes, the moment you move you will be shot. Ajit, open the window facing the street the police are waiting outside. Beware"

The doctor got up in a panic and tried to escape through the door, but immediately Atul's big fist hit his jaw like a hammer and pinned him down. The doctor sat up on the floor and said, "Enough, as you wish." But what is my crime!"

"Have you committed only one crime, doctor, that I will tell you verbally. All the crimes that you have committed are being documented now at the police station. In the meanwhile-"

Suddenly the daroga and Inspector entered the room with four or five constables.
Atul said, "For now, you tried to kill Satyanweshi Byomkesh Bakshi, I am handing you over to the police for this crime. Inspector Babu, this is the accused. "The inspector handcuffed the doctor silently. The doctor said with a poisonous look in his eyes, "This is a conspiracy! The police and that Byomkesh Bakshi have framed me in a false case. But I will see. There are law courts in the country. I am not short of money either."

Byomkesh said, "Why would you be. Where will the money from the sale of cocaine go!"
The doctor said with a contorted face, "Do you have any proof that I sell cocaine?"

"Indeed doctor, I do! The proof is in your sugar-of-milk vial."
The doctors' eyes began to rain down upon Byomkesh with powerless anger.

Anukul babu no longer seemed to look like a simple polite man. He looked like a dreaded criminal who had committed a ghastly act. What a man he is, till date this hardened criminal was living among us under the garb of a homeopathy doctor. This man has various skins which he sheds like a snake to suit the occasion. A chill ran down my spine when I realised that I was spending my time with a criminal mastermind and even for an iota of time I didn't suspect him of any wrongdoings.

Byomkesh asked, "What medicine have you given to both of us? Tell me, doctor?" Powdered Morphine? Tell me? Well, don't say it, the contents of the medicine will be determined post its chemical analysis." Holding a cigar and sitting comfortably on the bed, he said, "Darogababu, now note down my statement."

After the first information report was recorded, the doctor's room was searched, and cocaine was found in two big bottles. The doctor remained silent all this while never uttering a word. It was almost dawn by the time the police recorded our statements and took Anukul babu to the police station.
After the police departed, Byomkesh said, "Everything is a mess here. Come to my place, we will have some good tea.

After reaching the second floor of a building in Harrison Road, I saw a brass-plated name plate on the door.

The name plate read "Shri Byomkesh Bakshi Satyanweshi"

Byomkesh said, "Welcome! Please enter my humble abode."
I asked, what is Satyanweshi?
That is my professional title. I don't like the term detective nor the word private investigator, hence I have kept my professional title as Satyanweshi. Doesn't it sound good?"

All entire second floor consists of four or five small rooms; the place is spanking clean. I asked, It seems that you stay alone?"
"Yes. My only companion is my servant Puntiram"

I took a breath and said, "Your place is very good. How long have you been here?"

"I have lived here for almost a year only for a few days had shifted to your hostel."

Puntiram served us some tea and snacks. Byomkesh sipped on hot tea and said, it was a great experience to spend a few days in disguise in your hostel. But the doctor caught it at the end. Of course, that was my fault!"

"How come?"

"I made a mistake by telling the police about the window. Didn't you understand? Ashwini babu died due to that window."

No, no, say it from the beginning."

Byomkesh took another sip of tea and said, "Well, then let's start from the beginning." Last night itself I told you a piece of the story, now hear the rest."

"For the past couple of months many murders happened in your neighborhood. The police authorities were quite embarrassed with the situation. The Bengal Government on one side and the news journalist on the other made the police more impatient by poking them in and out. During this time, I went to meet the head of the police department. I said to him that I am a private detective, and I believe I can solve all these murders. After much discussion, the Commissioner gave me permission on one condition that no one will know about this except him and me."

"Then I went to your hostel in search of accommodation. While doing any investigation it is important to have your base of operation in the vicinity of the crime scene. Hence, I chose your hostel. At that time, I had no idea that the culprit had the base of operation at the same place."

"The doctor seemed to be a very good person, in fact he so good and generous that I had doubts. It is very convenient for a cocaine dealer to run his business under the garb of a homeopathy doctor. I had some doubts about the doctor but was not sure that he is the mastermind of the cocaine drug business and the reason behind all murders."

"The doctor caught my suspicion on the day before the murder of Ashwini babu. You remember the day before the death of Ashwini babu a man was found murdered in front our building. When the doctor heard that a thousand-rupee note had been found on the murdered man, for a moment his face showcased an image of failed greed. I saw it and all my doubts fell on the doctor."

Then the incident of Ashwini Babu snooping on our conversation in the evening. Actually, Ashwini Babu did not come to listen to our conversation, he came to talk to the doctor. But when he saw that we were there, he quickly left with an apology."

"After seeing the abnormal behaviour of Ashwini Babu, I thought that he might be the real culprit. I overheard the doctor and Ashwini babu's conversation lying down on the floor the night, but it did not make any sense. I only understood that he had seen something terrible. Then that night when he was murdered, there was nothing left to understand."

"It was Anukul babu who had killed the poor man in front of our doorsteps and Ashwini Babu happened to see the scene from his window. And that's what he secretly told the doctor." Now you understand the matter quite well. The doctor used to deal in cocaine but did not let anyone know that he was the mastermind of this business! If anyone had found out, he would have been killed immediately. This is how he has saved himself so far."

"This poor man was probably the doctor's broker, maybe through him cocaine was supplied to the market. This is my guess, may not be correct. That day he had come to the meet the doctor in the middle of the night, for some reason there was a discord between them. Maybe the guy tried to blackmail Anukul babu or scare him saying that he would tell the police about the matter. After that when the man left the room, the doctor followed him and stabbed him from behind. Ashwini babu himself saw this scene from the window and went to tell the doctor with great reluctance."

I don't know what his intentions were. He had benefited from the doctor and revered him, so maybe he wanted to warn the doctor. But the result was exactly the opposite. In the eyes of the doctor, he no longer had the right to live because he knew about his illegal business and had witnessed the murder.

At some point that night Ashwini babu must have gone to the washroom, this is when the doctor must have entered and hid in his room. After his return from the washroom, his throat was slashed by his own razor. After murdering Ashwini babu, the doctor kept the razor is Ashwini babu's fist and locked the door."

"I can't say whether the doctor initially suspected me or not, but when I told the police that Ashwini babu's death was a murder and not suicide and the reason behind the murder was the window, then he understood that I for a fact have come to know of all his heinous crimes. Then he decided that I should also be dealt with and silenced. But I was not at all anxious to leave this world so, I started taking precautions for my life."

"Then the police made a big mistake when they arrested me. Anyway, the Police Commissioner came and released me, I came back to the hostel. The doctor then realized that I was a detective; he showed great kindness by letting me stay in the hostel for the night. Beneath the kindness was only one motive to somehow kill me because, as much as I knew about him, no one else knew. "

"There was no real evidence against the doctor till then. Of course, his room could have been searched and cocaine seized, and he could have been jailed, but he would not have been proven in a court of law to be a ruthless murderer. So, I also started tempting him. I damaged the lock on our door by dropping a nail in the door lock. The doctor got excited when he got the news that we can't sleep with the door closed at night."

"Then when we went to get the medicine, he found the perfect opportunity to murder me. He gave us both two packets of powdered morphine, he thought after taking the same we will fall into a deep slumber, and he would murder me with ease.

"After that the tiger came and stepped into our trap. The rest you are aware off."

I said, "Now I will take your leave, brother."
You won't seem to be going there?"
"No."

"Are you going back to the hostel."
"Yes."
"Why?"
"What why? Don't I have to head back home."

"What I was saying is, you have to leave that room, why don't you join me here? This room is not bad."
I remained silent for a while and said, "I understand you are repaying me for my help."
Byomkesh put his hand on my shoulder and said, "No brother, not repayment. Over the past few days after staying and bonding with you It seems that we are meant to stay together.
"Is it so?"
"Yes, it is."
"Well then so be it, you stay here, I'll go and bring my belongings here."
Byomkesh said cheerfully, "Don't forget to bring my belongings too."

Adwitiya
(The Inquisitor)

When by natures inviolable law Satyawati had a conjugal quarrel with Byomkesh I used to take a neutral position and enjoy it. But when the topic of relative excellence of women and men came up in marital disputes, I was forced to side of Byomkesh. Still, we two friends being united could not always defeat Satyawati. In the history of the vast human race, the example of male violence has been recorded so vividly that it is impossible to refute it. At last, we had to break the war of words.

For some time now there has been some unique criminal activities taking place in the city of Calcutta, which Byomkesh and I were discussing one winter morning over tea along with the newspaper. The following is the modus operandi of such criminal activities that have happened recently: sometimes one, sometimes one or more classy young women head out at noon. During the afternoon the men are off to work, the women at home take a siesta after completing lunch. During this time the young women go and knock on the door of middle-class households. If the housewife is alert, she asks without opening the door. Who is it? A young woman says from outside, "I am selling good petticoat and blouse made of chikan, the price is very cheap. will you buy it? The housewife thinks it's a hawker, and she opens the door. Such young women enter the house, brandishing knives or pistols they loot the household of all cash and jewellery.

This kind of event has happened several times before and the accused have not been caught. That day I read about a similar crime in the newspaper. The previous day at noon a similar burglary happened in the house in Kashipur. I read the news to Byomkesh. He laughed a little and said what is there to be surprised about! "Girls do robberies in daylight."

At this very moment Satyawati entered the room, stood near the door, and looked angrily at Byomkesh. She said, "OK! Girls rob in daylight, and all you men are all saints?"

Byomkesh did not say the words for Satyawati to hear; But when Satyawati has heard and answered, there is no turning back. Byomkesh said, I did not say that all of us saints, but women are neither.

Hence the argument began. Satyawati sat on the edge of the dewan and said, "It is the nature of you men to insult girls. What have we women done?"
Byomkesh said, "Not much, robbery in daylight.
I read aloud the news of the burglary to Satyawati.
Satyawati said, well, I accept, they have done wrong. They have done this to feed their hunger. But the killings and violence you men are doing, killing thousands of people by starting a war, is nothing? These burglaries are nothing compared to the crimes that you men commit.

Seeing no way out, Byomkesh said, "You women have been locked in the house for so long hence could not commit such heinous crimes. With the passage of time and more freedom you women will show your true colours. Long ago Bankim Chandra wrote about Devi Chaudhurani. Devi Chaudhurani was born in the yesteryears and see what she did, if she was born in this era then think what would have happened?

Satyawati waved her hand and said, "You can't fool me by saying such nonsense. Can you show a real example where a girl has killed a person?"
Byomkesh said, "Looking for a true example? Just a couple of months back a female inmate murdered the jail guard and escaped from jail.
Satyawati smiled, "Two months ago, a girl committed a murder, and in these two months have you counted the number of murders that you men have committed?
Today's newspaper has a story of a man-perpetrated murder, but I suppressed it. Instead, I said, "Today's paper contains a serious instance of female brutality. A washerman my mistake made a tear in a woman's expensive silk saree, the woman cut off her nose with a knife. The condition of the washerman is pathetic, he is in the hospital, it is doubtful whether he will survive."

Satyawati said with a merciless smile, all you guys are incorrigible liars. You are all liars, thieves, robbers, and murderers.
It is not possible to say how far our argument would continue, but at this time, there was a loud knock on our door. I stood up to attend to

the door. Satyawati went inside with a victorious smile. I opened the door and saw a postman. The postman handed over a thick fat envelope to me and walked away.

The Envelope was in the name of Byomkesh, sender's name was not mentioned. When the envelope was brought to him, he glanced at it and without opening the package said, "Seems to be a manuscript from a new aspiring writer. Please send it to Prabhat.

Ever since we got into the book publishing business, aspiring budding writers do often send us their manuscripts, so Byomkesh cringes at the sight of letters in thick envelopes.
I said, "It may not be a Manuscript. Just open it once and check the contents."
He said, "You open it and see."

I opened the envelope. It is not a manuscript, but someone wrote an extremely long letter to Byomkesh, almost like a short story. Byomkesh felt very relaxed and stretched out on the dewan saying, "It's definitely not a love letter." So, you read."

I pulled a chair next to the dewan and started reading the letter. The handwriting is not very clear, it is difficult to read; But the language is neat.

To Mr. Byomkesh Bakshi,
My heartiest greetings,

My name is Sri Chintamani Kundu. The police are trying to implicate me in a murder case, hence in desperation I seek refuge with you. If I had the strength, then I would have personally met you and narrated my story. It would have been clearer if I had narrated the story myself. For the past several years I have been crippled by paralysis, the left side of my body is paralysed hence I am immobile. I can only walk around a little that too with great difficulty. Hence, I am forced to write this letter.

Before explaining the serious matter that has happened, I would like to introduce myself. I am now fifty-seven years old; have no wife or children. I have only three houses which I have rented. I stay in one of the houses on the first floor. I have two rooms for myself, and I have a servant Ramadhin who attends to me.

By looking at the address in the title, you will understand that I live in the Southeast region of Calcutta. The road is quite wide; The house where I live is on one side of the road, my other two houses are almost opposite to it on the other side of the road. These two houses are relatively small and single storied. They are alike, you can call them twin houses. Between the two houses there is a narrow lane leading to the rear door of the house.

I am now crippled by paralysis; my life is contained in these two rooms. Before the onset of paralysis, I used to be a broker. I used to run around a lot; I am used to running around. So now I sit in front of the window all day long, watching the movement of people on the street. I have bought a binocular to see things happening at a distance. Many indoor scenes are also visible through these binoculars, I can also keep an eye on the tenants of my twin house. Those who are physically capable go to the cinema; I sit at the window and watch the stream of life with these binoculars. You will be surprised to know how many strange things I have seen through these binoculars. But let that be for some another day.

A month and a half ago, in the middle of Poush month, a boy came to meet me. He had a short frame, well-trimmed copper-colored hair, swarthy face a small butterfly moustache under the nose. He was wearing expensive English clothes and a camel hair fabric coat. Standing near the door, he said, "My name is Tapan Sen. Can I come inside?"

I was sitting near the window reading the newspaper, I raised my face and said come inside.

Tapan Sen came inside, pulled a chair, and sat in front of me. I said, tell me what do you need?

He pointed his finger outside the window and said, "One house of your twin house is vacant, so I came if you allow me to be your next tenant. The house had been vacant for some time. The previous tenant had made a mess of the house. I repaired and whitewashed the house and had decided that I would not give it for rent until I find a good tenant. The boy looked a gentleman and from his clothes I guessed he was well to do. I asked, "What do you do for a living?"

He took out a cigarette pack from his overcoat pocket and put it back; seemed that he did not light the cigarette out of respect for an elderly person like me. He said, "I work in the newspaper office. I am the Night editor. I work all night and sleep all day. He said and smiled a little.

I asked, "Who is there in the family?"
He said, I have just started a family. Me and my wife only two souls.
I felt happy that Tapan does not have kids, cause kids ruin the house they make crayon painting on the walls and destroy the paint. I said, "Fine I will rent the house to you. The rent will be a hundred and fifty rupees per month."
Tapan said hesitantly, "It's a little too much for me.
I said, "It is a Furnished house. You will get bed, table, chair, cupboard everything.
He said, "well, then I agree. Can I see the house once?"

I handed over the keys to Tapan, he went to see the house. He returned after a while and handed me a hundred and fifty rupees and said, "Here is one month's rent.
I wrote the receipt and said, "When will you take possession?
He said, 'Tomorrow is the first of the English month. The house is lying empty, if you allow me, I would like to shift today itself.

I said, "Fine, come whenever you want. Tapan Sen took the keys and left. I was happy thinking that I had found a good tenant. I sat at the window all afternoon and looked at the house, but Tapan did not shift. I opened the window in the morning and saw they had come. The front door was open. They must have shifted in the night.

My curious eyes started looking in the direction of the new tenants. Around 9:30 in the morning, a young woman came and closed the front door from the inside. Then after a few minutes she came out through the rear door from that narrow lane. Then I got a good look at her appearance. She had a slim frame and her hair arranged on the neck in the form of a bun. She had a small attaché case in her hand.
I thought, after working all night, Tapan was sleeping, so his wife was going to market.

The entire morning passed but she did not return. She returned at about four o'clock. She did not knock on the front door; she went through the alley to the rear door. It seems that she did not want to disturb her husband's sleep.

After a while I sent Ramadhin to the new tenants. They are new tenants I have to check if they require anything. I sat at the window and saw Ramadhin knock on the door. The girl opened the door and after talking with Ramadhin, the girl raised her eyes once and looked at my window, then came up to me on the second floor with Ramadhin.

I has seen her from afar, now I saw her close. She was a beautiful tall lady with long flowing hair and not a speck of fat on her. She had a lentil like red mole on the left cheek which indeed increased the beauty of her face. I noticed one thing, the husband and wife are of almost the same age i.e., twenty-three or twenty-four. Maybe fell in love and got married. These things are very prevalent these days.

She did a namaskar to me and said, "My name is Shanta. We are facing no problems; It is a very nice house." Her manner of speaking is as sweet as her voice is soft.
I said, "Sit down."
I asked, you have come to a new neighborhood, if you need a servant then let me know.
She said, "No need for a servant. We are a family of two, I alone can handle all the work.
I Asked," you were out all day, just returned now. Where were you all day?"
She said, "I teach in a school. There is a small girls' school towards Chetla, I work as a teacher there. She said, well, I will go now, have to prepare food for my husband. He will go to work later in the evening. Shanta smiled a little and went away.

I like both of them. At present my life consists of my tenants. They live in my house, pay rent, do their own thing, no socializing. There is a Madrasi family in the other twin house; they don't understand my language. Every month they come, pay rent, take rent receipts and leave. I have no heartfelt connection with them. But this young Bengali couple has attracted my heart.

I sat at the window and saw, after nightfall Tapan exited the house from the rear door. He was wearing a coat, a pant and an overcoat. He came out through the narrow lane, stood under the lamp in front of the house and lit a cigarette. Then he went towards the main road. He would stay out all night, finish work and return early morning.

Then their routine life began. At half past nine in the morning, Shanta would leave for school and come back in the afternoon. Tapan would go out in the evening, I don't know when he came back at night. Their life is very quiet; no guests come to their house, maybe they don't have friends and acquaintances around. The lights in the house go out after Tapan leaves for work, only a candle burns in the front room which too is extinguished at eight in the night. I think Shanta sleeps early after a tiring day.

I have enough curiosity about them, so I look at the house with binoculars. But nothing can be seen of the interior of the house from the outside, as the front door is closed also the front window. Only the soft light of the candle can be seen at night through the curtains.
One Sunday morning, Shanta came and chatted with me for a while. I asked jokingly, " Is your husband still sleeping?
She said smiling, "Yes, he doesn't get to sleep all night.
I said, "You don't switch the electric lamp at night?"

She said "My eyes are not good; I cannot tolerate bright light for long. Tapan does not see well in low light. So, when he leaves, I turn off the electric light and light candles.
Did you notice this?
Yes Shanta. I sit by this window from morning till night.
She said in a sympathetic tone: "True, you have nowhere to go. I will come sometimes here to have a chat with you and send him too.
Life went along like this. One evening Tapan came to me on his way to work and we spoke for a couple of hours.

Then one day late at night I noticed something. I usually go to bed at 9:30 pm. But I have insomnia, sometimes I have difficulty sleeping at night, on such days I am awake most of the night. Two weeks ago, I went to bed on time, but I couldn't sleep at all. I tried my best to sleep but could not. Finally at midnight I got up and thought a cup of hot cocoa would make me sleepy. I turned on the stove and started preparing cocoa. Ramadhin sleeps in front of the door outside my room. I didn't wake him.

It was quite chilly that day, hence the window was closed. Suddenly, I lifted the window blinds and looked outside. There were no people on the street in the dead of night. the streetlight was burning in front of the twin house.

I saw a man walking along the footpath. He was covered from head to toe in a black shawl. He walked up to the twin house and then stopped, turned his head and looked around and then strode down the lane between two houses. I could no longer see him. After a while, the electric lamp in Tapan's room lit up and went out again.

I was sipping the cocoa and thinking. Who is this man? Why were his movements so cautious? That narrow lane leads to the backdoor of the Madrasi's also, but the Madrasi's are large in number, after evening they lock their door and go off to sleep. This man has undoubtedly gone to Tapan's house. Tapan is not home at night, Shanta is alone, and this man sneaked in quietly. What's the matter?
In the middle of the night, husband is absent, no one but a young lady at home. At this time an unknown man come wearing a shawl. It looks shady to me.

I became upset. Shanta seemed like a good girl; But it is difficult to understand a woman's character by looking at her. Let it be. Why should I be concerned about what the tenant's wife doing? I will be happy if get the rent on time.

Once I thought to sit at the window and see how long the man stays. But after drinking cocoa I was feeling a little sleepy, hence I went to bed. If I don't sleep now, I may have to stay awake all night.

Two weeks have passed since this incident. Last Sunday, Tapan came and paid the rent, nothing significant happened. I did not tell Tapan about the unknown man visiting his quarters. Why shall I.

Then suddenly the day before, again I was gripped by insomnia and twisting and turning in bed till twelve o'clock. I got up to prepare some cocoa and opened the window blinds. It was as if the man was waiting for me. I saw the same man in the shawl. He was walking swiftly across the footpath and entered the lane in between the twin houses as before.

Then I saw another man walking the same route as if he was following the unknown man wearing the shawl. This man was wearing a comforter and he walked up to the twin houses and stopped right in front of the narrow lane between the houses. This new man started looking around as if he was searching for the other man.

Then I saw the man in the shawl come out from the lane surreptitiously. He removed the cover from his face. I realised it was none other than Tapan. Tapan drew a shining knife from his shawl, then in no time he jumped and stabbed the comforter wearing man in his chest. The man lay on the footpath writhing in pain and blood oozing out of his heart. In the meanwhile, Tapan ran inside the lane and hid in his house.

I was shocked to witness these scenes. I felt my veins freeze. The man now lay motionless in the footpath. I was sure that the man was dead by now.

I have a telephone in my room. After coming to my senses, I called the police station. The police station is very close to our house. The police came within five minutes. Darogababu heard my story and surrounded Tapan's house, But Tapan was not found at home. Shanta was sleeping, she could not know anything. There is no doubt that Tapan had come home by opening the rear door, He changed his clothes at home and escaped quietly without waking up Shanta. The body could not be identified that night; It was later learned that the deceased was identified as Bidhu Bhushan Aich from Burdwan, who had recently come to Kolkata on leave.

Tapan's house is under police guard. Tapan has not been caught yet. Darogababu has been interrogating Shanta continuously. But the poor girl is innocent. I am ashamed that I suspected her unjustly. Now I understand that Tapan used to come back home in the middle of the night wrapped in a shawl.

Meanwhile, my situation has become miserable. I don't know why Tapan committed a murder, but daily new police officers are coming and interrogating me hour by hour. I am a crippled man, but the police seem to suspect that I am responsible for the murder. My crime is that Tapan is my tenant and I have witnessed the murder.

Now I humbly request you to save me from this misery. My soul is exhausted, the police may arrest me on suspicion of murder and lodge me in jail. I will definitely die if such a thing happens. I have money; If you can save me, I will pay you handsomely.

I have nothing more to say. Please save me from this police trouble as soon as possible. I will be forever grateful to you.

Yours Faithfully,
Shri Chintamani Kundu.

After I finished reading the letter, Byomkesh grabbed the letter from me and started reading it in again. I headed towards the kitchen for another cup of tea, Satyawati may be angry, she needs to be cooled down.

I came back after half an hour and saw Byomkesh sitting with the letter in his lap and smiling to himself. I asked, "Why are you smiling?"
Byomkesh said, 'Chintamani Kundu made a mistake in one thing, he did not pay attention to the time when the electric lamp would go off in Tapan's house.
How do you know?
"If my conjecture is true, then he must be wrong. He has made yet another mistake but that's normal." Byomkesh smiled again. Then he turned and said, "Ajit, 'Chintamani Kundu has a telephone in his house, please find his number from the directory and call him. I need an answer to an urgent question. Ask him how Tapan's voice was.
How Surely a very urgent question. Want to know something else?
Nothing more. Tell him, not to worry, I'm going to visit him soon.

I called Chintamani babu, then came back and said, "Tapan's voice is very feeble."
Byomkesh said, "Tender! Then I guessed it correctly."
I said, "You know only what you have guessed. But Chintamani babu's voice is also feeble.
Byomkesh said, "What's surprising about that?" Chintamani babu is paralysed and is fearing that the police will incarcerate him. Let's go to Chintamani babu's house and help the poor soul. We will return in time for lunch.

Chintamani babu's lives is in the outer fringes of the city, hence the place is relatively secluded. The locality has quite wide new roads. Tapan Sen's house was easily identifiable by the police guard outside. On the opposite side of it is Chintamani Babu's two-storied house. We went up to the first floor to meet him. Just before we knocked on the door, the Hindustani servant i.e., Ramadhin opened the door and stood aside. Chintamani babu was sitting on a chair next to the open window. He eagerly raised his voice and said, "Byomkesh babu." I recognized you when I saw you on the road. Please come inside."

Ramadhin bought two chairs for us to sit, we sat down. Chintamani babu's face is not what I had imagined after hearing his voice on the telephone. Chintamani babu was a stout man of dark complexion, due to his sitting posture he did not appear to be paralysed. There lay an expensive pair of binoculars next to him on the table.

Chintamani babu said, "tell me first what will you have. Tea, Cocoa or Ovaltine?"
Byomkesh said, "There is no need now. Did the police come to you today?"
Chintamani babu said, "They come every day, even today they came and questioned me!" Once they question me then they rush to question Shanta. I don't understand what they want. They ask me the same questions repeatedly.
Am I paralyzed? Can I go down the stairs? Why did I keep the binoculars? why did I rent the house to Tapan Sen? Tell me, Byomkesh babu, what to do, I am tired of answering the same questions again and again? "Now only you can save me."
Byomkesh said, "don't think much, everything will be fine. Now I need to meet Darogababu. Who is the Darogababu here?"
As we were speaking, Darogababu entered the room.

We had met Bijoy Bhaduri almost ten years ago when he was still a junior inspector. Bijoy had a thin, bamboo shaped frame, but a very active and skeptical person. In ten years, he has become a senior inspector, but his appearance has not changed a bit. It can be guessed from the look in his eyes that he was still as skeptical as before. After inspecting the surroundings, he entered the room and said in a dry tone. "Ohh Byomkesh babu."

Byomkesh smiled and said, "I see that you have recognized me. Have you caught the accused, I mean, Tapan Sen?
Bijoy Bhaduri looked at Chintamani babu with a crooked glance and said, "Not caught yet, but will be soon. How come you are here Byomkesh babu?
Byomkesh said, "Chintamani babu is my client. There has been a murder in front of his house, his tenant is the murderer, but you are disturbing him. So, he has appointed me in his own interest."

Bijoy Bhaduri looked at Byomkesh's with crooked eyes, maybe he was thinking whether to grab his throat and shove him off. Then when he spoke his tone changed completely. He leaned towards Byomkesh and said with a stern voice, "Will you come out once. Need to speak to you alone?"

We went outside the room to a corner of the long veranda and stood. Bijoy babu brought a forced smile on his face and said, "Look, Byomkesh babu you have good connections with the top police officials, if you want to get involved in this case, I will not be able to stop you, but I beg you not to help Chintamani Kundu. I believe, he and his servant Ramadhin are involved in this murder.

Byomkesh sat still and listened to Bijoy babu, then said, "Do you know who committed the murder?" Bijoy Babu said, "Of course Tapan Sen did, but the old man is also in it.

Byomkesh replied, If the old man was also involved then why would he have brought murder charges on Tapan.
Bijoy babu then said, this is a ploy of the old man, to bring charges on Tapan and free himself.
Byomkesh said in an irate tone, "I am sorry to say Bijoy babu, you have not understood this mystery."

He raised his eyebrows and said, "what do you mean Byomkesh Babu?"
Byomkesh said, "I will tell you later. First please answer few of my questions."
"Has the knife with which the murder was done been found?"
No. Tapan ran away with it post murder.
Did you find anything after searching Tapan's house?

No, I did not find anything? But the chest is not opened yet, its key is with Tapan.
Have you interrogated Shanta?
Yes, we did but she was not of much help. They were married four months ago but she does not know anything about Tapan's work.

Hmm. But I know everything. I know who did the murder, I even know where the accused is.
Bijoy babu jumped up, he said, if you knew it, why did you not say anything.
Byomkesh laughed, "I will tell you when the time is right. Before that, I want to visit Tapan's house once. And I would like to ask Shanta a few questions." You have of course, cross-examined her sufficiently and received satisfactory answers. I will only ask her a couple of questions.

That's fine," said Bijoy Babu. "But the murderer?
You will find murderer also.
Where? In that house? I don't understand what you're saying.
You will soon. Let's go to that house first. Be ready to catch the murderer.
You mean to say that Tapan Sen will return home or is hiding in the house.

Let's go said Byomkesh and we started to exit the room, Byomkesh stopped near the door and looked back at Chintamani babu and said, "Chintamani babu, don't be afraid. We are going to Tapan Sen's house within an hour this mystery will be solved.
Then we went down the stairs to Tapan Sen's Place.

Police are guarding the front and back of Tapan's house. I have noticed a strange thing; the intelligence of the police increases when the thief runs away. When the criminal has committed a crime, then what is the use of putting a strict guard around the place, I don't understand this till today.
Byomkesh walked into the narrow lane between the twin houses and asked, is there a way to escape apart from the front and back doors? Can't the accused escape by jumping the wall?
Bijoy Babu replied, No.

A watchman was standing at the rear door which was locked from the outside by a huge Lock. At Bijoy Babu's command the watchman unlocked the lock, and we went inside Tapan's house. The house had two rooms. Adjacent to the small courtyard was a kitchen and a bath next to it.
Byomkesh said, Bijoy Babu you and Ajit go and sit near Shanta, I'll take a look at the bathroom and the kitchen.

We entered the front room. This was the living room. The room was decorated with bamboo furniture. Shanta sat in distress in one of the bamboo chairs. Chintamani Kundu description of her appearance was true; At present the hair on his head was tangled; her eyes were swollen, probably she had been crying.

She looked up as we entered the room. She didn't notice me, she looked at Bijoy Babu with eager questioning eyes. Bijoy Babu did not say anything, he sat on a chair. I also sat. We all sat there silently. No one spoke a word. I thought that this girl has become tired after the continuous police interrogation.
If she is innocent, if she has nothing to do with her husband's crime, she is still not absolved. But why did Tapan kill that man? Was it Sexual jealousy? Did that man have an affair with Shanta?

Byomkesh entered from the bedroom; he had a smile on his face. He pulled a chair in front of Shanta and looked at her with a smile on his face. Shanta also looked at byomkesh with weary eyes, then slowly fear and caution appeared in her eyes. She sat up straight and said a little sheepishly, 'what? what?

Byomkesh cheerfully said, "I saw a small iron chest in your bedroom. What is in it?
Shanta said, "I told Darogababu, I don't know what is there. My husband used to keep the key to the chest with himself.
Bijoy Babu said, 'I have arranged to break the lock of the chest.
Very well said Byomkesh, you will find a lot of goods in it, looted cash, looted jewellery etc.

Byomkesh turned to Shanta, "Well, tell me, does not your husband shave. No shaving equipment was found in your house.

Shanta's face became pale, she mumbled, "He used to shave at the salon." Byomkesh said, "I see your husband was a remarkable man. He shaved in the salon but never wore sandals at home. Was there a reason?

Shanta lowered her eyes and said, "His indoor sandals were torn, he was yet to buy new indoor sandals. When he stayed at home, he wore mine. Byomkesh said, "Is that so? Both of you have the same foot size. Shanta said, "Almost the same."

Byomkesh said, " Wow what a convenience! I see that your husband and you are almost alike, only the hair color is different. Chintamani babu told Tapan's hair colour is copper. Right?
Shanta said, "Yes."

Bijoy Babu was listening to the questions patiently for a long time, he suddenly stood up and said in an intense voice, "Byomkesh babu! Byomkesh raised his hand and said, "Wait." Be prepared, this is my last question.

Shanta Devi, Chintamani babu saw that you have a red mole like a lentil on your cheek where did that mole go?

Shanta put her hand on his left cheek, then terrified she said, "Mole on my cheek, Chintamani babu has made a mistake. I have no mole on my cheek. Maybe there was a spot of red ink on my face which he thought to be a mole.

Byomkesh's face burst into a giant smile, he said, "I see you have prepared answers to all the questions. But what is your answer to this question?"

He quickly grabbed Shanta's hair and pulled at it. The wig that Shanta was wearing came out and we could see copper coloured trimmed hair inside.

Shanta also replied with lightning speed. She stooped a little and lifted the edge of the sari, attached to her right leg with a rubber band was a small knife. She took the knife in her fist and tried to stab Byomkesh's throat. I just went in a fearful hypnosis shock; it is unimaginable that a woman's beautiful soft face can turn so ugly and hard at the blink of an eye.

It is doubtful whether Byomkesh's life would have been saved if Daroga Bijoy Babu had not been ready. He jumped like a tiger and grabbed Shanta's wrist. The knife slipped from Shanta's fist and fell to the ground. She looked at byomkesh with venomous eyes as if she would kill him with her poisonous stare.

Byomkesh stood up with a smile, "Bijoy Babu, here is your fugitive murderer, and here is the murder weapon.
Bijoy Babu said a little hesitantly, "But Chintamani babu said Tapan Sen?"
Byomkesh said, "Tapan Sen does not exist, Bijoy Babu. There is only Shanta Sen. She is Tapan Sen by night and Shanta Sen by day. It's her who plays both characters with perfection. She is a great woman. Don't think that her only achievement is to kill Bidhu Bhushan Aich. Two months ago, she killed a guard of Burdwan Jail and escaped from jail. I don't know her real name, you can find the same as you are a policeman.

Bijoy Babu held Shanta's wrist in an iron grip and gazed at her with inquisitively, then he said, "Pramila Pal." Now I understand everything. You were sentenced to life imprisonment for poisoning your husband. After serving two years in jail, you killed the jail guard and escaped. You ran away and came here alone and hid yourself as a husband-and-wife. Then Bidhu Bhushan Aich saw you. Bidhu Bhushan Aich recognized you and followed you. You killed him that night here in front of the house." Turning his eyes towards Byomkesh, Bijoy Babu said, "This is what happened right?"

Byomkesh said, "Yes this is the crux of the story."
Bijoy Babu shouted in anger, "Jamadar."
Jamadar was standing outside the door; he entered the room. Bijoy Babu said, "handcuff her."

Byomkesh said, while sitting in Chintamani babu's room and drinking tea, "I was shocked to read your letter Chintamani babu. You have never seen the two of them together, even with binoculars you couldn't see them through Why? The man is short, the girl is tall. They do not use the front door; they use the rear door; Tapan Sen has a feeble voice. Why? I suspected that they were hiding something.

Broadly speaking Pramila Pal needed two things after breaking out of jail: A disguise and a livelihood. Her hair was of copper color which easily attracted attention. She needed a haircut to make her look like a man and avoid attention also a fake moustache. For doing robberies she needs a girly outfit hence she bought an expensive wig. Now began her double life.
Now winter season is very beneficial for women to wear men's clothes and pass of as a man. She put a little butterfly-moustache under her nose, put on an overcoat over her coat and trousers, then came home to you to take the house on rent. To pass off as a man she spoke to you in a coarse voice. It is very convenient to stay incognito in the city of Calcutta, the neighbors do not know about anyone. But she noticed that you sit by the window all the time with your binoculars. She must be careful to avoid your undue attention.

That night after you went to bed she moved in the house with her belongings. No one knew that only one person had arrived, not two. He had a small iron chest with her, which she kept in the bedroom.

Then began her daily routine life. In the morning she would go out as Shanta on the pretext of teaching in a school and look for promising targets, in the afternoon she would rob her targets and return in late afternoon. Post evening, she would come out dressed as Tapan to fool people specially you into thinking that there were indeed two people living there Shanta and Tapan. Before leaving she would switch off the electric lamp and light up an oil lamp. When the oil would run out, you would think that Shanta has blown out the lamp and gone to sleep. You just made one mistake; you did not notice that the electric lamp was switched off before Tapan would leave the house. You didn't notice because you suspected no foul play.

After you would go oof to sleep, she would come back home and sleep. She would probably go out carrying a shawl wrapped around her waist under her overcoat and would wrap it over the overcoat when she returned. So, the first night you opened the blinds and saw her return, you thought she was Shanta's secret lover. This was the regular routine.

Then Pramila suddenly faced a great danger. Bidhu Bhushan Aich a police officer, had seen Pramila before, he had come to Calcutta on vacation and saw Pramila and recognized her in a male disguise. He followed Pramila. Maybe the two met in a restaurant. Pramila must have tried to shake him off her trail, but when she couldn't."

Byomkesh stopped without finishing the sentence, took out a cigarette and held it. I said, "One thing. Why didn't Pramila leave the house after killing Bidhu Bhushan Aich?"

Byomkesh said, " She didn't get time to run away." She did not know that Chintamani babu had lifted the blinds and seen the murders hence she was not in a particular hurry. She thought she would escape with the looted jewelry and cash.

It was no longer safe for her to stay at that place. The body was lying in front of the house, she knew the police will surely come to question her. Pramila Pal was a fugitive from jail and a murder convict, anyone in the police may recognize her. So, she had planned to escape, but suddenly within five minutes the police came and surrounded the house.

She there was no way for her to escape, Pramila quickly put on the wig and dressed as a girl, but in a hurry, she forgot to paint the cheek mole.

Why did she draw a mole on your cheek?
To create a visible difference between Shanta and Tapan. As Tapan, she would put a butterfly moustache under her nose and as Shanta she would wear a wig and have a red mole on her cheeks.
Byomkesh said, Chintamani babu, we will take your leave now. Chintamani babu was very relieved after we solved this case and immediately wrote us a check for two hundred rupees.

It was almost two in the afternoon. We left for our home and the police took the accused. Surely Bijoy Bhaduri will surely earn a lot of praise for solving this crime. On reaching home, I saw Satyawati standing anxiously near the door, she raised her eyebrows and looked at us with questioning eyes as if asking, where were we the entire afternoon.

Byomkesh suddenly burst into laughter. Then he raised his hand and shook Satyawati's chin a little and said, "You women are also not far behind."

Dustu Chakra

(Wicked Plan)

Doctor Suresh Rakshit said, "You must come once, Byomkesh babu. The patient is in a very bad state, if you don't give him your assurance, the patient may not live through.

Doctor Suresh Rakshit is about forty years of age, he is of a very thin frame, these new and expensive western clothes don't suit him. But he seems very sharp and intelligent. Today morning he has come to meet Byomkesh and has put forward a weird proposal.

Needless to say, Byomkesh has no desire to visit the patient. He looked at the doctor Rakshit with half-closed eyes and said, "What is the disease?"

The doctor said, 'Paralysis. About three months ago he was diagnosed with paralysis. He managed to survive the first shock, though he is of sound mind, but his blood pressure is too high. He sent me if I could bring you to his abode. Please come once, if he gets your assurance and advice he may be saved from untimely death.

Byomkesh said, "are you treating him?"
The doctor said, "Yes yes. I am his tenant and reside on the ground floor of his house. I am his family physician as well. The man is very rich money lender. You may have heard of his name Bishu Pal." Byomkesh said, "What name did you say, Shishupal?
The doctor laughed, "Bishu Pal." But some people also call him Shishupal, I don't know why. The man is a moneylender but not heartless. Especially in the last three months he has become completely helpless due to paralysis."
Byomkesh said, "But what can I do? I am not a doctor."

The doctor said, "Let me tell you the truth. Bishu Pal has a debtor named Abhay Ghosal. The man is a rogue. He borrowed a lot of money from Bishu Pal now he is not paying back. Bishu Pal pressurised him to get his money back, so Abhay Ghosal threatened to kill him if he ever asked for money. Bishu Pal had a stroke and has been bedridden for the last three months. Of course, there is no danger of life and if he gets good medical treatment then he may be able to walk again. But the real thing is not that, fear has crept into his soul that Abhay Ghosal will kill him, even if he waives-off the debt, he will kill him. You don't need to give him medical treatment. Bishu Pal's wants to speak to you to combat his fear and if you may give some advice on staying safe."

Byomkesh looked a little downhearted and said, "If someone is determined to kill Shishupal it is impossible for even Shiva to stop him. However, when the gentleman is so anxious for my company, I will go. Of course, one should maintain good relations with money lenders in this world and even the world beyond. What do you say, Ajit?
I replied, "Yes Indeed."

The doctor stood up, smiling he said, "Thank you. Here is our address. When will you come?" He took out a card and handed it to Byomkesh. Byomkesh looked at the card and handed it over to me. Bishu Pal's house is not far away, in an alley of Amherst Street. Byomkesh said, "today at five o'clock in the evening we shall visit him. Now you may go." As the doctor left, Byomkesh said with a smile, "This is my first time to console a paralysed patient."

The alley is spiral; It is flowing like a mountain river, bending here and there with sharp turns. The alley was lined on both sides with multi stories houses. No matter how narrow the alley is, I have never seen small houses on such alleys, the houses grow taller to compensate the lack of space.

We stopped in front of a three storied house after seeing the inscription of Dr. Suresh Rakshit. We understood that this is the house of moneylender Bishu pal. The doctor, saw us through the window, came out, and said, "Please Come in."

The house seems very old. On one side, a narrow verandah leads inside the house with a door on one side and two windows on the other side. The sparkling clean dispensary is visible through the door, but there is no rush of patients. A middle-aged compounder is standing near the door. Doctor Rakshit didn't take us to the dispensary, he said "we have to take the stairs, Bishu babu lives on the third floor."

Byomkesh said, "That's fine. Do you live in this house or only have your dispensary here?"
The doctor said, "There are three rooms. I live in one and the rest two have been converted into a dispensary. I am single hence a single room is enough for me."

There are Three rooms on the second floor as well. This is the office space meant for conducting the business of moneylending. The office does not have table or chairs instead it contains mattresses. It is like a Marwaris gaddi. Many clerks are sitting on these mattresses and managing accounts.
Byomkesh Asked, "What is this?
The doctor said, "Bishu babu's Office." It's a huge business, many kings and rich people are debtors to him.
Byomkesh said nothing more. I thought to myself, Bishu Pal is not only Shishupal but also Jarasandha.

We walked up the stairs to the third floor. At the entry to the third floor stood a Gurkha dressed in battle uniform and seated on a stool with a rifle in hand. He stood up hearing our footsteps and glanced sideways at us. The doctor said, "It's Okay." Then the Gurkha saluted us and stood back.

After a few steps through the balcony, we found a closed door. The doctor knocked on the door, from inside came a female voice. "Who is it."
The doctor said, "I am Doctor Rakshit. Please open the door."

The door was slightly opened, I saw the pale and frightened eyes of an old married woman. She saw our faces one by one, after getting convinced she the door opened completely. We entered a dark room. A male voice said, "Please switch on the lights." The lady switched on the lights and exited the room hurriedly.

Now I had a clear look at the room. It is a medium sized room with a bed lying in the middle. On the bed lay a ghostly man wrapped in a blanket. Next to the bed was a small table on which was kept few bottles of medicine a glass of water. The other furniture's in the room reminds me of a patient's room in a nursing home

The ghostly man, however, is Bishu Pal. He looked at us with two dull eyes in a worn-out face, his mouth was devoid of any teeth and his head is full of white hair. He looked very frail, he could be either fifty or sixty or even seventy years of age. He said in a weak voice, "Byomkesh babu you have come? It's my honour."

We went and stood beside the bed. Bishu Pal folded his shaking hands and said, "I have caused you great trouble. I should have gone to consult you, but you do see my situation."
The doctor said, "You don't talk too much."

Bishu Pal said in a weary voice, "I do have to talk. How will Byomkesh babu help me if I don't disclose the entire events to him in detail?"
"Say whatever you want but be brisk." The doctor took a medicine bottle from the table, poured some medicine into a glass, then mixed it with a little water and handed it to Bishu Pal saying, "Here, drink this first." Bishu Pal swallowed the medicine with an irritated face.
Then in a relatively normal tone, he said, "Doctor, please give these gentlemen a chair to sit."

The doctor pulled two chairs to the side of the bed for us to sit down. Bishu pal looked at Byomkesh and said, "I will not talk much else the doctor will get angry. I will be brief. You must have heard that I am into the business of moneylending. I have been in this business since the last twenty-five years, and I have loaned about twenty lakhs of rupees to my debtors. Various rich and popular people are my debtors."

"I never lend money without taking collateral. But two years ago, I did the unthinkable and now I am suffering its consequences. I lent thirty thousand rupees without collateral."

"You don't know Abhay Ghosal. I knew his father, Mr. Adhar Ghosal. He was a gentleman and extremely rich businessman. We had some business dealings hence I knew him. Abhay Ghosal died ten years ago; his only son Abhay Ghosal inherited his huge property."

"I had not seen Abhay Ghosal then. After his father's death I heard some news about him. When boys inherit their ancestral property, they do become a bit reckless and spendthrift but with the passage of time they fall back on the right track."

"I had forgotten about Abhay Ghosal, then around two years ago, suddenly one day he appeared in front of me. I was charmed by his looks and sweet talk. He was an incredibly handsome fellow and a very sweet talker. Introducing himself he said that his father was my good friend, hence he had come to me as he was in distress. He said he was in grave danger, his enemies had framed him in a false murder case and somehow after getting bail, he had come to me asking for thirty thousand rupees to carry on with the legal proceedings."

"You won't believe me Byomkesh Babu, A moneylender like me gave him the entire thirty thousand rupees without collateral, I just wrote him a hand note. They guy has just mesmerized me."

"In due course the murder case proceedings started in the court, excerpts from the proceedings started appearing in the newspapers. In due course I realised, there was hardly any crime which was not committed by Abhay Ghosal. He had blown away all the inheritance and had sold away almost all ancestral property. He had destroyed the lives of countless girls. He had charmed a married women and after staying with her for almost a year he had poisoned her to death. One day I went to see murder case proceedings in the court. Abhay Ghosal was standing in the courtroom's prisoner box, like a ferocious enraged cat. I was scared to see him. I cursed myself, to whom I lent money, that too without a collateral."

"But the lawsuit did not survive, Abhay Ghosal got away due to the loopholes in the law. He was declared innocent. The murder charge against him was not proved."

"Then another year passed. I had kept an eye on Abhay Ghosal, then I got news that he was trying to sell his residence. That was his last immovable property if he sells it too, I will have no way to recover my money."

"I started urging for my payments. First, I wrote him a letter from the office, but there was no reply. I send him three letters urging for my payments, but all went unanswered. Then finally I went to meet him one day, this happened three months back. We moneylenders do berate and abuse our clients to recover our money. I am good in this art, I thought that if I berate and abuse him, I may well recover my money without having to take legal steps."

"I had taken a Gurkha security guard along with me. Abhay Ghosal was sitting alone in a chair in his drawing room. Upon Seeing me, he did not even get up from the chair, did not speak a single word, just looked at my face."

"I got very furious at his antics. I started to denigrate and abuse him. I abused his entire family and lineage for almost half an hour. Then suddenly I noticed his eyes. Oh, God, what terrible eyes. His eyes were blood red and he stared at me as if he would kill me. Abhay Ghosal spoke not a single word, but his eyes told he what he had in store for me. A man who has been acquitted after killing once would not deter from doing the same again. I was extremely scared and unable to move an inch."

"I could not stand there any longer, I returned home with the help of the Gurkha guard. Even after returning home my hands and feet were shaking with fear. The shaking never stopped. Then I called for the doctor. The doctor came and gave me medicine and somehow my shaking stopped. I went off to sleep, during late night my body started shaking vigorously. Then the big specialist doctor was called; he came and found that I had a stroke, both my legs were numb. I have been bedridden ever since. But there is no peace in life. doctors assured me that I will not die of the disease, but I am not afraid of dying. Abhay Ghosal will not leave me. I don't come out of the house, I have put a Gurkha in front of the door, but I still don't get hope. Now tell me, Byomkesh babu, what can I do."

After finishing the story, Bishu Pal lay on the bed half dead. doctor tapped his wrist once to see the pulse but did not feel the need to administer medication byomkesh bowed his head and sat down. At this time Bishu Pal's wife entered the house Half veil on head, two cups of tea in both hands. We stood up, she gave us a cup of tea and left with a look of concern towards her husband. The lady was of silent nature, she did not speak to us. I saw that Bishu Pal was looking at byomkesh helplessly.

Byomkesh took a sip from the cup of tea and said, "You have been careful as much as you can be, what else is there to do. What is the arrangement of food?

Bishu Pal said, "We had a cook, but we have dismissed him, now my wife does all the cooking. No outside food comes here.
And servants?
We had a maid and a servant, but we have dismissed them as well. We have appointed a security guard. What else can be done?
How is the business going?
My money lending business is being taken care by my manager. He comes upstairs only in case of any emergency. But I don't let him enter the room, he stands near the door and talks. Doctor Rakshit is the only outsider allowed entry into the room.

After finishing the cup of tea, Byomkesh stood up, smiled and said, you have done everything that needs to be done, I don't know what else can be done. But does Abhay Ghosal really want to kill you.
Bishu Pal excitedly tried to sit up and lay down again said in a confused tone, "Yes, Byomkesh babu, my inner soul feels that he wants to kill me. Otherwise tell me why I will be so afraid!"

Byomkesh said, "I understand your situation. But how can you live like this in fear."
Bishu Pal said, "I know Byomkesh babu I cannot survive like this in constant fear. That is why I need your help. Byomkesh babu, please help me out. Please suggest me what to do.
Byomkesh said, 'I will think about it. If something comes to mind, I will let you know.

Bishu Pal called the doctor, Doctor Rakshit pulled out a hundred rupees note and handed it over to byomkesh. Byomkesh frowned and said, "What is it?" Bishu Pal said from the bed, "This is to honour your time. I have caused you a lot of trouble, wasted a lot of your time.
Byomkesh said, but I never asked for it.
Bishu Pal said, you have to accept it.
Reluctantly Byomkesh took the money. Then the doctor led us down the stairs. The Gurkha saluted us. Byomkesh said, "This man keeps a watch round the clock?"

The doctor said, "No, there are two of them. They are trustworthy guards. Previously they were guarding the first floor. One guard keeps a watch from ten o'clock in the morning to eight o'clock at night, the second man keeps a watch from ten o'clock in the night to eight o'clock in the morning.
Byomkesh said, "There is no watch for two hours in the morning and two hours at night?"
The doctor said, "No, that time I am present with Bishu Pal Babu."

As we descended the stairs, we saw the office had closed already and the clerks had left for the day. After we reach the ground floor byomkesh said, "Doctor, I want to ask you a couple of questions.
Doctor Rakshit said, well, please come to my dispensary, we can have a chat there.

We entered the dispensary. The front room, which is the patient's waiting room is furnished with new tables, chairs, benches etc. The compounder was slouching on one of the benches and went into the next room on seeing us. Byomkesh looked around the room and said, "Your dispensary is very well furnished.

The doctor replied, I have to keep the place well-furnished so that I can attract wealthy patients.
How long have you been practicing?
"I have been here for three years, before that I was practicing in the suburbs.
Seems its going well for you.
My practice is going good here. I am the family doctor for few families. Recently my practice has seen a good growth. If I can cure Bishu babu then my practice will grow by leaps and bounds.
Byomkesh shook his head, "Yes. Well Doctor, Bishu Pal's fear of death, is it phycological or is there really a reason for fear.

The doctor remained silent for a while and said, "There is reason to be afraid. Of course, those who have a lot of money are more afraid of death. But Bishu Pal's fear is not unfounded. Abhay Ghosal is a real murderer. I have heard that he has committed three murders. It is even suspected that he had poisoned his own father.

Byomkesh said, "Is that so! He seems to be a very talented guy. Now I remember two years ago, the snippets of his case appeared in the newspaper. Do you know his address The doctor said, "I know. It is close by, nearly a big mile away! If you want to meet, I can give you the address.

The doctor wrote the address on a piece of paper and gave it to Byomkesh, who folded it and put it in his pocket and said, "One more thing. Does Bishu babu's wife have any ailment."
The doctor said, "She suffers from a nerve ailment. She is a woman of nervous nature, also she does not have any children.
Understood, we will take your leave now. Bishu Babu has put me in a fix by paying me hundred rupees. I will think about his problem.

Outside, the streetlights were glowing. Byomkesh looked at his watch and said, "It's half past six. Come on, let's visit the accused murderer. When Bishu Pal has given the money, something needs to be done.

We boarded a rickshaw at the junction and proceeded towards Abhay Ghosal's residence. We noticed that there is less traffic on the Amherst Street; while in the other streets the crowd is flowing back and forth like a tidal sea, there is still less traffic on Amherst Street.

Coming to the northern end of the road, the rickshaw stopped in front of a house, byomkesh checked the address mentioned in the paper chit and said, this is address of the accused. We got off the rickshaw. The house is not right by the footpath, but there is a little open ground in the middle, with few large bushes hiding the house from the road. It was a two-storied house, the first floor was completely dark, and some light was flickering through the ground floor window below. We entered through a narrow gate.

The front room was furnished with tables and chairs, like an office. A man sat idly scribbling on paper with a pencil. As we approached the door, he raised his eyes and looked at us.

He was a handsome man. About thirty-five years old, fair complexion, curly hair with his hair parted in the middle. He looked like a work of art, it seemed as if his eyes and nose had been drawn by a painter. I was also mesmerized by his looks just as was Bishu Pal.

Byomkesh said from the door, "Can I come?" My name is Byomkesh Bakshi, and this is Ajit Bandyopadhyay.

Abhay Ghosal's eyes became alert. Then he flashed a smile a on his face said, "Satyanweshi Byomkesh Bakshi!" It's my lucky day today. Please come in."

We went and sat facing Abhay Ghosal. He put down the pencil and said, "tell me, what's the matter. I don't remember doing any bad deeds recently."
Byomkesh smiled and said I just here to see you.
Abhay Ghosal said, "Thank you! Am I a spectacular creature that you came here to see me? Have you come her all by yourself or someone sent you here?"
No one sent me but Mahajan Bishu Pal told me about his grief, so I thought I should give you a visit.
"Ohh Shishupal. Abhay Ghosal stopped for a moment and said, "I understood that someone had sent you, but I did not think of Shishupal. Byomkesh said, "You must be aware that Bishu Pal has been paralysed.

Abhay expressed surprise and said, "Is that so? I didn't know that. Three months ago, Shishupal came to my house. He abused me and my entire family. God is there hence he has faced such a fate. There was no speck of remorse in his face or voice. He picked up the pencil again and began to scribble on the paper.

Byomkesh said, "He had a stroke after returning from here. Since then, he has been confined to his home. However, paralysis is not the only reason he is confined to his house. He does not leave the house for fear of you."

"Fear of me? what do you say! I am his debtor, he is the moneylender, I am the one who is supposed to hide in fear of him." Abhay Ghosal raised his eyebrows and uttered the words in utter astonishment, but his smile continued to linger.
Byomkesh said, "He is afraid that you will kill him."

Look at this. Whatever happens people end up blaming me! I was once implicated in a murder case so everyone thought I am a murderer. No one thinks that I was acquitted of all charges. Abhay Ghosal, stopped for a second and said in a relatively low voice, "But one thing is true, those who have enmity with me do not live long. Are you leaving?

Byomkesh stood up and said, yes. I came to see you, now that I have seen you, I must leave. Let me tell you one thing, I will be very sad if Bishu Pal dies an unnatural death, and you too will be sorry in the end. Abhay Ghosal's face expression suddenly changed. The smile on his face was wiped away and a stream of brutal violence appeared in his eyes. He looked at byomkesh like a viper. My heart skipped a beat on seeing his violent eyes. This very sight must have scared Bishu Pal and left him disoriented with fear. I had never seen such violent eyes in anyone's eyes, as if he was swearing that he would kill us.
Byomkesh cast a contemptuous glance at him and said, "Come on Ajit, let's leave."

On reaching the footpath we saw a taxi standing across the road. As soon as I raised my hand to wave for the taxi, the driver started the taxi and sped away. I looked at byomkesh, he asked, was there anyone in the taxi. I said, I didn't see any passenger. I saw the driver was looking at us hence thought that taxi was for hire, but maybe there was a passenger in the back seat.

Byomkesh started walking and said, "someone must have been following us."
But who would follow us?
Apart from the doctor no one knows that we would be visiting here.
But why? What is the purpose?
I don't know that. Maybe the taxi did have a passenger and the taxi might have stopped for some reason and it left at the very moment you raised your hand to call for the taxi.
It was already Seven thirty in the evening and we walked towards our house. But the taxi incident still kept me thinking.

The next morning, I opened the newspaper and said, "Oh Byomkesh! He turned his back to me, 'What! Was Bishu Pal was murdered?' I said, "Not Bishu Pal, Abhay Ghosal was murdered."
Byomkesh stared at me for a while like a nincompoop, then snatched the paper from my hand and started reading.

The description in the newspaper was very brief. Last night, Amherst Street resident Abhay Ghosal, a wealthy man, was murdered in his sleep. The police have arrived at the scene; The murderer is yet to be apprehended. Two years ago, Abhay Ghosal was accused of murder and then acquitted of all charges.

My mind was prepared for other possibilities, so I remained abstracted for a long time. We had seen him alive last night at seven thirty. He had a war of words with byomkesh. What happened then all of a sudden? He had said sarcastically, he has many friends. Was any of his so-called friend waiting in the taxi and killed him after we left? Or was the man in the taxi Doctor Rakshit? But why would Doctor Rakshit go to kill him.

Daroga Rama Pati babu appeared before we could speculate too much about this incidence. We had a little acquaintance with Rama Pati babu, if not intimately. He has a reputation in the police department as a hard worker. He is of our age group, has a strong face, innocent voice and piercing eyes.

Byomkesh greeted him and asked him to sit and, said, "I saw in the papers today that Abhay Ghosal was killed in your area of jurisdiction. Rama Pati babu rolled his eyes and said, "You knew Abhay Ghosal?" Byomkesh said, "I didn't know him, we met yesterday evening. We went to his house to meet him.
Is it so? Why did you go to meet him?
Byomkesh nodded bravely and said, "First you tell me the news, then I will."

Rama Pati babu hesitated for a moment and said, "Well, I will talk first then." Abhay Ghosal was under the police's scanner for a long time. The man used to wear a mask of politeness, but such a big devil is rarely seen. He has destroyed the lives of several girls from well to do families. He had a wife, she died under mysterious circumstances. Then he eloped with the wife of a gentleman. The man divorced his wife. Then the woman may have pressurised him to marry her, and Abhay poisoned her to death.

"Abhay Ghosal was arrested by the police, the case went to court. But the case did not last as Abhay's crime was not proven. He was charged under Section 302 but was acquitted by the court. This is the history of

Abhay Ghosal. There are at least ten people in the city of Calcutta who would be happy to kill him."

Last night around 12 o'clock, Abhay's maid came to the police station and reported that Abhay was murdered. I was not at the police station at that time, on getting the news I went to his place to investigate. Abhay Ghosal's financial situation has now collapsed, he lives alone at home, with only a young maid to look after him. This maid came to report the death to the police station.

I went and saw Abhay lying on his side on the bed in the first-floor room, there was a knife protruding from the left side of his back. By questioning the maid, it was learned that Abhay went to bed after dinner at nine o'clock. She completed all the household work, had dinner then closed the door and window and went to check on Abhay in his room. She found Abhay lying dead in his room, while she was busy working someone had entered the house and killed Abhay. We have detained the maid, but she seems not to have committed the murder. Who killed him is not known. We have checked the alibi of people who had enmity with Abhay and also of people who had testified against Abhay in the case, but all have strong alibis. This is the current situation! Now tell me what you know."

Byomkesh said, "How do you know that I know something?"
Ram Pati babu took out a piece of paper from his pocket and handed it to Byomkesh,"This piece of paper was kept on the table in Abhay's living room downstairs.
I stooped a bit to see what was written in the piece of paper, the paper was full of illegible scribblings and two names Byomkesh Bakshi and Shishupal. I remembered last night Abhay Ghosal was sitting in front of us and scribbling in the paper.

Rama Pati babu said, "Looking at your name, I thought you might know something;hence I came. Byomkesh said, "Right. Now listen to what I know."

Byomkesh narrated all the events since the arrival of Doctor Rakshit yesterday morning. Rama Pati babu listened with deep attention; Byomkesh finished the story, Rama Pati babu said with a puzzled look on his face, "It is suspicious, but I don't see any motive of Bishu Pal. Also, the man is paralyzed. What do you think?

Byomkesh said, "I still don't understand. Do you know the time of death?
Rama Pati babu said, after nine at night and before twelve midnight.
Byomkesh thought for a while and said, "I think, we should check if Bishu Pal is really paralysed or not. Rama Pati babu said, "Sure and when there is no other suspect let us focus our attention on Bishu Pal. Byomkesh Babu you have a landline; May I please use it once?
Sure. Please come. Byomkesh took Rama Pati babu inside the room to use the telephone.

After a while, Rama Pati babu came back and said, I asked the police surgeon to go to Bishu Pal's house!" I'm going there too would you like to come?
Okay, let's go.

We got ready in five minutes and went out with Rama Pati babu. There was a commotion in front of Bishu Pal's house. The police surgeon was sitting in a police car infront of the door of the house. the street was crowded with people gazing at the police car. Doctor Rakshit was standing near the guarded door. When we arrived, surgeon Sushil babu got down from the car. Doctor Rakshit came towards us and said, "Byomkesh babu! What happened?

Byomkesh introduced the two sides. Rama Pati babu said to doctor Rakshit,"The police doctor wants to examine Bishu Pal. You have objection?" Doctor Rakshit was surprised for a moment, then said, "Objection! not at all. But why? what happened?" Rama Pati babu said, "Someone killed a man named Abhay Ghosal last night. Doctor Rakshit echoed, "Abhay Ghosal was killed! Oh, now I understand, your suspicion is that Bishu babu killed Abhay Ghosal." A dry smile appeared on his face, "you mean to say that Bishu babu's paralysis is not real paralysis, he is just pretending. Come on, check it out yourselves."

We went upstairs. The office on the first floor was busy. We climbed to the second floor and saw the Gurkha sitting on the stairs. The doctor knocked on the door. Bishu Pal's wife opened the door a little and gazed at us with fearful eyes The whole process was exactly like yesterday evening.

As Bishu Pal's wife went into the next room, five of us entered the room. The doctor switched on the lights. Bishu Pal was lying on the bed wrapped in a blanket. He said in a low voice, "what do you want? Doctor, why are there so many people here?

Doctor Rakshit bowed to his bedside and said, "This is the police doctor and wants to examine you. Bishu Pal's voice became sharper, "Why? Why does the police doctor want to examine me?"
Doctor Rakshit said in a low voice, "Abhay Ghosal has been murdered, hence your examination."

Bishu Pal's throat trembled, "Who has been murdered! What did you say, doctor?
The doctor said again, "Abhay Ghosal has been murdered.
Bishu Pal's face glowed with relief! After a moment, his face became dark again, he said in astonishment, "Abhay Ghosal has been murdered! But I lent him thirty thousand rupees, the interest-actually stands at thirty-three thousand. What will happen to my money?

Doctor Rakshit said bluntly, "Think about the money later. Now they have come to check whether you are really paralyzed or are you faking it?"
What do you mean? Bishu Pal turned his sharp eyes and looked at us.

Rama Pati babu went to the edge of the bed and calmly said, "Look, we don't have any personal agenda, our doctor just wants to examine you. Do you have any objection?
What's the objection! Can the police doctor can cure my disability?
Sushil babu said, "I can give it a try."

After few more questions and answers, Bishu Pal agreed. Sushil babu started the inspection by removing the blanket from his body. Bishu Pal's legs were numb from paralysis, but his upper body was active. Sushil babu poked a needle in Bishu Pal's feet but did not get any response. Then he inspected in many ways; He checked the pulse, checked the blood pressure, asked Doctor Rakshit various questions. Finally, he let a deep sigh and wrapped the blanket around Bishu babu.

At one point during his examination my gaze was directed inwards and I saw Bishu babu's wife looking at her husband with wide open eyes. Her anxiety was not normal anxiety, but an anxiety full of fear.

Sushil babu said, "I have inspected him, now we can leave."
As we turned towards the door we heard Bishu Pal's voice, "will my paralysis be cured?"
Sushil babu turned around and said, your paralysis can be cured, your doctor is doing a good job.

On the way back home in the police car, Byomkesh asked, "Then the disability is real, not acting?"
Sushil Babu said, "No, not acting, He is paralysed for sure."

The entire day byomkesh laid on the dewan and stared at the roof smoking numerous cigarettes. When tea was served in afternoon, he still didn't get up. What are you thinking about so much? The police have not asked you to investigate the murder of Abhay Ghosal. He said, "Not thinking, Ajit, it's the sting of conscience." Then he suddenly got up and went into the next room. I heard him talking to someone over the phone. When he came back after a few minutes later, I saw that his face was brimming with enthusiasm.

Whom did you call?
Dr. Asim Sen.
We had met Dr. Asim Sen during the course of another case.
Byomkesh gulped down his tea and said, "Come on we need to go somewhere."
But where?
Bishu Pal's house.

At Bishu Pal's house, the clerks are coming down the stairs after finishing the day's work. Doctor Rakshit was sitting in his chambers smoking a cigarette with his feet rested on the table. when he saw us, he hurriedly lowered his feet.
Byomkesh said, "I see you have no patient. Let us go upstairs, I need to speak to Bishu Babu and ask him some questions. The doctor looked at Byomkesh and said," sure let's go." We reached the second floor; the Gurkha was nowhere to be seen and the Bishu babu's room door was

ajar. We entered the room there was no need to turn on the light as the room was well lit with the light coming through the open windows. Bishu Pal's death scare was over. He was half-asleep on the bed with a few pillows under his back, he turned his head on hearing our footsteps.

Byomkesh went to the side of the bed and for a while looked at Bishu Pal's face, then slowly said, "You have played a great game. Bishu Pal stared at Byomkesh like an owl. Byomkesh clenched his teeth and said, "You dragged the doctor into your team, because without the doctor, you would not have succeeded. But why did you pull me into the team? Because I will testify on your behalf?

The doctor had been behind us till now, he leaped forward and said in a loud voice, "what are you talking about! Why are you defaming me? Byomkesh looked towards Doctor Rakshit like an injured lion and said, have you heard of a drug named Procaine?"

The doctor went silent like a burst balloon. Byomkesh stared at him for a while longer and then turned to Bishu Pal. He took out a hundred rupee note from his pocket and threw it on the bed and said, "Here is your money. I can get both of you hanged for this crime, don't forget that. If we Keep you in jail for two days all your paralysis will wean away.

Bishu Pal almost cried, 'Byomkesh babu, please forgive me, I did it to save my life.
Byomkesh said, "Mercy only on one condition! You have to donate one lakh rupees to the defense fund. Are you ready?
Bishu Pal said in a low voice, 'one lakh rupees!
Yes, one lakh rupees, not one paisa less. Tomorrow morning you will deposit one lakh rupees in the reserve bank and send the receipt to me. If you don't deposit the money, then!"
"Okay, okay, I will give one lakh rupees."
Remember, I will wait only till 12 o'clock tomorrow to receive the receipt of reserve bank. Let's go Ajit.

Back home and after drinking a round of tea, I was thinking, donating one lakh rupees to the defense fund is very good act indeed, but why did Byomkesh let go of the murderers of Abhay Ghosal.

Byomkesh felt that he could understand my thoughts by seeing my mood; he said, there was no way without letting Bishu Pal walk free. Even if the case went to court, he would have been released. No one would have believed the motive of the murder.

I said, "But the motive is pure. Looking from Bishu Pal's side, his motive is pure, he killed Abhay Ghosal to save his own life. But the jury wouldn't believe it, they would have laughed it off.
Well, tell me one thing. Killing in self-defense is not a crime, the law says so. Then what crime did Bishu Pal commit by killing Abhay Ghosal.

People have the right to kill in self-defense, but if they commit murder after three months of conspiracy the law will not accept it. Bishu Pal knew that, so he carefully planned everything immaculately.
I understand. But still tell me the entire story.

Byomkesh then began to speak, we saw Abhay Ghosal yesterday. He had a smile on his face, but the cruelty of an executioner in his eyes. The man is a murderer. What we have heard about him is not a lie. Bishu Pal was mesmerized with his sweet talk and loaned him thirty thousand rupees. Then when the time came to repay the loan, Abhay Ghosal was nowhere to be seen.

Bishu Pal did not know Abhay Ghosal well at that time, he went to his house one day and abused him so that he can recover his loan. Abhay Ghosal did not say a word, just stared at Bishu Pal. Bishu Pal got scared seeing his deadly stare. He realized what kind of a person Abhay Ghosal was; he had killed before, now he will kill him.

Bishu Pal is also shrewd. When he realized that Abhay Ghosal would definitely kill him, he decided to kill Abhay Ghosal first. He was not afraid of losing his money because Abhay Ghosal has a house which can be auctioned to retrieve his loan. Bishu Pal had an advantage, he knew that Abhay Ghosal wanted to kill him, but Abhay Ghosal was not aware that Bishu Pal also wanted to kill him. Hence Abhay Ghosal did not take any precautions.

Bishu Pal stopped coming out of the house. He deployed a Gurkha at his doorsteps. Then Bishu Pal sat down to draw a plan to kill Abhay Ghosal. Doctor Suresh Rakshit is his tenant on the ground floor. It is evident that his practice was not doing good. He was unable to pay the house rent and been a debtor to Bishu Pal. Bishu Pal called him and told him his plan. Being a debtor is like having a noose around the neck hence he agreed.

Bishu Pal bought new furniture and arranged the doctor's dispensary, so that it seems that Dr Rakshit is a good doctor and has a good practice., he has a lot of money. Then Bishu Pal started his faking his paralysis. These days medical science has improved a lot. Earlier, chloroform had to be given to make the patient unconscious for operation now it is no longer necessary. Drugs like procaine are available in the market which when injected into the spinal cord, numbs the body and then the operation on that part of the body can be done comfortably, and the patient does not feel any pain.

Dr. Rakshit did so, Bishu Pal's legs became numb. Then a famous doctor was called who diagnosed Bishu Pal with paralysis. The effects of Procaine drug last for five to six hours. Then no more. But outsiders don't know this, only Bishu Pal's wife and doctor Rakshit know. The clerks come to the work on the first floor they came to know that the owner is paralyzed. No one apart from his wife and doctor Rakshit were not allowed to enter the room. No one had a clue that Bishu babu was faking his paralysis.

But Bishu Pal is a shrew man, to make his story more believable he needed an impartial witness; he wanted a witness whom no one would disbelieve. Yesterday morning he send the doctor at our place so that we could visit him and help strengthen his lie. I agreed to go. The doctor gave Bishu babu an injection of procaine at around one in the afternoon.

We went at five o'clock and found Bishu Pal lying in bed, powerless. He told me about his grief, then sent me away with a hundred rupees as my consulting fee. His intention was to kill Abhay last night. Doctor Rakshit told Bishu babu that we had taken Abhay's address. He thought if we would stay at Abhay's place till late at night then his plan would be ruined hence, he sent Doctor Rakshit to keep an eye on us.

The Doctor kept an eye on us and waited in front of Abhay Ghosal's house in taxi and when he saw us exit Abhay's place, he sped away in the taxi. By seven o'clock in the evening, the effects of procaine waned away from Bishu Pal's body, and he gained mobility. One Gurkha leaves at eight o'clock, the second Gurkha arrives at ten o'clock. Bishu Pal came out of the house at around nine, wrapped in a shawl and a knife in his hand. For the past three months, he had been keeping a track of Abhay Ghosal's movements at home. There is no one but a young maid. Abhay Ghosal goes to sleep after having dinner at nine in the evening. The front door is not bolted, the maid seems to bolt the front door after completing the kitchen work at around ten in the night. So, there was no problem for Bishu Pal.

After killing Abhay Ghosal, he returned to his house before ten o'clock; No one did know anything. if someone had seen him, it still would have been difficult to break Bishu Pal's alibi. Can a person who is bedridden with paralysis for three months just hop off to kill someone? Where is the motive to kill?

This morning Bishu Pal took another injection. He had to be careful cause he had suspected that the police doctor might examine him. We went with the police-doctor. The police-doctor examined and found that he was indeed suffering from paralysis. I had a lingering doubt in my mind from the very first day. Why would a usurious moneylender spend a hundred rupees just to tell me his woeful tale? That was where Bishu Pal made a grave mistake. Then this morning when I read the news of Abhay Ghosal's death in the papers, there was no doubt in my mind that it was Bishu Pal who caused Abhay Ghosal's death. But how?

I had three suspects: Bishu Pal himself, his wife and Doctor Rakshit. Doctor Rakshit is a debtor to Bishu Pal, he can help Bishu Pal indirectly, but will he kill with his own hands? I don't believe so.
Bishu Pal's wife is a woman, she can poison Abhay Ghosal to save her husband, but it is not possible for her to go that far and wield a knife. The knife is not a woman's weapon. Only Bishu Pal remained, but he is crippled by paralysis.

I left both the Gurkha's out of my list of suspects at the very beginning. They are not averse to killing animals and they can wield a knife as well. But Bishu Pal is not an idiot that he will ask the Gurkhas to kill Abhay Ghosal. Gurkhas are very simple and honest and will blabber away the truth if caught.

Suddenly the real manipulation flashed in front of my eyes. If I had knowledge of medical science, I would have understood long ago. Bishu Pal's paralysis is not true paralysis, but a temporary paralysis, created by medical procedures.

I called Dr. Asim Sen in the afternoon. He is a senior doctor, he explained to me that by using a drug procaine temporary paralysis can be set in.

I have just one grief, that along with Bishu Pal I have to pardon Doctor Rakshit as well, being a doctor, he should never have been accessory to such a crime. He does not deserve mercy for what he has done. However, one lakh rupees donation in the defense fund is not bad. Is it?

Heyalir Chonde

(Cryptic Story)

Byomkesh went to Cuttack on official work, I also went along with him there. After spending two days in Cuttack, we realised that based on the mountain of documents of the government offices it would take much longer to uncover the truth. Then Byomkesh decided to stay in Cuttack while I came back to Kolkata as a male member is required for managing the day-to-day life of a Bengali household.

Since coming to Calcutta I am sitting idle. Byomkesh is not here; without him I feel a little helpless. Winter is setting in; the days are getting shorter; still am not able to pass my time. Sometimes I go to our publishing house, supervise Prabhat's work, read new manuscripts from bussing writers, but still, I have enough idle time.

Then suddenly an opportunity arose to spend my evenings Our building has three floors. We live in the top floor occupying all the five rooms. The middle floor houses a hostel where ten or twelve working men are staying. The ground floor houses the manager's office, storeroom, kitchen, dining room. Only one gentleman lives on the ground floor in a corner room. We are familiar with all residents, but not particularly close.

That evening, I was sitting reading a magazine, there was a knock at the door. I opened the door and saw a middle-aged gentleman standing with a polite smile. I have seen him on the first floor of the house a couple of times before, he has been living in the mess for some time. He occupies an entire room on the first-floor hostel. He is a fashionable man and was wearing a silk kurta and pajama along with a Jawahar coat. He had a head full of hair.

After bowing, he said, "Sorry to bother you, my name is Bhupesh Chatterjee, I live on the first floor.

I said, "I have seen you several times. I didn't know your name. Come on inside.
He came inside and said, "It's been a month and a half since I came to Calcutta. I work in an insurance company; I have to travel around a lot for my work." I get transferred a lot due to my work profile.
I felt a little uncomfortable and said, "You work in an insurance company!" But I've never got a life insurance, and I don't plan get one.

He laughed and said, "No, that's not what I came for. I work in the office of an insurance company but I'm not a broker. I came to... He paused a little and said, "I'm addicted to playing bridge. I could not play since I came here. I found two gentlemen to play bridge with great difficulty. They live in room number three on the first floor. But couldn't find the fourth person yet to make a complete team. We spent a few days playing cutthroat bridge, but that is nothing like playing real bridge. Today I came here because I wondered if Ajit Babu would like to play bridge.

At one time I was fond of playing bridge. Not a hobby, but a heavy addiction. I haven't played for along time, and hence the addiction has died. I thought it is better to play bridge than spending the evening alone reading a dull magazine.

I said, "Sure would love to become your bridge playing partner, but I have lost touch with the game because I have not played for a while. Bhupesh babu said, then there is no point in wasting time, "Let's go to my room, I have already set up my room for playing bridge."

I said, I will join you in a while after having tea.
I smiled at his enthusiasm. At one time, I was also so addicted to playing bridge in the evenings, that one day without playing bridge seemed to be a day wasted.
I went downstairs with Bhupesh babu after informing Satyawati.

Bhupesh babu's room is the first room on the first floor right next to the stairs. Bhupesh babu stood near his door and shouted, "Ram babu, Banamali babu, come. I have brought Ajit babu today to play bridge."

Two faces appeared from the third room in the gallery and disappeared in an instant saying "I'm coming." Bhupesh babu took me into his room and switched on the lights.

Bhupesh babu's room is quite spacious. There are Two mullioned windows on the two walls. There was a bed on one side of the room, On the other side, on top of an empty almirah was kept a gleaming stove, tea equipment, etc. In the center of the room lay a low table surrounded by four chairs, clearly meant for playing cards. Apart from this, the room has a dressing table, a chest of drawers and other small furniture. The room clearly showed that Bhupesh babu has a taste for luxury.

Bhupesh babu sat me on the chair and said, "Let me prepare tea, it will be ready in five minutes. He lit the stove and boiled the water. Meanwhile Ram babu and Banmali babu came and sat inside.

Although I knew Ram babu and Banamali babu still Bhupesh babu introduced them to me.
"This is Ramchandra Roy, and this is Banmali Chanda, both live in the same room and work in the same bank.

I noticed; they have various similarities. I had never seen them together hence guess I didn't notice the similarities. Both were between forty-five and fifty years of age, both were stocky and medium built. Both had similar facial features, thick nose, sparse eyebrows, broad chin. The similarity is clearly genetic. I wanted to surprise them. After all I am a friend of Byomkesh.

I said, "Are you both maternal brothers? Both of them looked surprised and said No. Ram babu said rudely, 'No. I am Vaidya while Banamali babu is Kayastha. I felt awkward. I was trying to give an explanation for my act when Bhupesh Babu brought a plate of Samosa on the table and rescued me. Then came the tea. After finishing the tea party quickly, we sat down to play bridge.

The topic of maternal brother got suppressed. Sitting in the game, I realised that I have not forgotten the skill of playing bridge. I was still good at playing and calling in bridge. We started playing with small bets.

The bet amount was very negligible and also without bets the game would not remain interesting.

Ram babu and I became partners in the first rubber. Ram babu lighted a thick cigar, Bhupesh babu and I lit a cigarette, Banmali babu only put betel nut and cloves in his mouth and then the game started. When a rubber would end, the cards would be shuffled, the partner pair was changed, and the game continued. All three are good players; There was not much conversation, everyone's mind was occupied with the game. Only cigarettes and cigars keep burning. Bhupesh Babu once got up, opened the window and sat quietly.

When the game was over, it was nine o'clock at night. The hostel servant had come twice asking for us to have dinner. We tallied the accounts of the game and I realised that I had won two annas.
I pocketed my winning and got up. Bhupesh babu asked with a smile, "Will we have a game again tomorrow?" I said, why not.
I came up home and was admonished by Satyawati. It was already quarter past nine and in winters that is quite late. But after a long time, my heart was full after playing bridge, I gave no heed to Satyawati's admonishments.

From then on, we started playing bridge almost all evenings. We would sit for a game as soon as it was evening, and the game lasted until nine at night. In the last five or six days I have made few observations and formed my opinion of these three men. Bhupesh babu was a kind hospitable person, fond of playing bridge. Ram babu is of serious nature; does not speak much, doesn't argue when someone makes a mistake in the game. Banamali babu respects Ram babu very much, tries to emulate him, but can't. Both are men of few words; deeply addicted to playing cards. Both have a slight East Bengal accent in their speech.

We played bridge in peace for 6 straight days, playing bridge and gossiping in the evening became a part of our daily lives. But this enjoyment and happiness was short lived, an incident happened in ground floor that wrecked our enjoyment. The sole resident on the ground floor i.e., Natbar Naskar was suddenly murdered one day. We have no relations with Natbar Naskar, but as he lived in the same building his sudden death wrecked our lives as well.

That day, at half past six, I put on a shawl and went out to join our bridge club. I was running a bit late, so I hurried down the stairs. When I reached the last step, I heard a loud sound and was startled. I couldn't figure out where the sound came from. Some car motor may have backfired on the road, but the noise was very loud.

I stood still for a while, then I got down again and entered Bhupesh babu's room. I saw Bhupesh babu was peeking out of the window and trying to figure out something. Ram babu and Banamali babu were standing behind Bhupesh babu and were also trying to look out of the window. When I entered, Bhupesh babu was saying in an excited voice, Look, look there, he ran out of the street, did you see Him? He was wearing a light brown color shawl.
I asked from behind, "What's the matter?"

All three turned inwards and looked at me. Bhupesh babu said, "Did you hear the sound? It came from the alley below. As I opened the window, I heard a loud bang from near the window in the alley below, I saw a man wrapped in a brown shawl exit the street hurriedly.

Our house is on the main road. A brick-paved narrow lane runs along the side of the house connecting the main street with our building's rear door. The servants of the house usually use this narrow lane. I felt something fishy. I said, "A gentleman lives in the room below this room. Did the sound come from his rooms?

Bhupesh babu said, "Maybe, it's possible?" There is a gentleman who lives in the room beneath mine, but I don't know his name.
Ram babu and Banamali babu looked at each other, then Ram babu cleared his throat and said,"Natbar Naskar lives in the lower room.
I said, "Let's go. If he is at home, he can tell what the noise is all about.

These three men were not particularly interested to go, but I am a friend of the truth-seeker Byomkesh why should I leave without searching for the source of the loud boom? I said, "Let's go, let's go, once we see it, we can come and start our game." If the sound was a normal sound, it wouldn't have mattered, but what if a man came down the street and threw firecrackers or bombs in Natbar babu's house? It is necessary to investigate this matter.

Reluctantly, the three followed me Downstairs. Manager Shiv kali babu's office was locked, the door to the storeroom was also closed, the dining-room was empty only Natbar babu's door was not locked from the outside. So, there is high probability that he is in his rooms. I called, 'Natbar babu." There was No response. I called out his name again loudly, still there was no response. Then I slowly pushed the door open. The door was ajar. The room was dark, nothing could be seen; a faint smell came to my nose. The smell of gunpowder, we exchanged glances.

Bhupesh babu said, "There must be a light switch next to the door. Wait, let me switch it on." He pushed me away and peered into the room, then reached out to find the light switch. After a click sound, the light flickered on.

The first thing that caught my eye in the room was Natbar babu's dead body. He was lying in the middle of the room with his arms and legs spread out; he wore a white sweater and a dhoti. Dark blood dripped from the sweater's chest. Natbar Naskar was not a handsome man by any means, he was fat guy with a heavy ugly face full of scars. But post death his face looks even more scarier. I will not describe the horror of his face. The fear of death is such an ugly emotion that can be understood by looking at the face of a dead body.

We froze for a while, Ram babu made a sound like hiccups in his throat. I saw him staring at the dead body with eyes filled with disbelief. Banmali Babu suddenly grabbed one of his hands and said in a low voice, "Dada, Natbar Naskar is dead." I could not understand was his expression of sadness or surprise or joy. Bhupesh babu said, "There is no doubt that he is dead. Dead by gunshot. Look there at the window sill.

A mullioned window stands open, a pistol on its sill. The picture became crystal clear, standing in the alley outside the window, the assailant shot Natbar Naskar, then left the pistol on the window sill. At this moment, I heard footsteps behind me and turned my back. Hostel manager Shiv kali Chakraborty had arrived. He had a very thin physique, his eyesight unreasonably confused. He came to us and said, "You people are here?" What happened here? what happened?" I said, "See with your own eyes." We stood aside for him to see what had occurred. Shiv kali Babu saw the bloody corpse and exclaimed, "Oh God! What is this? Natbar

Naskar's been murdered. Blood, blood everywhere! Oh my God!" How did he die?
I pointed my finger towards the window and said, "You will understand if you look there."

On seeing the pistol, Shiv kali Babu said again, "Ah, pistol Natbar babu was killed by the pistol! Who killed him? When was he killed?
I said, "We done know who killed him, but he was killed just five minutes ago." We Briefly explained the situation to him. He looked at the dead body with dismay. I didn't notice it for a long time, but suddenly realised that Shiv kali babu was wearing a brown shawl. After suppressing my palpitations, I said, "Were you at home or did you go out?
He said, "Well, I went out for work. But but, what needs to done now. What should we do?"
Our first duty is to inform the police.
Shiv kali babu said, "That's right, that's right. But I don't have a telephone, Ajit babu, you have a telephone, if you can please call the police. I said, "I am calling the police now. But you don't enter the room please stand here itself until the police comes.
I came up quickly. On entering the room, I saw my reflection in the mirror, I realised I was also wearing a brown shawl.

I was acquainted with Pranab Guha, the inspector of our area. An able old man, but he was not pleased with Byomkesh. Of course, his displeasure was not expressed through any harshness. He spoke to Byomkesh with extra respect and laughed a little at the end of the speech. Both byomkesh and Pranab were from separate school of thoughts. Pranab babu did not like an outsider like byomkesh meddling in government affairs.

After listening to my message on the phone, he said sarcastically, "What did you say! A murder under the very roof of the truth seeker! Why do you need me when byomkesh is there? He himself can do the investigation."
Annoyed, I said, "Byomkesh is not in Calcutta, but he would have investigated if he were here?"
Pranab Babu said, "Well, well, then I am coming." He chuckled and hung up the phone.
I went downstairs again.

Half an hour later, Pranab Babu came with his team. He smiled when he saw me then he took a hard look at the dead body. He walked up to the window and discovered the pistol; he wrapped the same in a handkerchief and put it in his pockets. The dead body was taken for postmortem, Pranab babu sat in the lone chair kept in the room and started his interrogation.

I told everything what I knew. The statements of all the rest are summarised below –

Manager Shiv kali babu is a celibate man, meaning unmarried. He has been running this hostel for the past twenty-five years. Natbar Naskar has been staying in this hostel since the last three years. His age is estimated to be fifty years and he did not have much acquaintance with anyone. Ram babu and Banamali babu used to visit him sometimes in his room. Shiv kali babu had no issues with Natbar because he used to deposit the hostel dues on the first day of every month. Shiv kali babu got news this afternoon that in a warehouse cheap Potatoes were available, so he went to buy potatoes. But the potatoes had already been sold, so he returned empty- handed.

Bhupesh babu works in an insurance company and has been staying in this hostel for the past one and a half months since he got transferred to Calcutta. He is about forty-five years of age, and a childless widower. He has no place to call home, he travels throughout the country related to work affairs. He told the police accurately the events of the card game and the events of the evening, also mentioning having seen a man wearing a brown shawl hurriedly exiting the narrow lane post the loud boom sound. He could not see the man's face well; the face of a moving man cannot be seen from behind; in the future it is unlikely that he will be able to recognize him.

Ramchandra Roy and Banamali Chand's statements are almost alike. I noticed that although Ram Babu replied slowly, Banmali Babu was a bit rattled. They were previously residing in Dhaka and working together in a foreign company. During the uproar of the division of the country, all their family was killed, and they fled with great difficulty. Ram babu's age is forty-eight, Banamali babu's age is forty-five. Since the last three years they are residing in this hostel in Calcutta and work in the same bank.

They have a hobby of playing bridge, but after coming to Calcutta they did not get a chance to play.

A few days ago, Bhupesh Babu arranged to play bridge in his room, since then they were playing bridge every evening. Then today, five minutes after they entered Bhupesh babu's house there was a sudden loud noise in the street! They knew Natbar Babu from Dhaka but did not have much acquaintance. Natbar babu used to do various brokerage work in Dhaka. As they used to stay in the same hostel and knew each other from before hence they used to have an occasional chat in Natbar babu's room. They were not aware if Natbar babu had any other friends. They had seen a man in a brown shawl hurriedly exiting the alley for a blink in the evening light, and if they saw him again, they would not be able recognize him.

The others in the hostel could not say anything about this incident. At the other end of the second floor, few people were sitting in a room playing dice. Four players and a few spectators were present there; they did not hear gunshot. Although they had seen Natbar babu but hardly had any acquaintance.

Only Hostel staff Hari pada said something that could be either important or meaningless. He said that around six in the evening Suren Babu from the first floor had asked him to bring some potato savouries from the market. When Hari pada returned from the market and entered the building through the rear gate, he heard someone speaking to Natbar babu in a low voice in his room. Natbar babu's room door was bolted hence he could not see who was inside, nor could he recognise his voice. Since no one visits Natbar babu hence this caught his attention.

This means someone visited Natbar babu's room half an hour before his death, it was an outsider because no one in the building admitted that they had gone to Natbar babu's room. Maybe the man in the brown shawl or anyone else. Nothing concrete could be figured out from Hari pada's statement.

After everyone's written statement was taken, Pranab Daroga said, "You can all go now we will now search the entire building. Yes, I must inform

you Ajit babu and Shiv kali babu, that until we solve this case both of will not try to go out of Calcutta without my permission.
Surprised, I said, "But why?"
Pranab Daroga said, "because both you and Shiv kali babu are wearing a brown-coloured shawl. He smiled and shut the door in our faces.

We came back to our respective rooms. We didn't feel like playing cards. The next day passed uneventfully. There is no response from Pranab Daroga. He had searched Natbar babu's house last night, locked the door and left with some documents. The man is hostile towards us; But he expresses hatred so sweetly that there is nothing to say. He knows that I have an irrevocable alibi, but he ignored me and imposed a ban on me from leaving Calcutta! I am a friend of Byomkesh, so his only intention is to harass me.

In the morning, everyone went to their work. No one was least affected by the fact that a resident staying for over three years was murdered by a gunshot. no one had any regrets. Everyone had accepted the fact that you are born to die, it's inevitable.

In the evening I went to Bhupesh Babu's house, Ram babu and Banamali babu were already present. Everyone was a little dull. No one mentioned the game today. While drinking tea we discussed the death of Natbar Naskar and condemning the inaction of the police.

An idea came to mind while climbing up the stairs. Pranab Daroga does not have the skill to be able to find the killer of Natbar Babu. Byomkesh is not here, and the cards games won't resume soon, if I write down this incident then I can keep busy and not spend time idly. When Byomkesh comes back and reads my writing, he can maybe solve the murder.

Same night I sat down to write. I started writing in such a way that Byomkesh does not find any flaws, I recorded all the details minutely and also from my point of view, starting from the introduction of the incident. The writing was finished by the next afternoon. The writing is over, but the story is not over. When and where will Natbar babu's murder story end, no one knows. Maybe we will never find the murderer. I was slightly dissatisfied at the turn of events and lighted a cigarette, when I heard footsteps on our stairs. Suddenly the door was thrown open and entered Byomkesh.

I jumped up in joy, "Hey! You are back! Your work is finished?"
Byomkesh said, the work has not started yet. There is a quarrel in two departments of the government. First, let them sort out their internal issues, then only I will be going.

Satyawati could hear Byomkesh's voice from inside and came running to greet him. Their married life is not new, but whenever Byomkesh comes from outstation, Satyawati's eyes light up with joy. When the turn of marriage reconciliation was over, I brought up the important topic and let byomkesh read my notes. Byomkesh read the text while sipping tea.

At six o'clock in the evening, he returned the notes to me and said, "Pranab Daroga has put you under city arrest." The man hates me from the core of his heart! We will go and meet him tomorrow, now let's go and talk to Bhupesh babu. I understood that Byomkesh is attracted to this mystery. I said happily, "Let's go." We may meet Ram babu and Banamali babu also.

I took Byomkesh to Bhupesh babu's room on the second floor. My guess was correct, Ram babu and Banamali babu were also present. I did not have to introduce Byomkesh, as everyone was familiar with him. Bhupesh Babu greeted Byomkesh with respect and asked us to be seated. Ram babu's anger remained unwavering, but Banamali babu's eyes began to wander around in tension.

Byomkesh sat down on a chair and said, "I was also addicted to bridge once but then Ajit taught him to play chess. But now I don't enjoy these games anymore.
Bhupesh babu turned back to him as he was preparing tea and said, "Now I only play the game of death."
Byomkesh said, "yes you are right. After playing with death all my life, I have reached such a stage that I can no longer play such light games."

Bhupesh babu said, " I also deal with death. I am in insurance business, what else can you call but the business of death? But I still love playing bridge.
Although Byomkesh was talking to Bhupesh babu, but his eyes were following Ram babu's and Banamali Babu because they were completely uninterested in such enriching talk.

Bhupesh babu placed a cup of tea and a cream crackers in front of him. Byomkesh said thoughtfully, "You too are a man of individual nature. Bridge is a game for the intelligent, naturally intelligent gravitate to this game. Some play cards in the hope of a momentary escape from the trappings of life. I knew a man long ago who used to play bridge to mourn the loss of his son.
The eyes of all three turned to Byomkesh, as if they were robots. No one said a word but looked in amazement and drank tea in silence. Then Byomkesh wiped his face with a handkerchief and broke the silence, he said "I had gone to Cuttack. I returned today in the afternoon. As soon as I returned, Ajit informed about Natbar Babu's unfortunate death. Although I had no acquaintance with him still, I was intrigued at someone being murdered in our building. So, I thought I would talk to you.

Bhupesh babu said, "Fortunately due to the murder we have this opportunity to meet and talk to you. But I do not know anything about Natbar Naskar, I did not even see when he was alive. He had little acquaintance with Ram babu and Banamali babu though.

Byomkesh looked at Ram babu's face. Ram babu's face seemed to look tense, he wanted to say something but didn't. Byomkesh then turned his eyes to Banamali babu and said, 'You must know what kind of person Natbar babu was?

Banamali babu said, he was quite a good man but, by this time Ram babu regained his speech, he cut short Banamali babu and said, Look, we were not very close with Natbar babu. But when we were in Dhaka, Natbar babu used to live next door hence his face was familiar to us though we don't know anything about his character.

Byomkesh asked, "How long ago were you in Dhaka?
Ram babu took a gulp and said, 'Five-six years ago. Then the partition riots started, and we fled to West Bengal.
Byomkesh asked Banamali babu, "You two used to work in the same office in Dhaka I believe?"
Banamali babu said, "Yes. Ever heard the name of Godfrey Brown Company, It's a big multinational Company. We were working there. Even before he finished speaking, Ram babu immediately stood up and said,

"Banamali! Remember today we have to visit Narayan Babu at seven in the evening? today we will take your leave. Both Banamali and Ram babu quickly exited the room. Byomkesh turned his head and watched their hurried departure.

Bhupesh babu smiled lightly. He said, "Byomkesh babu, your questions were very innocent but Ram babu took offence, I guess.
Byomkesh said, "I didn't understand why it hurt him." Do You know something regarding them?
Bhupesh babu shook his head and said, "I don't know anything. I was in Dhaka during the riots, but I did not know them at that time, nor do I know anything about their past.
You were also in Dhaka during the riots.
Yes. I was transferred to Dhaka a year before the riots. I came back after the partition of the country.

There was no conversation for a while. Byomkesh lit a cigarette.
Bhupesh babu asked, "Byomkesh babu, the story you told, that a man started playing bridge in bereavement of the death of his son, is that a true story?

Byomkesh said, "Yes, a true story. Long ago when I was still studying in college. Why do you ask? Bhupesh babu did not answer, got up and brought a photograph from the desk and handed it to byomkesh. The photo was of a nine-ten-year-old boy; the face of the child was very innocent. Bhupesh babu said in a heavy voice, "This is my Boy."
Byomkesh looked at Bhupesh babu and said, But I knew you are a widower and childless?

Bhupesh babu shook his head, "He is Dead." He went to school the day the riots started in Dhaka and never came back from school.
Byomkesh broke the awkward silence and asked loudly, "Your wife?"
Bhupesh babu said, "She is also dead. Her heart was weak, could not bear the grief of her son's death. I didn't die, I couldn't forget them either. Five or six years have passed, the grief should have subsided by now, but it hasn't. I work, play cards, laugh, and play, but I can't forget them. Byomkesh babu is there any medicine to erase the memory of grief.
Byomkesh took a deep breath and said, "The only medicine is Death."

Next morning, while drinking tea, Byomkesh said, "Let's go and visit Shrimad Pranab Ananda Swami. Hearing the tragedy of Bhupesh babu's life last night, I was a little sad. On hearing that we are going to visit Pranab daroga I asked, is it really necessary to visit Pranab daroga today?
Byomkesh said, 'If you don't want to be free from the suspicion of the police, then there is no need.

At half past nine, I went down the stairs to the second floor and saw Bhupesh babu's door was locked. He must have gone to office. Ram babu and Banamali babu were coming out of their room, dressed in office going clothes, they saw us and entered the room again. Byomkesh looked at me and gave a wicked smile.

Shiv Kali babu was sitting in the office on the lower floor and looking at the account books. As soon as he saw Byomkesh, he rushed to him and asked, "when did you return from Cuttack? Have you heard of Natbar Naskar's murder? The police are dragging me into this case."
Byomkesh said, "Not only you, but Ajit too.
"Yes, yes. Brown shawl and what not! They don't have any clues hence are targeting us." Please help.

After exiting the building Byomkesh said, Let's inspect the narrow lane. He meant the lane right next to our building, the lane through which the man hurriedly escaped wearing a brown shawl after having shot Natbar babu. It is a very narrow lane, two people cannot walk side by side. We first entered the back lane; Byomkesh walked slowly, keeping his eyes on the surroundings. I don't know what's on his mind, but after three days no trace of the killer will be found.

The window of Natbar babu's room is closed. Byomkesh went there and cast a searching eye on the surroundings. The window is four feet above the street, and if the panes are open, one can easily stand in the street and shoot into the room comfortably.

What's that stain said Byomkesh. I followed his fingers directions, and I saw, just below the window, on the brick-paved floor, a pale-colored stain; A star-shaped spot three inches in diameter. Sometimes there is dust in the street, but despite the efforts of the cleaners, the stain has not been removed. The stain looks two or three days old.

I said, "What about this stain? Byomkesh didn't answer. Suddenly, byomkesh laid on the street and started smelling the stain.

Jokingly, I said, "Why are you rubbing your nose on the ground."
Byomkesh stood up and said, 'I didn't rub my nose I was sniffing the stain.
You were Sniffing! what it smells like?
If you want to know then go ahead and sniff.
I don't need to.
Then let's go to the police station.
"We went out of the street and walked towards the police station. I caught a glimpse of Byomkesh's face a couple of times, but he didn't tell me what he smelled in the stain.

Pranab Daroga was sitting in his room; He is of good built but only five feet and three inches tall and a dark face. Seeing Byomkesh, his eyes lit up with amazement, then mocking us, he said, "Byomkesh babu! I just got up and saw your face. What a blessing!

Byomkesh said, my luck is no less. You know what the scriptures say if you start your day by seeing a short man. I doubt I will get a rebirth as a human.

Pranab Daroga was startled at Byomkesh's mean words. Byomkesh has always ignored Pranab Daroga's sarcasm but today his mood is different. He is ready to retaliate.
Pranab Daroga said gruffly, "I admit that my face is not bright, but you cannot ridicule me like this." Byomkesh laughed, "I can't help but admit that neither your face nor your brains are bright. Pranab babu's face turned black, he gave a wry smile and said, "Not everyone is bright in face and brains. Do you need anything?"

Byomkesh said, "Indeed there is. First of all, I have brought Ajit along with me as proof that Ajit will not be a fugitive. Be not afraid, I have my eyes over him, he cannot escape from my sight.
Pranab Babu tried to smile in advance. Byomkesh said mercilessly, "I don't know what the Commissioner will say when he hears that you have kept Ajit under city arrest, but I am interested to know his views on the same. There are courts in the country, even a police officer can be punished for interfering with the rights of a common man. Anyways

leaving this aside, my second question is whether you have been able to make any breakthrough about Natbar Naskar's death?"

Pranab Babu wondered if he would give a harsh answer to this question. But realizing that Byomkesh should not be played with in his current state of mind, he said slowly, "Byomkesh babu do you know the population of this Calcutta city?"

Byomkesh said, have never counted it myself but it should be in the vicinity of fifty lakhs.
Pranab Daroga said, suppose it is fifty lakhs, is it easy to catch a person wearing a brown shawl among this half a crore people? Would you be able to catch him Byomkesh Babu?
If I have all the details, I surely can.
Although we cannot tell a common person all details pertained to any case, but for you I will make an exception.

Ok tell me have you found any trace of Natbar Naskar's relatives?
"No. We have advertised in the newspapers, but no one came forward yet.
What are the results of the post-mortem examination?
"The bullet penetrated the chest bone and entered the heart. The ballistic report has confirmed that the bullet matches the pistol that was found on the window sill."
And thing else?
"Natbar Naskar was in good health, but he had signs of cataract in his eyes."
Whom does the pistol belong to?
"It is US military pistol, easily available for purchase on the black market.
Did you find anything from searching his rooms?
"Whatever we found useful is on that table. A diary, five rupees, a bank passbook, and a copy of a court judgment. You can see if you want.
There was a table in the corner of the room, Byomkesh got up and went there, I didn't go. Pranab Daroga is not a good person, if he would have objected an unseemly situation would have arisen. Byomkesh took a look at the diary, the passbook and read the court documents in detail and then he came back.

"Pranab Daroga's evil mind had been raised again by now, he asked mockingly, Whatever I saw, you saw the same. Did you figure out who the killer is?"
Byomkesh said, "Yes, I did."
Pranab Babu raised his eyebrows and said, "What did you say?" You already have figured out who the killer is. You are very smart! If you have figured out who the killer is then pray tell me the name, I will arrest him right away.

Byomkesh said with a firm jaw, "I will not tell you the name of the accused Darogababu; That is my own discovery. You get paid for this job; you have to find out on your own. But I can help a little, you will get a clue if you inspect the narrow lane next to the building.
Pranab Daroga laughed and said, "has the killer left his footprints there?"
No said Byomkesh, He has left much more important mark than footprints. Let me tell you one more thing, I am leaving with Ajit for Cuttack in the next few days, and I dare you to stop me.
Ajit, Let's go.

As we came out of the police station, I asked in an excited voice, "Who is the killer, have you found him." Byomkesh shook his head and said, "I knew before coming to the police station, but Pranab daroga is an adamant fellow. It's not that he doesn't have intelligence, it's the opposite. With his antics he can never catch Natbar Naskar's killer.

I asked, 'Who is Natbar Naskar's killer? A familiar person?
I will tell you later. For now, know this that Natbar Naskar's profession was blackmailing. You go back home; I am going to the office-neighborhood." Godfrey Brown also has a large business in Calcutta, some inquiries must be made at their office. Well, I shall be late in my return." He waved and left while I returned home alone.

Byomkesh returned at half past one. After finishing lunch, he said, "There is some work to be done; In the evening you will go and invite Ram babu, Banamali babu and Bhupesh babu for tea in our room." The meeting will be held in this room.
Sure. But what's the matter! Why did you go to Godfrey Brown's office?

One of the possessions of Natbar Naskar, lying in the police station was a court order. I read the court order and understood that two brothers named Rash Bihari Biswas and Bana Bihari Biswas were working in the Dhaka branch of Godfrey Brown Company in the finance department. They were caught stealing office money and a case was filed against them. Bana Bihari was jailed for two years and Rash Bihari for three years. Natbar Naskar had somehow acquired the judgment of that case. Then I opened his diary and saw that every month he receives eighty rupees from Rash Bihari Biswas and Bana Bihari Biswas. I went to Godfrey Brown's office to check if the theft case is a true story or not. No doubt Natbar was blackmailing them.

But who are Rash Bihari Biswas and Bana Bihari Biswas? Where and how will you find them?
You don't have to look far; they can be found in room number three of this hostel!
What! Ram babu and Banamali babu?
Yes. You guessed close. They are not maternal cousins; they are blood brothers.
But they could not have killed Natbar Naskar, cause when Natbar was killed ---
raising his hands, Byomkesh said, "Be patient. You will hear the rest of the story during our tea party.

Arrangements have been made for guests to be entertained with tea and various types of fried food from the Marwari's shop. Bhupesh babu appeared first wearing Dhoti, kurta with a shawl draped over shoulder, and an eager smile on his face. He said, "Is there an arrangement to play bridge?"
Byomkesh said, "If you want to play, arrangements can be made.
After a while Ram babu and Banamali babu came. They were wearing Collared coats and had a wary look in their eyes.
Byomkesh said, "Come on inside."

Byomkesh started a lively conversation with everyone. After a while, I noticed that Ram babu and Banamali babu's tense expression was wiped away. They joined the conversation with eagerness.

Twenty minutes later, after finishing tea and refreshment, Ram babu lit a cigar; Byomkesh gave Bhupesh babu a cigarette and held the cigarette tin in front of Banamali babu and said, "Please take it, Bana Bihari babu."

Banamali babu said, "Actually, I don't smoke cigarettes. After saying this his face turned very pale. He said my name is---

Byomkesh said, I know the real names of you two brothers Rash Bihari and Bana Bihari Biswas." Byomkesh went to his chair, "Natbar Naskar was blackmailing you. You were paying him eighty rupees every month."

Rash Bihari and Bana Bihari sat frozen like statues. Byomkesh lit a cigarette, puffed out the smoke and said, "Natbar Naskar was a very big devil. When he was in Dhaka he worked as a broker and ran a small blackmailing business. When you two brothers went to jail, he kept copies of court judgments thinking about the future. He did so to extort money from you when you join a new job after getting out of jail.

Then one day the country was divided. Natbar's business did not continue in Dhaka, he fled to Calcutta. But here he hardly knew anyone. He could not start any business whether legal or illegal, he had no one to blackmail as well hence his business collapsed. He came to this hostel and took a room with the little money he could bring along with him.

While staying here, suddenly one day he saw and recognized you. He fetched information about you and realised that you both work in the same bank using a pseudonym. Natbar Naskar found a way to earn good money. Fate put you guys in front of him.

Natbar started blackmailing you, he told you, give money, otherwise he would reveal your real identity to the bank. You started giving him money month after month. The money is not much, only eight rupees per month. But for Natbar, that was enough to pay his rent here. It went on like this for many years. There was no happiness in your life, there was no way to get off his clutches. The only way out was if Natbar was dead.

Byomkesh stopped. There was pin drop silence in the room. Suddenly Bana Bihari started howling and crying. He said, what you say is true, but we did not kill Natbar. We were in Bhupesh babu's house when Natbar died.

That's right! Byomkesh leaned back in his chair and blew smoke upwards, saying nonchalantly, "I don't care who killed Natbar. It's the headache of the police. But you work in a bank and if there is ever a discrepancy in the bank's accounts then I will have to reveal your true identity.

Now Ram babu aka Rash Bihari babu said, "We will not steal banks money. We will not repeat the same mistake we made once."
"Good then I and Ajit will remain silent." Byomkesh looked at Bhupesh babu's and asked, "You Bhupesh babu?"
Bhupesh babu's face was lit with a strange smile, he said softly, "I am silent too. I will not open my mouth about their affairs.

Then the room remained silent for a while. Then Ram babu stood up, folded his hands and said, "I will never forget your kindness in my life." Well, I will go now, am not feeling great."
Byomkesh led them to the door, then closed the door and came back and sat down.
I saw Bhupesh babu looking at Byomkesh and smiling softly. Byomkesh also smiled. Bhupesh babu said, "I didn't know Natbar Naskar was blackmailing Ram babu and Banamali babu. I guess you know the entire truth and have solved the mystery.

Byomkesh took a deep breath and said, "I didn't understand everything, but I understand the crux of the matter.
Bhupesh babu said, "Then you tell the story. If I have anything to add, I will add it later.

Byomkesh handed Bhupesh babu a cigarette, took one himself then looked at me and began to say slowly, "You have written an account of the death of Natbar Naskar. It raised few doubts in my mind. A pistol shot is not so loud. But the sound you heard was more like a bomb bursting. But Natbar died due to a pistol shot.

You noticed the similarity in appearance between Ram babu and Banamali babu. I spoke to them and saw that they were trying to hide something. They used to visit Natbar's house, hence I was curious about them.

But when the gunshot was heard they were both in Bhupesh babu's room on the first floor. The situation in Bhupesh babu's room was very calm and normal. He was in his own room. At five past six Rash bihari and Bana bihari went there to play bridge. But until Ajit comes the card game cannot commence. Two minutes later Ajit's footsteps were heard on the stairs. Bhupesh babu stood up and opened the window facing the street. At that very moment there was a loud boom sound in the lane below. Rash bihari and Bana bihari went to the window. Bhupesh babu shouted, "There, there, see a man is wearing a brown shawl is running out of the lane into the main road.

There was a lot of movement on the main road, lot many people were walking down the road. Rash bihari and Bana bihari looked towards the road and saw several people walking in the main road and many were wearing a shawl. They had no doubt that Bhupesh Babu was speaking the truth. They also thought they had seen a man wearing a brown shawl leaving the alley. This kind of illusion can be created easily.

Later the pistol was found on the window of Natbar's house. Naturally, the question arises why did the assailant drop the pistol? There is no good reason to drop the murder weapon. I suspected that behind this simple picture was a great trickery.
Hostel servant Hari pada had heard someone in Natbar's room in the evening. Had that man killed Natbar? Maybe to create a strong alibi for himself he tricked everyone into believing that the death happened a bit earlier. A difference of fifteen-twenty minutes is not detected in the autopsy.

My firm belief was that whosoever committed the murder is not an outsider, but a member of this hostel. But who? Bhupesh babu? Shiv Kali babu? Rash bihari or Bana bihari babu? Or someone else? I didn't know who had a motive but only Shiv Kali babu has a chance, all others have irrefutable alibi. My mind was clouded, I could not comprehend anything clearly. I noticed that Natbar's room is below Bhupesh babu's room and Natbar's window is below Bhupesh babu's window towards the street. But I didn't consider crackers at all. Yes, crackers. The cracker that makes a sound when the cracker is thrown from a height on the hard floor.

I was going to the police station this morning, hoping to get some fresh updates. While going out, I thought, let's see if I can find any clues near the window of Natbar facing the lane. I got a clue; I saw a stain on the floor beneath Natbar's window. I sniffed the stain and it smelled of gunpowder. The picture became crystal clear to me. All my doubts vanished. A beautiful Alibi has been created. Who had created his alibi? It can be none other than Bhupesh babu because he opened the window himself. Rash bihari and Bana bihari came to the window after hearing the noise.

That eventful evening Bhupesh babu sneakily went to Natbar's room. The pistol had been procured earlier, he entered Natbar's room and introduced himself and shot him. He opened the window facing the street and left the pistol there and returned to his room. Fortunately, no one saw him entering or leaving Natbar's room. But if someone has seen it, then an alibi is necessary. He came to his room and started waiting. Ten minutes later Rash bihari and Bana bihari came to play cards. But Ajit still did not come, so the three started waiting.

Then Bhupesh babu heard the footsteps of Ajit's on the stairs. He was ready, he took a marble-like cracker in his fist and went to open the window on the pretext of the stale air in the room, he opened the window facing the street and immediately threw the cracker out of the window. There was a loud noise below. Rash bihari and Bana bihari ran to the window, Bhupesh babu showed them the imaginary assailant in a brown shawl.

Then Bhupesh babu didn't have to do anything else; As usual, the body was discovered on time. The police came, took the body and left.

Byomkesh went silent. Bhupesh babu had been listening to byomkesh calmly.
Byomkesh looked at Bhupesh babu and said, "Do you want to make any corrections to my story.

Bhupesh babu now sat down, shook his head with a smile and said, 'No, no corrections to be made. All happened exactly as you said. Byomkesh babu, I made only one mistake, I never realised that you would return from Cuttack so soon. I thought by the time you return the case would have been cold and closed by the police.

Byomkesh smiled a little, and said, "Two questions remain unanswered. One, what is your motive?

Two, how did you suppress the sound of the pistol? Even if the pistol is fired in a closed room the sound is likely to escape. Did you not take any precautions in this regard?

I will answer your second question first. Bhupesh babu took the jute shawl from his shoulder and held it in front of us with both hands; I saw that there was a small hole in the shawl. I shot Natbar from inside the shawl; the sound of the bullet was buried it could not come out.

Byomkesh slowly shook his head in agreement. "And the answer to the first question? I guess it is related to your son's photograph which you showed us yesterday. Anyways you continue."

Bhupesh babu's forehead pulsed, but he said calmly, I showed you my son's photo, because I understood that you would eventually find out the truth. Hence, I made my confession beforehand. On the day of the riots in Dhaka, Natbar kidnapped my son away from school. After that evening, he came to my house and said if I give him ten thousand rupees, he will release my son from his clutches. I did not have ten thousand rupees in cash, but I gave him everything I had, my wife took off all her jewelry and gave it to him.

Natbar left with everything, but I did not get my son back. I didn't even get to see Natbar. Then a few years passed, I lost my wife and son and moved to Calcutta, suddenly one day I saw Natbar on the street.

Then Byomkesh said, "Understood. No need to say more, Bhupesh babu remained silent for a while and finally said, "I have taken my revenge you can do whatever you wish to."

Byomkesh remained silent for a while then said, " Natbar was an evil person. God knows how many people's lives has he destroyed. I guess a lot many people are relieved hearing that Natwar is dead cause he was a master blackmailer. I don't think the world will miss such an evil man."

"Be rest assured I will not tell this to the police. It's their duty to apprehend the killer not me. I am a truth seeker and am contained in getting to know the truth."

Khuji Khuji Nari

(Esoteric message)

Byomkesh's has been in acquaintance with Rameshwar babu for the past fifteen years. But in the past fifteen years I doubt whether I have seen him fifteen times. I have not seen him at all in the last five to six years. The fact that he has not forgotten us, I got the proof of the same twice a year. Every year on Bengali new year and Bijoya, he used to send his greetings to Byomkesh.

Rameshwar Babu was a rich man. He had eight or ten houses in Calcutta, and he had huge cash reserves in his banks; Most of the income from the rent of the houses was accumulating in his bank account. His family members included his second wife Kumudini, first son Kusheshwar and his daughter Nalini. He always had an endless flow of humor.

Rameshwar babu was humorous. As he could open his heart and smile, he could also make people laugh. I discovered a natural law through a lifetime of observation, that those who have humor in their souls can never be rich, Maa Lakshmi loves only the serious kind. Rameshwar babu did defy this observation of mine and I realised that this rule is not universal.

Another great quality of Rameshwar Babu was that he never removed from his mind the people whom he became intimately acquainted with. He first met byomkesh over a petty incident involving a burglary at his house. Although the affair had ended in a humorous farce, but he was highly impressed with Byomkesh. We have been invited to his house a few times. He was a little older than us, and his body was falling apart in the past few years. Though in bad health still he was extremely humorous, this was evident from the letters he wrote to us.

Today I am penning the story of Rameshwar Babu's last letter. The incident happened a few years ago; At that time, the law did not recognize the equal rights of daughters in paternal property.

On the first day of baisakh, we received Rameshwar babu's greetings. Thick antique paper envelope, with name and address written in neat handwriting. Byomkesh smiled as he took the envelope. I have noticed that people smile when they remember Rameshwar babu. Byomkesh carefully examined the envelope and said, "Ajit, how old do you guess Rameshwar babu is?

I said, "ninety maybe". Byomkesh said, "Not that much, but eighty for sure. But still, he is not mentally disorientated. His handwriting is also quite clear.

Byomkesh tore the envelope and took out the letter. It was a Double-folded expensive paper with a monogram printed at the top.

Rameshwar babu wrote –

Hey Sea of Intelligence,

Byomkesh babu and Ajit babu please accept my New Year's wishes. May Your intellect grow day by day and may Ajit Babu's get more appreciation as a writer.
It's time now that I should leave for heavenly abode. Yamaraj's summons has arrived, soon the Yamadut's will arrive and take me to Yamraj. Soon I will go to Vaikuntha. My only sorrow is that I will not be able to send you my greetings next Bijoya.
I have prepared my will and allocated my possessions to my dependents. Please see to it that my last wish is fulfilled, and my will properly executed. I have great faith in your intelligence. Farewell. Please do not ignore this letter of mine. I will observe from Vaikuntha whether you received the sum of Rupees five thousand or not.
Yours faithfully,

Shri Rameshwar Ray.

Byomkesh read the letter and sat with furrowed brows. I also read the letter. A man joking about his death, this man has some strong character, but I could not make sense of all the words written at the end of the letter. My last wish to be fulfilled. What wish? We do not know anything of his last wishes, nothing is written in the letter. Then – did you receive five thousand rupees or not. Which five thousand rupees? Was this letter written in humour or else has the man become senile.

Byomkesh suddenly said, "Let's go and see Rameshwar babu tomorrow morning." Don't know which day will be last."
I said, "Okay, let's go. After reading the letter, don't you think that Rameshwar babu's has become senile. Byomkesh remained silent for a while and said, "Did Pitamah Bhisma become senile?

Recently Byomkesh has started reading Ramayana and Mahabharata, and when there is no work at hand, he sits down with the epics. This is nothing to do with his proclivity towards religion or understanding religious literature. There may be other motive of his reading such literature. But sometimes he quotes Ramayana and Mahabharata in his speech.

I said, "Is Rameshwar babu, Pitamah Bhisma?
Byomkesh said, "There is some similarity. But his similarity is more with Dasharatha from Ramayana. I said, "Dasharatha did become senile."
Byomkesh said, "Perhaps he did. It was not due to age, but to his nature. But if Rameshwar babu lives to be a hundred years old, he still would not be senile.

Our knowledge of Rameshwar babu's family situation is very sketchy. He lives in a house of his own in the northern part of Calcutta. His second wife Kumudini is now in her mid-fifties, she is childless. He has named his son from his first wife as Kusheshwar to rhyme with his name Rameshwar. Kusheshwar is also not less than fifty years old and has white hair and bald patches in his head. He is married, but I can't say if he has any children or any property. He looks like a helpless person without any backbone. His younger daughter Nalini fell in love and married someone, Rameshwar babu has no relation with her. His family is not very big, so there is less room for unrest. Rameshwar is very rich and has endless humour. However, it is suspected that his family life is not happy.

I arrived at Rameshwar babu's house at nine o'clock the next day. The house is narrow and long; there was a car standing in front of the door. We knocked on the bolted door. After a while a woman opened the door. She seemed to be expecting someone else so his fierce look softened when he saw us. She covered her hair with the saree and asked us in a low voice, "Whom do you want to meet?"

Although I don't have acquittance with the two women in Rameshwar babu's house, but I have seen them. This was the wife of Kusheshwar; Short stout with a strong built and about forty years of age. Byomkesh said, "My name is Byomkesh Bakshi, I have come to meet Rameshwar babu.

The woman's jawbone hardened; she seemed to have opened his mouth to bid us farewell from the door itself, when the sound of shoes was heard on the stairs. The woman raised her eyes once to look at the stairs, then turned away from the door and entered a room. The room must be the kitchen, because the sound of utensils and cutlery was coming from there.

Two people came down the stairs, one was Kusheshwar, the other person was a well-dressed aged doctor. The doctor said, "The patient is doing well now, presently I don't see any fear. If any issue arises, you can call me.

The doctor went to his car and left. Kusheshwar did not notice that we were standing outside the door. Kusheshwar seems to have grown a larger bald patch. Byomkesh said, I think you don't recognize us, I am Byomkesh Bakshi, and I am here to meet your father.

Kusheshwar was surprised and said, 'Byomkesh Bakshi! Oh, yes, I know. Father's health is not good. Byomkesh said, "What happened?" Kusheshwar said, "He had a sudden heart attack last night. But now he is stable. You want to meet him? He is on the second floor.

I was startled by hearing a loud knocking sound coming from the direction of the kitchen. We all three looked there; An invisible hand from inside the kitchen is tapping the cupboard with tongs. I looked at Kusheshwar and saw that his expression had changed. He cleared his throat and said, "I am afraid you can't meet father; his health is very bad.

The knocking stopped then. Byomkesh smiled a little and said, "Understood." What is the name of the doctor?
Kusheshwar said, "Dr. Asim Sen. Don't you know him? He is a great heart specialist.
I don't know him personally, but I have heard the name. He has his Dispensary on Vivekananda Road, right?
Yes

Then we won't be able to meet Kusheshwar Babu today?
I mean there is a strict directive from the doctor that no visitors should be allowed to see him. Kusheshwar looked at the from the corner of his eye and let a sigh of relief.
For how long has Kusheshwar babu being keeping ill?
He has no health issues, but he has is getting old. He can't move much and stays alone in his own room. He wrote several letters yesterday morning, then suddenly this happened.

Then we heard an impatient rustling at the kitchen door; Kusheshwar stopped halfway. Byomkesh said, seems like your wife is angry. We will take your leave now.

We went down the footpath and turned back to see the front door was already closed. Byomkesh stood silent for a moment and said, "Dr. Asim Sen's dispensary is not far, let's go and meet him.
Fortunately, Dr. Sen was in the dispensary, there were also three or four patients. Byomkesh wrote his name on a note and sent it to the doctor. Doctor Sen sent it back saying - we have to wait a little.

After half an hour, Doctor Sen called us after sending the patients away. We entered him chambers. The doctor sat behind a big table in the middle of a large room decorated with medical equipment. He looked at Byomkesh and said, "Are you Byomkesh babu? Didn't I see you today at Rameshwar babu's house?

Byomkesh said, "Yes. We have not come here for a medical examination. We have some other work. Byomkesh started to introduce himself when Dr. Sen laughed and said, "No need to introduce yourself. Sit down." Tell me what you need." We sat across the table.

Byomkesh said, I have known Rameshwar babu for a long time. I got his New Year's greetings yesterday, in which he expressed his doubt that he would not live much longer, hence we went to see him this morning. We came to see him and heard that he had a heart attack last night. We were not allowed to see him, so to you I have come to inquire about his health. Are you Rameshwar babu's family doctor?

Doctor Sen said, "You can say that I am his family friend. I have been examining him for thirty years. His heart is not strong, also he has grown old. He was facing health issues every now and then; Then yesterday suddenly he had a heart attack. Anyway, he is doing fine now.
So presently there is no danger of death?"

I can't say that. Nothing can be said about such patients; he can live for two more years or can have a second heart attack today itself. In case of a second attack, it would be hard for him to survive.
"Dr. Sen, do you think that Rameshwar Babu is being cared for?"
Dr. Sen thought for a while and said, "I understand what you are implying. Is there any good reason for you to think likewise?"

Byomkesh said, "I know only Rameshwar babu, I don't know anyone else in his family. But today I have a doubt that his family does not want him to meet any outsiders."

Dr. Sen said, "That's right. You don't know Rameshwar babu's family well, but I know. It's a weird family, No one seems to mentally stable apart from Rameshwar babu. His wife Kumudini is sixty, she has grown fat and is unable to move or do any activity. She still plays with dolls and is not concerned about the family. Kusheshwar is spineless and is controlled by his wife. Only Kusheshwar's wife Lavanya seems normal, and she drives the family.

But why is there no servant or cook in the family, they are filthy rich?

Lavanya cannot stand any servants hence sent everyone packing. She cannot cook herself, so she has employed a dumb cook, and does all the other work herself. She sends Kusheshwar in the market to buy household stuff and other chores. But why? What is the reason for such behavior?

Dr. Sen thought for a while and replied, "I believe, Nalini is at the root of all this!
Nalini! Rameshwar babu's daughter?

Yes. It happened a long time ago, you may not have heard. Nalini married a boy against the wishes of everyone in the house, hence everyone was angry on her. Lavanya was very angry at her. Rameshwar babu was very angry at first, but gradually his anger subsided. But Lavanya's anger did not subside. She does not want to let Nalini enter the house; she does not allow her to meet her father. Lest Rameshwar babu establish contact with the girl through servants so he removed them all. Rameshwar babu is kept confined to his house, but there is no lack of care for him.

Byomkesh remained silent for a moment and said, now I understand the situation. Well, can you tell if Rameshwar babu has made a will?

Doctor Sen looked at Byomkesh seemingly surprised, "He Did." I believe he has bequeathed a portion of the property to Nalini. I didn't know, But I found out last night.

Last night at ten o' clock Rameshwar babu had a heart attack. His family called me, and I went to attend him. After almost an hour, Rameshwar gained consciousness. Then I asked everyone to relax and have dinner. Rameshwar babu opened his eyes and looked around, then whispered "Doctor, I have made a will. If I die, please inform Nalini." At this time Lavanya entered the room again and we spoke nothing more.

Byomkesh said, "It is clear that they are not allowing Rameshwar babu to make a will, lest he gives a share of the property to Nalini. If he dies without making a will, Kusheshwar and his wife will get the property according to the rules of general inheritance." Nalini will get nothing. Who is Rameshwar babu lawyer?

Doctor Sen said, "I have not heard he has a family lawyer."

Byomkesh got up and said, "I have wasted a lot of your time. By the way, how is Nalini's family life.

The doctor said, they are a middle-class family. Her husband Debnath does a small job, earns three or four hundred rupees a month. But they have a lot many children.

Then we bid farewell to Dr. Sen and left. The family life of Rameshwar Babu became more vivid, but not pleasant. Rameshwar Babu is indeed a jovial man but in his last years is facing family trouble, but we have no way to help him out.

Eight days later, I saw the news of Rameshwar Babu's death. It appeared in a corner of the back page of the newspaper. He is a not famous person, but he had tons of money, so it seems that the news of his death reached the pages of the daily papers.

Byomkesh read only advertisements in newspapers, so I showed him the news. The name of Rameshwar babu did not bring a smile on his face today. He remained silent for a long time then he went to the next room and spoke on the telephone. When he came back, I asked, "Who was it?"

He said, "Dr. Asim Sen. Rameshwar babu died last night after another heart-attack. He was attended by Dr. Sen; But could not be saved. Doctor has issued a certificate of natural death.

I asked, "Did you suspect of unnatural death?

He said, "No exactly. But you know, in such a situation, a little carelessness, a little willful negligence can become fatal. If Rameshwar babu dies none of them will lose anything, but everyone stands to gain. Now the thing is, if Rameshwar babu has made a will and decided to give some of his property to Nalini, will Kusheshwar and his wife keep the will? They will destroy it the moment they find it.

One afternoon Nalini and her husband Debnath came to meet us. Nalini's age is around forty; her body is somewhat thin, but the beauty of youth has not been completely erased from the body. Debnath's age is about forty-five, in his youth he must have been very handsome. Debnath raised his hand and did a namaskar.
Nalini said with teary eyes, "Dad is dead. His last wish was that he wanted us to meet you." So, I have come. Byomkesh greeted them and seated them.
When they were all seated, Byomkesh asked, when did you receive Rameshwar babu's last order?

Nalini said, "First day of Boishakh." See this letter.
On the envelope was written an address of a relatively poor area of Calcutta. The monogrammed paper is similar to the letter written to Byomkesh. This letter is briefer.

Greetings!

You all take my New Year's blessings. If anything, good or bad happens to me, please meet Mr. Byomkesh Bakshi.

Your Well wishing
    Father.

The letter was very brief without any specifics. If Kusheshwar and Lavanya had opened the letter they would not have found anything suspicious. "If something good or bad happens" does not mean that someone is fearing the possibility of one's own death. It is very generic hence they allowed the letter to be posted.

Byomkesh returned the letter and said, when was the last time you met Rameshwar babu?

Nalini said, "Six months ago." After puja, I went to pay my respects to my father, that was the last time I saw him. Lavanya stood near us all the time eavesdropping on our conversation, hence could not speak to father alone nor could understand if he was facing any difficulties.

Don't you have good relations with Lavanya?

Good Relations! Lavanya hates me from the core of her heart.
Is there any reason for the hatred?
Yes, indeed there is! She is jealous of me. By god's grace I have many children, but she is infertile and has none.
Have you met Dr. Sen recently?
Yes Dr. Sen came by our place yesterday and said that father has made a will.
Do you know where the will is?
How can I know?
They kept the father as a prisoner in his own house. Father cannot move around due to his age; he cannot leave his house at all; they have kept a strict vigil on him allowing no one to meet him. They read all the correspondence that he sends or receives. If they do not like the letters, then they tear it up immediately. Even if father has made a will, is it still there? Lavanya must have torn it up.

Byomkesh said, Rameshwar babu is a very clever man. If he has made a will, he has probably hidden it somewhere where no one could easily find it. Now the task for us is to find it before they do.

Nalini eagerly said, "Yes, Byomkesh babu. If father has made a will, he must have given us something, otherwise there is no point in making a will, but we don't know what to do in this situation. Nalini was looking at Byomkesh with tearful eyes.
At this time, Debnath cleared his throat and was about to say something, when Byomkesh turned his eyes on him. He said a little awkwardly, "I remembered something." I have heard that two witnesses are required for making a will. But where will my father-in-law get two witnesses.

Byomkesh said, "What you say is true, but there is an exception. If the testator writes the will from the start to the end in his own handwriting, then there is no need for a witness?
Nalini asked her husband with bright eyes, "Do you hear? This is why father asked me to meet him.
Byomkesh babu, please help us in this matter.

Byomkesh said, "I will try. The will must be in the house, the house must be searched. But why would they let anyone search the house? The police will be required also Doctor Asim Sen will be needed. It will take two or four days. You go home, I will do what is required. If the will exists, I will it find out.

When Byomkesh used to visit the government offices, he didn't take me with him. I also didn't like wandering in the maze of government offices. I don't know where Byomkesh wandered for two days. On the third day in the evening, he returned home and let out a deep breath and said, "Everything has been arranged.
I asked, 'What has been arranged.
He said, 'The search warrant has been obtained. Tomorrow morning, we will go with the police to search Rameshwar Babu's house.
The next morning, we arrived at Rameshwar Babu's house with five-six policemen and an inspector named Mr. Halder.

Kusheshwar threw tantrums first, his wife Lavanya looked at us with her fiery red eyes as if she would burn us down with her looks. But nothing they did deterred us. Inspector Halder took Kumidini, Kusheshwar and Lavanya and made them sit in the kitchen along with a policeman, while we searched the entire house. Two men searched the lower floor, while two searched the first-floor rooms of Kusheshwar and Lavanya. Byomkesh, Inspector Halder and I went to the second floor. Rameshwar babu used to live there, so it is more likely that it will be found there.

The second floor consisted of two rooms. The small room is the wife's bedroom, the big room is Rameshwar babu's bedroom and office. On one side lay the bed, on the other side, table, chair, bookcase etc. From this room a narrow door leads to the bathroom.

We started searching the rooms. We had to search for the will in this room containing several furniture's, beds, tables, chairs, cupboards etc. We searched the entire room minutely and realised that the rooms have been searched once before us probably by Kusheshwar and his wife who were also searching for the will.
Byomkesh heard me and said, "Yes now the question is, have they found the will before us?

After two and a half hours of searching, we sat down tiredly. On one side of the table was a small brass mortar and pestle. Rameshwar babu used to use the mortar pestle for grinding betel leaf. Byomkesh pulled it forward and was examining it. In the meanwhile, the policeman searching the lower two floors came and reported that they had found nothing during their search of the lower floors.

Inspector Halder said, "There is nothing to be found in this house. That means either Rameshwar babu didn't make a will or Kusheshwar and Lavanya have already found the will.
Byomkesh said, "I have no doubt in my mind about the existence of the will.
But.
Meanwhile Inspector Halder lifted the lid of a container with a lazy hand. The table was strewn with papers, pens, envelopes, pincushions, glue bottles, etc. We had examined the table and its drawers, but the container which Inspector Halder opened let off a pungent smell.

"Smell of Raw onions!
Byomkesh stood up and said, what smell. It smells like raw onions. Let me have Look!

Pulling the bottle close. He smelled it deeply. He tilted the bottle and looked inside, looking at the dark white substance, it looks like a sticky paste. But why does it smell of onion? Where did the onion come from?

Byomkesh sat motionless for a while with the bottle. He was thinking deeply it can be guessed from the intense look in his eyes. I exchanged glances with Inspector Halder. What mystery did Byomkesh find in the bottle containing onion pulp?
Inspector Halder, please call Kusheshwar's wife once.

After a while Lavanya entered the room with rebellion. Byomkesh got up and pointed to his chair and said, "Sit down." I will ask you a question.
Lavanya sat down. Her jawbone was clenched, his eyes are fiery red. Seeing three unknown men, her look did not soften.

Byomkesh asked, "Did your father-in-law like to eat raw onions?"
Lavanya looked at Byomkesh in surprise, the rebellion on her face subsided a lot. She said, "He didn't love it, since the last few days, he had a craving for raw onions. He was in a terrible state, he didn't have a single tooth on him; he grinded the onions using a mortar and pestle.

Byomkesh asked, since when did Rameshwar babu start this weird habit?
"Since the last Ten-twelve days ago he started this habit of consuming raw onions, during the latter half of Chaitra month.

Byomkesh folded his hands and said, "Thank you" Please forgive me for troubling you. Come on Ajit, let's go Inspector Halder. We are done here.

I didn't understand anything how our work ended; we came out of the house. Byomkesh got down on the footpath and said, "Inspector Halder, you come along with us to our house, your companions will no longer be needed.

Upon reaching home, Byomkesh asked me, "Ajit, where is the letter that Rameshwar babu sent us?"
I looked around and said, 'I have not seen that letter anymore.' Must be lying around somewhere here. We don't store any of personal letters, once the letters are read, they are kept for a few days then they are thrown away.

Byomkesh was very upset and said, "Look, please look for it, the letter is very important. Rameshwar babu wrote in it, "Please do not ignore this letter of mine."
Then Inspector Halder said, "But what is the matter, why suddenly has the letter became so important." Byomkesh said, "You did not understand!" That letter is Rameshwar babu's will.
"What. Is it?"
Yes. "Today I saw the onion juice in the bottle and realized. Rameshwar babu wrote the will in invisible ink and sent it to me. "
What invisible link?
I'll tell you later.
Ajit, look around for the letter, call Puntiram and ask him to search for the letter. If the letter is not found, then Nalini and Debnath will lose a fortune.

Puntiram was called, he could not say anything. Byomkesh sat with his hands on his head, then he raised his face and said, "Stop, stop. Don't search outside, search within your memory.

Byomkesh sat in an easy chair and started gazing the roof and began to smoke. He smoked a cigarette after another. We also lit a cigarette. Fifteen minutes later he staggered and sat up and said, " Do you remember which book I was reading that day?"
I said, "When? Which day?
The day Rameshwar babu's letter arrived. First day of Baisakh, afternoon. Don't you remember?

I tried to picture the scene of that day in my mind. The postman knocked on the door, Byomkesh was sitting on the dewan and reading a thick book, either Kali Singha's Mahabharata or Hem Chandra's Ramayana.
Byomkesh said, "The Mahabharata, the second volume. Don't you remember us talking about Pitamah Bhisma? I rushed and took out the second volume of Mahabharata from the shelf, and as I opened the book fell out Rameshwar Babu's letter.
Byomkesh shouted with joy, 'found it! found it! Puntiram, make a coal fire in a brazier and bring it here.

Dr. Asim Sen has come along with Nalini and Debnath after getting a phone call from Byomkesh. The fire from the brazier kept on the floor of the house has made the environment even hotter.

Byomkesh took the letter carefully and started saying' Rameshwar babu was a funny and a very intelligent man. But physically he had become very weak. He did not have the ability to work independently, he became a puppet in the hands of his son and daughter-in-law.

When he realized that he was nearing deathbed, he wanted to give a share of his property to Nalini.
But if he wants to give her a share of the property, then he has to make a will. According to the current law, the daughter has no natural claim on her father's property. Rameshwar babu decided that he would make a will.

But just making a will is not enough; how to make sure that his will be executed after his death. After his death Kusheshwar and Lavanya will never give Nalini a share of his property, they cannot see eye to eye with Nalini. They do not allow Nalini to meet her father. They always keep a watch on Rameshwar Babu. They open and inspect all the letters he writes, and if there is anything suspicious in the letter, they tear it up.

But Rameshwar Babu used his wits to find a way out. Not everyone knows this fact that when you write a letter with onion juice, there is no stain on the paper, the writing disappears. But there is a way to reveal that invisible writing, a very easy way. When the paper is heated, visible writing emerges. When I was in school, I had a hobby of performing magic tricks, many times I have shown this magic to my classmates. Rameshwar babu knew this magic trick. He asked to eat raw onion. Kusheshwar and Lavanya thought that the old man has become senile. They did not object. Rameshwar Babu was fond of eating pan but had no teeth hence he used to keep a mortar and pestle. He used the same to grind the onions and make onion juice. No one knew! He had humor in his soul, while doing this he must have laughed a lot.

On the first of Baisakh, he used to write letters wishing his close people the New Year greetings. He realised that new year was near hence he started writing his will with the onion juice. He used to send his greetings every year. This year he did the same but on the rear of the letter he wrote his will with the invisible ink. Here is the letter and his will.

Byomkesh opened the envelope and carefully took out the letter, opened the fold of the letter and held both ends of the letter with both hands and began to move it slowly over the fire in the brazier. We held our breath and looked at it.

After holding our breath for a minute, a loud breath came out of our collective nostrils. The invisible ink was coming to life, brown letters were oozing out on the back of the paper. After Five minutes, byomkesh removed the paper from the fire. Byomkesh glanced at it once and then raised it towards Dr. Sen and said, "Dr. Sen this is the will that Rameshwar Babu told you about. Please read, we will all listen.

Dr. Sen once read the will in silence, a smile of remembrance appeared on his face Then he cleared his throat and started reciting the will.

Namo Bhagavate Vasudevae. I Sri Rameshwar Ray, Resident of No. 17 Shyamdhan Mitra Lane Bag bazar, Calcutta, being in good health and sound mind am writing my last will and testament. It was not possible for me to get a witness to sign the will hence I will write the entire will from the start to the end in my own handwriting. Dr. Asim Sen is a witness to the fact that I am of sound mind. Now I am recording my last will and testament.

Out of my eight houses in Calcutta and all the money in the bank, the house in Harrison Road and seventy-five thousand rupees in cash shall be given to my daughter Smt. Nalini. My wife Mrs. Kumudini shall enjoy the tenure of my Shyampukur house for life. After her death my daughter Nalini will inherit that house. All the rest of my property, six houses and the remaining money in the bank will be given to my son Sri Kusheshwar Ray. Renowned truth-seeker Sri Byomkesh Bakshi and the renowned doctor Asim Sen will act as the executors of my will. They will make the necessary arrangements and will receive a remuneration of five thousand rupees each from my estate.

Date: 1st Baisakh 1360
Signed by Self
    14th April 1953.
Shri Rameshwar Ray

When Dr. Sen finished reading the will, no one spoke for a while, then we all stood up together. Nalini came running with teary eyes and touched Byomkesh's foot and said in a happy voice, "Byomkesh Babu you gave us a new life."

Byomkesh smiled a little and said, but will the court accept this will? Inspector Halder came to the rescue of byomkesh, he said, please don't worry about this, they won't dare contest this will! If they do, I will be a witness.
Dr. Asim Sen said, "Me too."

Lohar Biscuit

(Iron Biscuit)

Kamal Babu said, "I live in this neighbourhood, on the edge of Hindustan Park, I have seen you many times, wanted to speak to you but didn't have the courage. I got a reason today, so I thought I will meet you and talk about it. A small problem has come in my life.

A problem! Byomkesh held out a cigarette case and said, pray tell me, it's been quite a while that I have solved any problems.

This discussion was happening in Byomkesh's Keyatala house on a warm Sunday Afternoon.

Kamal babu looks like Narugopal, but his face is bright and intelligent. He smiled and lit a cigarette, then began his story, "My name is Kamal krishna Das, I am the cashier at the nearby Branch of Central Bank of India. I came here a year and a half ago after being transferred from Purulia.

"When I came to Calcutta, I fell into trouble; I was unable to find to find a good house on rent anywhere. Finally, a kind man rented me a room on the ground floor of his house. I was unable to bring my Family alongside, I left my wife and daughter in Purulia and started staying here all by myself.

"The landlord's name is Akshay Mondal. The house is two-storied; there are two rooms on the lower floor and two on the first floor. We both have separate entrances. Akshay Mondal lives alone on the first floor and has some occasional visitors. Akshay Mondal is a sweet-spoken man, but I not aware of what he does for a living. Sometimes Akshay Mondal used to come down to my room to have a good chat, but he never invited me to his rooms upstairs. He hardly spoke to any of his neighbour's. He had a savings account in my branch hence he used to speak with me.

However, after spending three months like this, one day I had a dinner invitation at my Office colleague's place. I was late to return home that night. Once back home, I saw Akshay Mondal coming down from the second floor and locking the door of the stairs, he had two suitcases on him. I asked, "Where are you going at this time of the night?"

Akshay Mondal was bewildered to see me. He came to me with two suitcases in both hands, and said in a deep voice, "Kamalbabu, I have to leave immediately due to some urgent work, I don't know when I will return."

His eyes were bloody red. I asked, "what is the matter, where are you going?" A smile appeared on his face He said, "Well too far, I should leave immediately."

I stood surprised. He went a few steps and stopped, then came back and said "Kamalbabu, you work in the bank, and you are a gentleman, let me propose you something. "If I do not return within a week, you can use my entire house and you must pay Rs.150 as rent. I have a savings account in your bank you can deposit the rent in the same account. "Are you fine with this agreement?"

"Akshay Mondal was gone in no time. I stood stunned for a while. Then I realised that Akshay Mondal did not give me the key to the first floor. "However, the hope that I will be able to use the entire house and bring my family from Purulia was exhilarating. It seemed from his words that Akshay Mondal would not be returning for a long time.

The next day I wrote a letter prematurely to my wife – "be prepared to pack up the family belongings and shift to Calcutta. There is a possibility get a good house soon."

Two days passed in hope that I would finally get my family in Calcutta. After three days, some rotten smell started coming out from the first floor. It was a strong rotten smell, like the smell of decaying fish or chicken.

I got suspicious and informed the police. The police came, broke the lock, and went upstairs. I followed the police upstairs and witnessed a horrible scene. On the floor lay a dead body drenched in blood with a hole in the middle of his temple. I understood what had occurred. That night when I went for dinner at my colleague's place, Akshay Mondal had shot dead this man in my absence and fled away with his valuable belongings. Hence, he said that he would not be returning soon as he is now a fugitive.

Soon a group of policemen came and surrounded the house. The body was sent for post-mortem. Then Darogababu interrogated me and started searching the entire house. A gentleman from the neighbourhood and I were asked to help conduct the search as impartial witnesses.

But nothing special was found in the police search. Only in one of the drawers were found a few small boxes made of sheet iron; similar to Cigarette cases. These boxes were empty. Darogababu fiddled with them anxiously but could not understand the use of such iron cases.

The Police left after conducting a thorough search of the house. I was feeling uneasy after this incidence. I went to the police station after three or four days and enquired about the incident.
I went there and got the news that the identity of the deceased had been established from the fingerprints and other physical attributes. The deceased was Harihar Singh; A hardened criminal, who was known for smuggling drugs, gold, silver, and other illegal items.

His connection with Akshay Mondal was yet to be established and a look out notice has been issued for Akshay Mondal. Akshay Mondal seems to have vanished in thin air as police have no clue about his whereabouts.

While returning from the police station, I asked with fear. Can I occupy the whole house?
Darogababu said, "With ease." When the fugitive has left the house in your custody then you can use the entire house with ease. But one thing, if you get any information of the accused then you must immediately report to the police station.

Then about a year passed without any issues. I brought my wife and daughter from Purulia and started occupying the whole house and was living in comfort. The house rent is paid monthly in Akshay Mondal's account. I use his table chair etc. but I don't touch his wardrobe and cupboard.

Suddenly, two months ago, a problem appeared. In the morning, I was sitting in the ground floor room reading the newspaper, when a stranger came along with a woman. A middle-aged gentleman and a married woman. The man pointed his finger at the woman and said, "This is Akshay Mondal's wife, I am her elder brother. I have fed and supported her financially for a long time, but I no longer can support her, and she also wants to stay in the husband's house. You must leave the house immediately."

It was as if lightning struck me. I kept wondering what to do now. Then an idea struck me, I said "I have never heard that Akshay Babu has a wife. If what you say is true go to court and prove your claim, then we will see."

After some bickering, they left. My suspicion is that they are scumbags who want to take over the house by stealth. Such a beautiful double storied house who would not want to have it for free.

I went to the police station and reported the news. Darogababu said, "we don't know if Akshay Mondal has a wife. However, if they come again, sneakily bring them to the police station. We will also keep an eye on the house."

I have a pistol, and I keep a dog. A fierce mountain dog, called Bhuto, he eats from no one's hand but mine. I unchain him when I go to office and let him roam the house unhindered at night. He guards the house. With Bhuto roaming the house unhindered at night no one has the guts to break in, if anyone tries breaking in, Bhutto will chew him up. However, after this incident, there is an uneasiness in me. Akshay Mondal is not a good person, maybe he is playing some crooked games to get me out of this house.

After ten days, I received an anonymous letter, "Leave the neighborhood, otherwise you will be in danger." neighborhood means house. I went to the police station and showed the letter. Darogababu said "don't budge an inch. I am increasing the guard on your house."

Since then, no one has come, not even any anonymous letter. I feel quite safe now. But a problem has arisen. I came to you to solve this problem. I could have gone to Darogababu, but he would have given advice that we would not have liked.

I have accrued a month's leave in my office. My wife wants to go on a pilgrimage to Haridwar, Hrishikesh etc. One of my bank colleagues is also taking leave with me to go on a religious trip in Kundu Special. There are many benefits to go if we go along. My wife is very enthusiastic about this pilgrimage. I am not less enthusiastic too.

But if we want to go, we must lock the house. Bhutto also must be put in a kennel for a month. The house will be unprotected. While we are away if that imposter who claims to be Akshay Mondal's wife breaks the lock and enters the house and occupies the house, then what should I do? I have no right without Akshay Mondal's verbal permission. Currently I am in possession of the house, if they want to dispossess me, they will have to go to court. But if they occupy with force or trickery, then where will I go?

"This is my problem. It is a domestic problem not suitable for your attention. However, I have come to you with the intention of going for a religious tour while keeping the house safe. Now tell me should we leave home and go on pilgrimage?

Byomkesh sat for a while with his hand on his cheek, and finally said, "It would be a sin to interrupt your pilgrimage, and it is not advisable to leave the house empty. Do you have any acquaintance who is strong enough to guard your house while you take a pilgrimage?

No. Everyone has a home. Those who do not have, I don't have the courage to let them guard my house, they may be ones to capture the house and dispossess me.

Byomkesh stood up and said, "Then let's see your house." Kamal Babu asked with cheerful eyes, "Sure let's Go! What luck! My place is not far from here."

Byomkesh said, please wait for a while, although your place is not far away, but the sun is quite harsh. Let me bring an umbrella. Byomkesh went inside and brought an umbrella. This umbrella is Byomkesh's favourite, The umbrella was bent and corroded with discolored cloth and innumerable holes. This umbrella is apt for an investigator, as covering your face and head you can follow the suspect and still be invisible. You can see through the innumerable holes, but the outsider can't see the umbrella holder's face.

Let's Go! Kamal Babu said Byomkesh.

Kamal babu's house was five minutes away from Byomkesh's house. Sometimes while passing this way, the house caught the eye of Byomkesh. A small two-storied house; but one whose features draws attention. The entire roof was covered with iron rods like a huge iron cage. It is not possible to climb the roof from outside.

Byomkesh wrapped his umbrella and entered the house. Kamal Babu first took him to the downstairs living room. There was nothing special except a cot covered with a beautiful bedsheet and two chairs. Byomkesh looked around the room, he seemed to be looking for a clue, but couldn't find anything interesting in the naked room! He said, "There is another room downstairs, isn't it?"
There is. The room was not used during Akshay Mondal's tenure, I made it a kitchen,will you like to see? "No need, your wife seems to be cooking now. Let's go upstairs, said Byomkesh.
Let's go.

Adjacent to the house on a narrow balcony were stairs to go to the first floor, On the top of the stairs was a door. On the door was hanging an Iron horseshoe. After looking at it for a while, Byomkesh picked up his umbrella and pointed to it, "What is that?

"That is a horseshoe. According to foreign superstition, hanging a horseshoe on the door brings in a lot of money. The tip of Byomkesh's umbrella got stuck in the horseshoe, he pulled it out and said, 'Did you put it on or was, it's from Akshay Mondal's time?"

Byomkesh looked at the horseshoe and started wondering. Kamalbabu called. Please come in.

Kamal babu's ten-year-old daughter was studying on a mat on the floor inside the house,
a handsome dog was pawing outside the mat, looking up at
Byomkesh with beadless blue eyes. Kamalbabu said, "Khuku, go
ask your mother to make tea, and some fritters."

Byomkesh objected a little, but Kamalbabu did not listen. Khuku went downstairs and Bhuto followed her.

Byomkesh then surveyed the room and said, 'Is there any furniture of the Akshaya Mondal in this room? Kamalbabu said, "There was but I moved it to the next room. There was a cot and a table with drawers.

The next room was rather large, a cot towards the window and a table in the other corner. Byomkesh went to the table and said, "The iron cases that were found in the police search, have they been taken away by the police "The police took just an iron case away, the rest are in this drawer." Kamalbabu opened a drawer and bought out an Iron case. It's like a cigarette case. Putting it down byomkesh said with a smile, "Very funny stuff! Just put two whole biscuits in it and tie it with a thread, and it is safe to carry around." Let's see the roof now.

"But there is nothing on the roof".
So be it. Emptiness can become meaningful.
"Come on then?
There was really nothing on the roof. The iron-clad roof stands like an empty tiger cage. On a high pedestal in one corner is a red-colored iron water tank. Tap water is supplied to the house from this water tank. Byomkesh walked around the roof and said, "Don't you use the roof?

Kamal Babu said, "If it's too hot, we come and sleep on the roof. It's a safe place, there's no way that thieves can get in here.

Byomkesh said, I am done inspecting the roof, now let's go downstairs.

Just then Khuku came and said, "Father, Tea has been served in the living room." Byomkesh said while drinking tea with poppadum and fried aubergines, "What is the name of the Darogababu of the police station that you go to?"
Kamalbabu said, "His name is Rakhal Sarkar."

Byomkesh smiled. After finishing his tea, he stood up with the umbrella and said, I will take your leave now.

Kamalbabu said, "But what will happen to our pilgrimage, whether we should go or not, you didn't say anything?

"Surely do the pilgrimage. When are you planning to leave?'
From next Saturday
"Then don't delay, buy your tickets! Do not fear, you will not be evicted from your house, you have my assurance." Well, then I will take your leave now.

Ah is that so! Thanks, Byomkesh babu. Let me walk you to your house. Byomkesh said, 'There is no need for him, I will go to the police station now. I must chalk out a plan with Mr. Rakhal the Darogababu.

On Saturday morning, the police guard was lifted from Kamal Babu's house. Kamalbabu took Bhuto to a kennel.

In the evening, Kamal Babu locked and left the house along with his wife, daughter, and belongings. On the way, he gave the keys to Rakhal Babu at the police station and said, "I have left the window unlocked. Now my fate is in your hands."
The house remained empty for the whole day.

At about 8:30 in the night, Rakhalbabu went to Kamal babu's house along with Byomkesh. Both of them were carrying pistols and electric torches with them. They had already taken a note of the surroundings. Both jumped the wall of the neighbouring house and entered Kamal babu's house through the unlocked window. After closing the window, they tiptoed up the stairs to the second floor.

Rakhalbabu shone his torch on the door and saw that the horseshoe was in the right place. He then whispered, "Let's go, it will probably be better if we wait on the roof. "

Byomkesh whispered in his ear, 'No. I am going to the roof, you hide in this room. If both of us go to the roof, the roof door cannot be closed from inside, the accused may suspect it is a trap.

"Well, you go to the roof and hide, I close the door from inside and wait next to the door. Byomkesh went and hid in the roof while Rakhal babu bolted the door from inside and hid near the second-floor door. They had no clue for what amount of time they have to wait, the accused may come today.

Byomkesh loitered around the roof for a while searching for the perfect place to hide. He then chose a spot opposite to the water tank. It was a moonless night only the twinkling stars. Byomkesh quickly disappeared into the darkness.

A long wait lay ahead. It was like tying a goat or a calf as a bait in the forest and waiting for the tiger. It was about two o'clock when Rakhal babu's grew restless in the vacant house. He thought there will be no action tonight. Just then he heard a soft sound outside the door, his nerves stiffened for a moment. He quietly drew the pistol from his pocket.

A man silently entered the house and walked up the stairs to the first floor. He was carrying a bag in one hand and an iron staff in another. The iron staff was covered with muga thread just like thread is tied on the fishing rod.

The man raised the stick towards the top of the door and brought down the horseshoe, then tied it to the end of the muga thread and climbed up the stairs to the roof. He was completely oblivious to the fact that two people were patiently hiding in the house to nab him.

Byomkesh was alerted when he heard the sound of the door opening. A shadowy figure came out of the darkness, went straight to the steps, and climbed on top of water tank. He opened the lid of the water tank and set it aside, then dipped the horseshoe tied to the tip of the iron staff into the water.

It looked as if the man was sitting in the dark and catching small fish. He was dipping the iron rod catching the fish, then throwing them in his bag. This continued for several minutes.

Twenty minutes later the man came down from the tank after completing his fishing expedition. He had a bag in one hand and the iron staff in another. He swiftly walked towards the door when suddenly a light shone on his face. Byomkesh yelled, "Akshay Mondal, how was your fishing expedition?

Akshay Mondal had a dark face and was wearing khaki pants and half-shirt. He looked bewildered and slowly put down the bag and hurriedly reached into his pocket. Byomkesh was quick to act, he swiftly struck Akshay Mondal jaw with his torch. Akshay Mondal fell to the roof and started grinning in pain. Rakhalbabu came up from below, he sat on Akshay Mondal's chest and said, "Byomkeshda, there is a pistol in his pocket, take it out quick."

Byomkesh took the pistol from Akshay Mondal's pocket and put it in his pocket. Rakhalbabu handcuffed the accused and said, "Akshay Mondal you are being arrested for murdering Harihar Singh. Byomkesh took a few wet iron cases from Akshay Mondal's bag and shone the torch on them. "Great! Here it is, just what I thought. These iron cases contain foreign gold biscuits."

The next morning, Satyawati said to Byomkesh, "Well, tell me, where were you last night?"
Byomkesh said, Me Lord, I did nothing untoward last night.
Darogababu Rakhal can vouch for my whereabouts.

Yes, an unscrupulous man will vouch for another. Well tell me the entire story of your expedition from last night.

'I will tell, I will tell. But first give me another cup of tea. I was awake all night and need another cup of tea to wash away the tiredness. Satyawati brought another cup of strong tea and sat on the chair in front of Byomkesh, "Now tell me, what do you do last night and why is your torch broken? Did you engage in a fight?"

Byomkesh said, "I did not engage in a fight, I just hit someone hard? Taking a sip of tea, he began his story.
Akshay Mondal was a gold smuggler; he made a lot of money from

these illegal activities. He built a house in a decent neighborhood according to his needs. He covered the roof of the house with iron rods in such a way that there was no way for thieves to enter the house. He had a special need to secure the roof of his house.

Akshay Mondal used to smuggle gold from foreign lands and sell them in the market. He had to store the gold, but there was no iron safe in his house. He devised a peculiar technique of hiding the Gold. Akshay Mondal lived alone at home; it is not yet known whether he had a wife. He did not socialise with his neighbour's but lest the neighbours should suspect anything, he rented a room downstairs to a gentleman named Kamal Das. He kept a few men to distribute the gold in the market, one of whom was Harihar Singh. Probably Harihar Singh had cheated Akshay Mondal. One day the two quarreled, Akshay Mondal killed Harihar Singh in anger. When he came to his senses, he realised that it would not be easy to smuggle a dead body by a single person that too in a watchful society.

He decided to leave the dead body in the house, take whatever gold and belongings he could lay his hands on and be on the run. But he could not take all the gold. Gold is a heavy metal, heavier than iron You women wear gold ornaments all over your body, but you do not understand the weight of gold.

Satyawati said, "Well, well, continue your story. Akshay Mondal became a fugitive, Harihar Singh's body was found a few days later; the police came but could not find anything substantial nor could find Akshay Mondal. There is no doubt that Akshay Mondal murdered Harihar Singh. Kamal Babu occupied the entire house.

Akshay Mondal must have been hiding somewhere in Calcutta. He remained silent for months.
But the gold hidden in the house which he could not move, had to be

recovered. The task was not easy. Kamal babu's wife and daughter were always in the house, and alongside them was a ferocious dog. Akshaya Mondal had a few tricks up his sleeve. He sent a woman as his wife and a man as her brother to Kamalbabu. The house had to be vacated to give his wife possession. Akshay Mondal may be a fugitive murderer, but his wife had committed no crime. Kamalbabu did not listen, he scolded them. Akshay Mondal then wrote an anonymous letter to scare him, but that too had no effect on Kamal babu.

So, Akshay Mondal then chalked out a new plan. He urged and sponsored Kamal Babu's bank colleague to go on pilgrimage with Kamal Babu. If Kamalbabu would be away with his family and dog from the house even for two-four days, that Akshay Mondal can easily break in and recover the hidden gold. This plan worked quite well, but for some reason Kamalbabu felt uneasy; He was not sure to leave the house vacant, hence he came to me for advice

After hearing his story, I became suspicious about the house, I went to see the house if I could gather any clues. The sun was scorching hot, so I took an umbrella. I went up to the first floor and saw that the horseshoe was loosely attached between three nails on the door. At first glance, it looked like a horseshoe, but indeed it was not. I extended the umbrella in that direction, instantly the umbrella got stuck in the horseshoe.

I Understood that my suspicions were true, it was not a horseshoe, but a very powerful magnet. With force I pulled at my umbrella. By questioning Kamal babu, I came to know that the magnet belonged to Akshay Mondal.

What does Akshay Mondal do with magnets? Why was it stuck to the top of the door? Why was it shaped like a horseshoe? Suddenly I remembered that few iron cases were found during the police investigation from the drawer of Akshay Mondal. The mystery gradually became clear to me. Then when I went to the roof and saw the water tank, nothing was left for me to understand.

No matter how strong a magnet is, it cannot pull gold, hence he wrapped the golden biscuit in an iron case and threw it into the tank water. Then, as, and when needed, Akshay Mondal would drop the magnet into the tank and lift it out the iron cases containing gold.

When he killed Harihar Singh and fled He could not take all the gold with him. Now he wanted to recover the rest of the gold. At the time of his escape, he did not think that the matter would become so complicated.

Anyways I got to know where he had hidden all the gold. Just as there are pearls in the bottom of the ocean similarly there was gold wrapped in iron cases at the bottom of the water tank. But only recovering the gold would not work, the murderer had to be caught.

I said to Kamalbabu, you should go on a pilgrimage with your family. Then I consulted with Darogababu, Mr. Rakhal and arranged the trap. Yesterday morning, Kamal babu and family went on a pilgrimage. Akshay Mondal had kept an eye on the house, he knew that his path was clear.

Yesterday after dusk Darogababu and I went to Akshay Mondal house and silently waited for him to arrive to retrieve the gold. We were not sure that Akshay Mondal would arrive on the very first night, but still we needed to be vigilant. At two in the night Akshay Mondal stepped into the trap. Then what, he was brought to justice by just a blow from the torch.

Satyawati asked in a low voice, "How much gold was found?" Byomkesh lighted a cigarette and said, "Fifty-seven iron cases, each containing two gold biscuits and weighing fifty grams each. Now Satya you calculate the price?"

Satyawati just took a deep breath.

Monimandan
(Diamond Necklace Theft)

A valuable diamond necklace has been stolen from the house of Rosomoy Sarkar. I had read the news briefly in the newspapers in the morning, I was featured under the delayed news section. The telephone rang at about eight o'clock.

Stranger's voice, Hello Byomkesh babu?
I said, "No, I am Ajit. Who is calling?
The voice over the telephone said "My name is Rosomoy Sarkar. Will you please call Byomkesh babu once?"
Hearing his name, I clearly understood that Byomkesh has been summoned to catch the thief.

I said, "He has gone to the bathroom, he will take time to attend the call. I read in the newspapers that a necklace was stolen from your shop.
Rosomoy Sarkar replied, "Not from the shop, but from our house. You are Ajit Bandyopadhyay, Byomkesh babu's friend, I guess?
Yes, I said. You can tell me what you want to say to Byomkesh?

After remaining silent for a moment, Rosomoy said, "Look, the necklace that was stolen is worth rupees fifty-seven thousand. I suspect that a servant of the house stole it, but no evidence is available. I have informed the police, but I want Byomkesh babu to investigate the matter. No one can recover the necklace save him.

Great! Why don't you come down here? Byomkesh will be out of the bathroom by the time you arrive.
Rosomoy Sarkar replied hesitatingly, Ajit Babu, I am a patient of Rheumatoid arthritis. I cannot move around freely at will. It would be really helpful if Byomkesh Babu can come and meet me.

Those who seek solutions to their problems come to Byomkesh, he doesn't go to anyone first. I said, "Okay, I will let Byomkesh know."

Rosomoy's plea became more desperate, 'No, no, you will surely come. I'm sending a car; you won't have any trouble.
Thank you, thank you. I'm sending the car now.

A few minutes later a Cadillac car came and stopped at our doorsteps. When Byomkesh came out of the bathroom, I explained everything to him and showed the car through the window. He didn't mind anything. We got into the Cadillac and left for Rosomoy Sarkar's house.

Rosomoy Sarkar has five jewellery shops across the city, but his house is in Boubazar. Soon the car stopped at his house. Rosomoy Sarkar's house was of old style, rising three stories from the very edge of footpath, in the middle were naked stairs connecting to the rest of the floors and rows of shops on either side, while the family occupies the top two floors.

The stairs door was closed from inside. As soon as the car stopped, the door opened and appeared a handsome young man, aged twenty-seven or twenty-eight. He bowed and said, "My name is Monimoy Sarkar. Father is eagerly waiting for you upstairs. Please come.
On the first floor there is a kitchen, a pantry, a servant's quarters and a living room with seating space. We went up to the second floor. In this floor, the Rosomoy Sakar lives with his family.

The second-floor entry had heavy doors embellished with silk curtains and a state-of-the-art lock. The floor was covered with fine Persian carpets. The drawing room was furnished with expensive furniture, expensive sofas and a table made of fine Kashmir wood. The room boasted of a huge bookshelf and the walls were adorned with Persian paintings and fine tapestries etc. But presently the room looked a little untidy. Monimoy showed us into the room and said, "Father, Byomkesh babu has come.

I saw Rosomoy Sarkar was sitting in a chair with his right leg stretched out and a young married woman sitting at his feet and using a hot water bag to provide relief to his pain struck fingers.

Rosomoy babu is about fifty years old, heavy built body, fleshy face still quite firm. He tried to get up to welcome us but quickly sat down again due to pain. Rosomoy babu joined both his hands and said, Please Come in, Byomkesh babu! I am overpowered by this pain and this theft. You have come, now I can be at ease. I know that you are the only person who can retrieve the necklace. Pray sit down, Ajit babu?

There is no doubt that Rosomoy is an intelligent man, he understood who Byomkesh is among us even without asking. We sat side by side on the sofa. Byomkesh said, "I see you have rheumatism in your legs. Though rheumatism is not fatal, but it is very painful.

Rosomoy said, "Don't say any more. I am in good health, but this rheumatism has made me helpless. I used to play football as a child, my right toe was broken. Now it stands like this, when a piece of cloud as small as a handkerchief rises in a corner of the sky, the right toe starts to crackle. But let that be, Daughter in law, please bring tea for the guest.

Rosomoy babu's Daughter in law was sitting at his foot and massaging it. A beautiful girl, but her face clearly showed signs of distress. As she was about to get up, Byomkesh said, 'No no, no need for tea, we have had tea before coming here. Please serve your father-in-law.

Rosomoy smiled a little, the bride sat down again. Rosomoy said, "Okay then. Moni, please bring some cigarettes.

Monimoy had been standing behind a chair for a long time, when he left Rosomoy cast a loving glance at the bride and said, "I am very fortunate to have her as my elder son's wife. My wife has gone for a pilgrimage with my younger son and this girl has taken over the reins of the family. She is very auspicious for our family. I don't usually ask her to massage my feet, But the servant- after saying this, he suddenly stopped, the tone of his voice changed and he said, "Let's not beat around the bush, let's talk about work. You have come on my request; I will not waste your precious time. Byomkesh babu, last night an incident happened at my house, something that has never happened before.

Byomkesh said, "tell me everything from the beginning. Don't summarize. Think that I don't know anything?
Monimoy entered the room with a tin of 555 cigarette and offered us. He stood in front of the window. We lit a cigarette.

Rosomoy began to say "I have five jewellery shops in Calcutta. It's a big business, we do sales of about thirty lakh rupees a year. We have many trusted employees who have been working with us for several years. I look after the business when I am physically fit. Since the last two years, Moni has started looking after the business as well.

We do business with jewellers across the country. Bombay, Madras, New Delhi everywhere where there are big jewellers, we deal with them. Sometimes they buy gems and stones from us and sometimes we buy from them. Apart from these large jewellers we have retails customers also from the royal families to the common folks, all are our customers.

A month ago, a big jeweler named Ramdas Choksi came to me from Delhi. He has received an order for making jewellery for a marriage in a royal family in Rajasthan. The order is worth ten lakh rupees. But he cannot make all the jewellery by himself, he wants me to make a diamond necklace for him. After deciding upon the design and diamond size, the price was determined at Fifty-seven thousand rupees. The jewellery should be made and delivered to Ramdas in Delhi within a month.

The jewellery was made. I wanted to go and deliver the jewellery to Delhi myself but since last Tuesday my arthritis pain has been bothering me. I was in a fix, what to be done? I cannot dare send such an expensive jewellery with my employees. Hence it was decided that Monimoy would go instead of me. He is supposed to go today.

I have not been able to leave the house for a few days, Moni is looking after the work. The necklace was made, it was kept in the safe of our big store. Moni brought it home yesterday afternoon.

Now let's talk about my house. My wife has gone on a pilgrimage with our younger son Hironmoy they have gone a pilgrimage in Southern India. I, Monimoy and my daughter in law are at home presently. The first floor is occupied by 2 servants, a cook, a driver, and my personal servant Bhola. Currently these are the people residing in the house.

Yesterday evening Monimoy bought the necklace home. At that time, I was sitting in this chair and Bhola was massaging my feet. Moni handed me the necklace and said, "Here it is, father."
I then excused Bhola from work. I opened the case and examined the necklace. Everything was fine. Then I called Bauma and said, 'Bauma, please sew the necklace well with a cloth. Bauma bought a piece of cloth and sew the necklace box with the cloth right here in front of me.

Byomkesh, who had been listening attentively for so long, now raised his face and said, how big is the size of the jewellery box?"

Rosomoy babu hesitantly looked around and said, "How big? Not big enough." Seeing his father hesitant, Monimoy took out a book from the bookshelf and said, "A box of this size." Rosomoy said, "yes, exactly this size. But the box is made of crocodile skin and the interiors lined with velvet cloth."

The book was crown sized of approximately three hundred pages. Byomkesh returned the book to Monimoy and said please continue.

Rosomoy started to speak again, "Then Moni went to the club after having tea. I took the necklace box and went to my office room. My office room is next door. When I need to work from home, I work from that room. I have a secretary desk in that room, I keep important documents in that desk. I placed the necklace box in one of the drawers of the secretary desk. We do have an iron chest, but my wife has taken the keys of the safe along with her."

"I made a grave mistake; I shouldn't have kept such an expensive necklace in a desk without lock and key. But such is the arrangement of our house that I never thought anything would ever be stolen. The servants live on the first floor and do not come upstairs unless called for; and no one else comes to the second floor. Hence, I never thought that the necklace could be stolen from here."

"I finished eating dinner by nine pm. Our dining room is on the first floor, but until since the last few days due to my arthritis pain I am having my dinner in my room only. Bauma bought me my dinner in this room. After finishing dinner, I sat down with a book, bauma also had her dinner. Moni's usually returns late from the club, hence bauma kept his dinner in their room.

"At around ten o'clock I rang the bell to call Bhola, then I prepared to retire for the night. I have severe arthritis; I can't sleep if someone doesn't massage my arms and legs. After massaging when I fall asleep, bhola goes away."

"Bhola is a very handy servant. He has been serving me for the last year and a half. He does all my work like brushing my shoes, washing my clothes, massaging my hands and feet and other menial jobs. Yesterday bauma opened the door, Bhola came and started massaging my hands and feet. I gradually fell asleep; I am not sure when bhola left yesterday."

"I woke up suddenly to Moni's call. He was leaning on my bed calling, Father, Father! I jumped up and said, what happened Moni? Moni said, 'Where have you kept the necklace? I said in the secretary table drawer. Why? He said, where? it's not there."

I ran and opened the drawer. There was no necklace box. I searched through all the drawers, but it was nowhere. You can understand my state of mind. I asked Moni, "How did you know so late in the night. He Said-
Byomkesh raised his hand and requested Rosomoy babu to wait. He looked at Monimoy as asked, what time was it then?
Monimoy hesitatingly said, "About twelve o clock. Maybe five or ten minutes before midnight."

Byomkesh said, 'At midnight for some reason you suspected that the necklace had been stolen. Tell me why you doubted. Please don't hide anything.

Monimoy cleared his throat, cast a furtive glance at his father and said, "Yesterday I was a little too late to return from the club. There was a bridge-drive going on at the club."
Byomkesh asked, "Where's the club? What's the name?
Monimoy said, "Name of the club is khela dhulo. It is very close, a five minutes' walk from our house. It has all kinds of indoor games facilities like cards, dice, ping pong, billiards etc. Last night the bridge-drive ended very late.
"Did you walk to the club?"
"Yes, it's very near, so I usually walk to the club. It was a quarter to twelve when I left the club yesterday. It was almost midnight. There is a lamp post right in front of the main door of our house. When I got within thirty-forty yards of our house I saw, all the shops in the neighborhood were closed, but there was a man standing right in front of our door. The man seemed to hear my footsteps, he looked back, then hurried into our house. From a distance, it seemed, it was bhola our servant. The main door was not locked. Normally I return from the club by ten or ten thirty and the front door is always locked by then. But it is open today. I was shocked, I locked the door and went upstairs and found that the servants were sound asleep on the first floor."

My wife came and opened the door as soon as I reached the second floor. You may have noticed that the second-floor door of is fitted with a bolt lock; if locked from inside you can never open it from the outside without a key. I told my wife; a man was standing in front of the house. she said, she had seen him too.

Byomkesh turned his eyes to the bride The bride was embarrassed; her face became scarlet red. Rosomoy encouraged her, don't be embarrassed. Tell all that you know to Byomkesh babu.
The bride then stuttered and said in a shy voice, "Yesterday my husband was late in returning from the club. I was standing near the window waiting for him. I stood for a long time, then I saw someone standing on the pavement right in front of our main door. I tried to lean over and see but couldn't see very well. Then the man disappeared. He seemed to enter our door. At that time, I saw him coming as it seemed that the man saw him and came inside. Then I went and opened the second-floor door.

Byomkesh asked, "Did you recognise the man?
The bride shook her head, 'No, his face could not be seen from above. But he seemed to be one of the servants.
Byomkesh said to Monimoy, "Then what happened?

Monimoy said, "Hearing what my wife said, my suspicions grew. I had brought the necklace in the evening, father must have kept it in the Secretary table drawer, because mother had taken the key to the chest with her. I quietly went to my father's office. I turned on the light and checked all drawers. No necklace case was to be found. I searched everywhere wherever it was possible to keep it. Alas it was nowhere to be found. Then I awoke my father.
After Monimoy finished, Byomkesh lit another cigarette and looked inquisitively at Rosomoy. He picked up the story from where monimoy had completed.

When we finally released that the necklace was gone, all my suspicions were on bhola.
Just think! our second-floor main door has a yale lock, to go from inside to outside is easy but not easy to come from outside to inside without a key. After ten o'clock at night of all servants only bhola was on the second floor. I fell asleep, I don't know when

Bhola left. Maybe he left at a quarter to twelve, took the necklace from the drawer and slipped quietly down the stairs. Maybe he had accomplice waiting outside the house.

Byomkesh asked Monimoy, "You saw only one person?
Monimoy said, yes. There was no other person.
Byomkesh turned to the bride and said, " and you?"
The bride said, "I also saw one person. I was looking down all the time, if there was anyone else, I would have definitely seen?
Rosomoy said, "It was already twelve o'clock then. I consulted my son and called the police station. Moni went downstairs and stood near the front door, so that no one could leave the house. I know Amaresh Babu, the senior daroga of the police station. He is a gentleman. Fortunately, he was present at the police station, immediately after receiving the call he came with three or four men.

First, the rooms on the first floor were searched. The servants were all asleep, bhola was also present but the necklace was not found. Amaresh Babu then searched the rooms on the second floor. It could be that the thief might have stolen the necklace and hidden it in the second floor itself. But the necklace was not found here either.

Amaresh babu then started interrogating Bhola. Bhola admitted, he had gone downstairs. He said, around eleven o'clock when he realised, I had fallen asleep, he went down to the first floor. The other servants were asleep by then. Bhola also lay down but could not sleep.
Then he went down in search of fresh air and stood on the pavement. He was not aware that monimoy had not returned from the club. As soon as he stood on the footpath, he saw monimoy coming. Then he quickly came back and lay down again

because there is a strict prohibition for servants to go out in the night. This is his statement. He doesn't know about the necklace.

Amaresh babu's interrogating also revealed that Bhola's has two brothers who live in Calcutta, their home is in Mecho bazar. He shares no special bond for with his brothers,but sometimes she goes to visit them at their house if there is no work at hand.

When Amaresh babu was interrogating bhola, his companions were searching the streets. They searched each and every dustbin and every nook and corner of the streets. Moni was also alongside them, but alas nothing was found. It was already dawn by then. Amaresh babu left a man on the first floor. He told Bhola that if he tries to leave this house, he will be arrested.
Then with the passage of time, my mind became restless. Amaresh babu is a workaholic, he will give his best to find the necklace. But I grew restless, Byomkesh babu then I decided to call you. Please find me my necklace. No one else can retrieve it except you.
Byomkesh smiled a little, "You have so much faith in me, I hope I can keep the faith! Bhola is still at home?
Yes, in the room on the first floor."
Please call him I need to ask him a few questions.
Sure. Rosomoy looked at Monimoy. Monimoy left and after a while came back with Bhola.

Bhola's appearance was not different from any other ordinary servant class person. Haggard with age, a thin and frail frame with a high nose and pointed chin. His body was twisted like bamboo and around forty-six years old. There was no sign of fear in his eyes, but a calm demeanour.

Byomkesh examined him closely and said, "I want to ask you a couple of questions?

Bhola simply said, "OK."
What is your name?
Bholanath Das
Where is your native place?
in Medinipur district
How long have you been in Calcutta?
It will be fifteen years.
Your two brothers live in Calcutta?
Yes, they live together in a house in Mecho bazar.
You don't stay along with your brothers?
No. I stay where I work.
Do you have good relations with your brothers?
Not that great. Both are educated and I am uneducated.
What do your brothers do?
One of my brothers works in the post-office, the other one is a Jamadar in the corporation.
Are you married?
I was, my wife is dead.
How long have you been working at this house?
One and a half years.
Where did you work before?
"I have worked in several places.
What work did you do?
I have worked as a house servant. I am not educated hence have no skills.
You might not be educated but have great intellect. Byomkesh said, everyone thinks that you have stolen the necklace.
Bhola was calm and replied, I have not even seen that diamond necklace.
Yesterday when Monimoy babu brought the necklace box and gave it to Rosomoy babu, you were massaging his feet, right?
He did bring a box, but I was not aware of its contents.
You were not able to guess the contents of the Box? Rosomoy babu

asked you to leave before opening the box? Still, you couldn't guess the contents of the box.

No Sir.

Byomkesh remained silent for a while then raised his eyebrows and asked.

Did you leave the house since yesterday evening?

Bhola's eyes had a little worried look, but he said in a simple tone, "Yes, I went out. I had to buy a towel, so I went out post taking permission from boudi.

Byomkesh looked at the bride, The bride nodded her head and agreed.

Rosomoy babu's face seemed like he didn't know about it. Neither did Monimoy, because he had already gone to the club by then. But how did Byomkesh know? Was he throwing a stone in the dark?

He asked Bhola, "How long were you out?

An hour.

It took you an hour to buy towels?

I loitered for a while after buying towels.

Didn't you meet anyone?

No.

Don't you have any friends?

I have acquaintance with two or four people, But no friends.

Last night after dinner you massaged Rosomoy babu's feet?

I massage his feet daily.

Last night till what time did you massage his feet?

I didn't see the clock. Guess till eleven in the night.

When you went down to the first floor, the other servants were awake?

No. All were fast asleep.

No one was awake?

No Sir.

Strange! What did you do next? You went to sleep as well?

Yes Sir.

Then why were you loitering on the street at midnight?

I tried sleeping but could not sleep, thought of getting some fresh air, thought that might help me sleep.

How long were you loitering in the footpath?

Not much, just a couple of minutes. I was not aware that monimoy babu was yet to return from the club. I saw him coming and rushed back to the house.

Did you lock the main door?

I saw monimoy babu was coming hence I did not lock the door.

Byomkesh again took a hard look at bhola, I think he appreciated his calmness. Then he said "Well, you can go now."

Bhola left. When he heard the front door closing, Rosomoy babu asked curiously "What do you think?"

Byomkesh replied with concern, He is very intelligent. He admitted that he went out yesterday evening.

What does it prove?

It proves nothing. Though he may have met his accomplice if any before stealing the necklace. Or else where would the necklace disappear.

Very true.

No further discussion happened about Bhola. Someone knocked on the door and Monimoy immediately went and opened the door. Entered the room a tall wide-faced, amiable man dressed in a khaki uniform. He was none other Daroga Amaresh babu. Rosomoy stood from the sofa and said, "Everyone this is Amaresh babu, do you have any news!

I had been to Mecho bazar to search the residence of Bhola's brothers! He stopped when he caught sight of us. Rosomoy stood up and introduced us. Inspector Mondal, this is Byomkesh Bakshi. I think you have heard his name.

Amaresh babu sat up straight, said in a surprised voice, "Wait! Byomkesh Bakshi? Who has not heard your name! I have also heard your name from Pramod Barat. Sir, do you remember Pramod? You had investigated the rose colony murders. Pramod is my friend.

Byomkesh smiled and said, 'I remember Pramod babu very much. A very intelligent man Amaresh babu said, "He is your ardent devotee. I have heard stories of your strange powers from him. So, are you also investigating this necklace theft? It's an honour to meet and work alongside you. I have heard from Pramod that you are not greedy for fame, you are satisfied only by searching for the truth.

Byomkesh tilted his face and smiled, Inspector Mandal, one who has what he has, he does not crave for it, this is the law of nature. Don't worry you will get the fame for this case. I will be satisfied if I get my remuneration.
Rosomoy babu said in a deep voice, "Please don't say remuneration, Byomkesh babu, Money cannot justify your services. If I get my necklace back, I will do anything to keep your honor.

Byomkesh turned to Amaresh babu, "You have searched the house of Bhola's brothers, did you find anything?
Amaresh babu said, "I did not find anything. His brothers went out to work. Their wives were in the house. But after searching, nothing was found.
Byomkesh thought for a while and said, "Then you suspect that Bhola has had an accomplice in his brothers in this necklace theft.
Amaresh babu said, bhola definitely has an accomplice if not his brothers, then someone else, or how would the necklace vanish in thin air. Monimoy and his wife did not see anyone else. By the time they saw Bhola, his accomplice might have moved away with the goods."

Byomkesh said, Monimoy babu's wife was standing at the window looking at the road for a long time. If bhola had an accomplice wouldn't have she see him.
Then Amaresh babu hesitantly asked, "Do you think it is not Bhola's work?"
I cannot comment anything as of now. You have done a thorough investigation. You have left no stone unturned. Now I just have to think.
Byomkesh stood up, "Now I will take your leave. I will let you know if I find anything.

On returning home I asked, "Whom do you suspect Byomkesh?"
Byomkesh said, "I have three suspects.
"Who are the three suspects?"

"Bhola, Monimoy and Monimoy's wife said Byomkesh as he went to bathe.

I sat and thought. All three can be suspected because they all had an opportunity. All of these there had the opportunity to remove the necklace from Rosomoy's drawer. And Motive? Rich man's sons always have the need for money. Monimoy went to the club and played cards and dice, surely, he used to gamble. Maybe he owes a lot of money, maybe he cannot tell his father because of fear. Monimoy's wife looks calm and polite, but her face shows concern. Women's greed for jewellery can become especially dangerous. But whoever stole the necklace, how did they remove the stolen goods without anyone knowing?

That afternoon, Byomkesh sat on the recliner and gazed at the roof and did not utter a single word. In the evening while drinking tea, he suddenly said, "Come on, let's go for a walk."
"Where to?"
On the footpath in front of Rosomoy babu's house. I have not inspected the place well.

It took us twenty minutes to walk from our house to the footpath in front of Rosomoy babu's house. Byomkesh walked around the footpath. Shops are open on both sides of the house door. A homeopathy medicine shop, a watch shop, two cloth stores. All the shops were busy with customers. The footpath was crowded with pedestrians

There were four windows on the second floor of Rosomoy babu's house. Monimoy's wife was looking out of one of them. I lowered my gaze and found that Byomkesh had suddenly stopped and was looking towards Rosomoy babu's front door. I followed his gaze and saw that Monimoy had opened the door and come out. He was wearing a dhoti, a vest, and had an envelope in his hand. He came out of the door and stood next to a letterbox on the wall. He dropped the letter in the box and started to go back inside!

Who did you write the letter to?
Monimoy was shocked at Byomkesh's appearance. Seeing us, he said, "Oh it's you! Is there any news?"

Byomkesh said, "I will give my news later. To whom did you write the letter?
Monimoy said in a slightly depressed tone, "I wrote to mother to come back soon. But today the letter will not go, the post has gone out early morning. This letter will be dispatched in tomorrow morning's clearance. But you must have received some good news. Pray tell the truth."

Byomkesh said, "I didn't have any news when I left home, but now I do.
"What news? Have you found the necklace?
Yes, I have. I'll tell you later, now I have to go to do some urgent work.
"Won't you come upstairs? Father is anxious to hear from you."
After thinking for a moment, Byomkesh said, "No, the urgent work must be done first. Ajit, you should go upstairs. Tell Rosomoy babu on my behalf that he will get the necklace back tomorrow morning." He said and left hurriedly.

I went upstairs with Monimoy. Rosomoy babu was looking sad and anxious, after hearing Byomkesh's message, he started asking me repeatedly. Will I get the necklace? Are you sure?

I said, "I have never heard Byomkesh give false assurances. When he said that he will retrieve your necklace, he will. After consuming tea, cake and 555 brand of cigarettes, I rode the Cadillac back home.

The evening passed, but Byomkesh still did not return. He returned after yet another hour. I asked, "Where did you go?" He said "to the police station. To meet Amaresh babu.
Why?
I had some urgent work with him. Finish your dinner and sleep early tonight. We must get up early tomorrow morning. Seeing that he did not want to satisfy my curiosity, I got up. Satyawati noticed my face when I sat down to eat and said, "Why is your face swollen? I said, 'Your husband is a turtle. Satyawati tilted her face and laughed, "Out of so many animals why turtle? Because a turtle does not talk.
Satyawati's face filled with sympathy, she said, "So true. I am also angry at him. Well, we may be less intelligent but that does not mean we have less curiosity."
We finished dinner early and went to sleep.

Byomkesh pushed and woke me up before dawn. "Ajit, wake up, we have to go out now. Tea was ready, I quickly cleared my throat and went out with Byomkesh. The streetlights were still burning bright as if guarding the sleeping city.

I still don't know where we are going; After advancing some distance, I realized that we were going towards Rosomoy babu's house. I asked, "Why do we need to visit Rosomoy Babu before dawn?

He said, "There is no need to meet Rosomoy Babu." Then why are we going to his place so early? "We have to strike right now." Please speak straight, don't riddle me.

Byomkesh said, the mail in letterbox on Rosomoy babu's house is cleared at five in the morning. We must be there when the letterbox is opened today.

Few lamps lit up in my clouded mind, but the darkness did not disappear completely. I said, do we expect some action today?

"Then Byomkesh raised his hand and said, "Be patient, friend, be patient?

After walking through a few lanes, we came across Rosomoy babu's house. Two men were hiding there, where the lane met the main road. Byomkesh whispered something in their ear. Then we also hid ourselves in the corner of the lane.

I checked my watch it was ten minutes to five o'clock. The road was still devoid of any traffic, an occasional truck laden with vegetables rumbling by. The inside of Rosomoy babu's house was dark, the front lamppost was shining and throwing light on the front door. The red letterbox next to the main door was hardly visible due to the pamphlets stuck on it. Due to the innumerable pamphlets the letterbox was vaguely visible to the untrained eye.

Every minute was passing so slowly. I could hear the vibration of the hands of my pocket watch in my chest clearly. It was already five o'clock and my body stiffened expecting some action.

Out of the blue someone silently arrived in front of the letterbox. It felt unreal. The man was wearing a khaki uniform with two large bags slung on each shoulder. He lowered the bags on the street and bought out a bunch of keys from his pockets and tried to unlock the letterbox.

Byomkesh waved his hand and beckoned, we advanced like hunters. I peeked from the corner of the street and saw two pair of plain clothed policeman approaching the letterbox.

The man opened the letterbox, and we went and surrounded him. He covered the open letterbox with his back and said in a soft tone, "Who are you, what do you want?"

Byomkesh said in a stern tone, "Your name is Bhootnath Das? You are the elder brother of Bhola?" Bhootnath Das's face was distorted with fear, his eyes almost gouged out and he asked us in a trembling voice, "Who are you?"
Amaresh babu shouted, "We are the police."
Suddenly I realised that Amaresh babu was also clandestinely waiting for the culprit. He came forward and firmly put his hand on Bhootnath's shoulder in a little dramatic manner so as to scare him. The effort was fruitful. Bhootnath was completely disoriented.

Bhootnath cried out loud, Oh Bhola, what you have done to me, you have ruined my life! I will lose my job; I will go to jail.
Amaresh babu shook him vigorously and shouted, where have you kept the stolen necklace? Tell me quick.
Bhootnath fell on Amaresh babu's feet, "Sir, I have not touched that necklace yet. It is still in the letterbox.
I was numb for a while. The necklace was lying in the letterbox on the wall of Rosomoy babu's house since day the before.
Amaresh babu shouted, "Bring out the necklace now Bhootnath.

Bhootnath got up and turned towards the letterbox. There were many letters piled up in the letterbox, he put his hand in and took out a parcel from the rear of the box. A brown package stitched in white cloth, about the size of a crown sized book.

Bhootnath handed over the package to Amaresh babu and said, please take it babu, God knows what is in the parcel, I haven't checked it yet.

At this very moment, Rosomoy babu's front door opened. Rosomoy babu came out leaning on a walking stick and behind him Monimoy and his wife. Their tired and worried eyes spoke that they did not have a good sleep. Rosomoy babu exclaimed, Amaresh babu! Byomkesh babu! What happened? Any news of my necklace?

Byomkesh took the packet from Amaresh babu's hand and handed it to Rosomoy babu, "Here is your necklace. Open it and check."

At around 9:30 in the morning, we were sitting facing each other on the couch in our living room. We requested Satyawati for another round of tea and started discussing the necklace theft.

> Byomkesh said, it unnecessarily took so long, had I noticed that the letterbox was next door, everything would have been settled in five minutes. In the city of Calcutta, there are numerous letterboxes on the walls, but they are not easily visible to the eye. The letterboxes have become almost invisible due to the numerous pamphlets being pasted on them. For those who know It's location, it is not a problem for them, but it is difficult for those who do not of its existence.
>
> When I first heard about the theft of the necklace, I suspected three people. Bhola, Monimoy and Monimoy's wife, one of them was the thief or it may be that two of these may have conspired to steal. Monimoy and Bhola may have conspired, or the husband and wife may have conspired. I could not even rule out any affair between Bhola and Monimoy's wife.
>
> But whoever stole the necklace, where did they hide the stolen goods? Within an hour of the theft, the police came and searched the entire house, but the stolen goods were not found in the house. Only Bhola was on the road in the middle of the night. But he was standing in front of the house, did not go far. He did not meet any other person. If Bhola stole it, what did he do with the necklace? Same question about Monimoy and his wife, if they stole the necklace where did they hide it?
>
> Although I had three suspects, but my prime suspect was bhola. When

monimoy gave the necklace to his father bhola was present there. I was not difficult for him to guess that the case contained expensive jewellery. In the evening he went out to buy towels, this raised my suspicions on him. If he was planning to steal the necklace, he must have had an accomplice outside and he might have gone to inform his accomplice. But how did he steal the jewellery and give it to his accomplice?

Now let's think of monimoy. What if Monimoy and his wife were involved in the crime. What if Monimoy returned home from the club at eleven o'clock at night, stole jewellery from his father's drawer and went out again; Then he hid the jewellery somewhere and returned home at quarter past twelve. Not impossible; But if that is the case, then wouldn't Bhola know about it? Would he have remained silent? At this time, Satyawati entered with tea and placed the cup in front of us and said with a smile, "Look, finally the turtle has uttered a word.

Byomkesh looked angrily at Satyawati. But Satyawati ignored his gaze completely and said, "narrate your story now but you will have to say it again later."

After Satyawati left, we sat in silence for a while and drank tea. It was not difficult to understand that byomkesh did not like the turtle analogy. I felt very happy. Now on I will call him a turtle if I get a chance.

However, after a while he started saying again, "The doubt that was cast on Monimoy and his wife, was only because they had an opportunity to steal. I didn't think about their motive yet. Monimoy may have needed a big sum of money, his wife may have lust for jewellery; But from what I saw of their family life, there doesn't seem to be any need to steal. Rosomoy babu is a loving father, loving father-in-law. He owes nothing to his son and daughter-in-law. No one steals what is available.

But bhola both had the opportunity and motive. The man is very cunning and has a calm demeanour. Maybe he was planning to steal from the very day he joined work and had the whole plan chalked out in his mind. Yesterday evening, he got a chance to make a big heist. Expensive jewellery has arrived at home, but Rosomoy babu's wife has gone on a pilgrimage with the key to the chest.

Bhola had an accomplice in his elder brother Bhootnath. Now remember Bhoothnath works in the post-office; His job is to collect letters from roadside letterboxes and take them to the post-office. He currently works in the Boubazar area; he used to clear the letterbox every morning afternoon and evening.

On the pretext of buying a towel bhola went to Bhootnath. He was told that while cleaning the mail in the morning, he would find a packet in the letterbox, he should not take it, but let it remain in the letterbox. Then after the police investigation is over, he should retrieve it. No one drops packets in a letterbox, so there would be no difficulty in recognising the packet. This packet may not contain an address.

Bhootnath is a good man. But he fell into greed. Greed is sin, sin is death. He will lose his job and probably may go to jail for being an accomplice in theft.

I was groping in the dark until yesterday evening. Then when I saw Monimoy dropping the letter in the letterbox, everything became crystal clear. Bhola had said that one of his brothers works in the post-office. Suddenly everything became crystal clear to me, who is the thief, what has been stolen, where are the stolen goods. Bhola went down the stairs, dropped the packet in the letterbox and went upstairs again. Maybe he stood in front of the door for a minute to catch his breath. Monimoy had not returned from the club and that Monimoy's wife was standing at the window looking for her husband.

When I understood the matter, I rushed to Amaresh babu. I went to the post office to know where Bhootnath works and what are his duties. Now all that was left was to trap the accused and extract their confessions.
I heard a knock on the door and opened the door. It was monimoy at the door.
Byomkesh said from inside, "Come Monimoy babu, Monimoy came in and sat down, he said, father asked me to come here and give this to you. He took a small blue velvet packet from his pocket and placed it in front of Byomkesh. He would have come himself, but his leg.

Byomkesh said, "No, no, why should he come as an old man when there he has a worthy son?
Is he happy to get back the necklace?

Monimoy laughed and shook his head, "indeed he is." He told me, this little thing is not worthy of your talent, but you must take it.

What little thing? Byomkesh opened the packet, A pea shaped diamond sparkled.
A Diamond ring! Exclaimed Byomkesh.
Byomkesh inspected the ring and said thank you. Tell your father that I have accepted the ring though it looks like I'm not fit for it.

Monimoy babu, where are you going? Wont you have some tea? Monimoy said, "I am in a bit of a rush today. I have to board an afternoon flight to Delhi to deliver the necklace to Ramdas Choksi.

Once I am back from Delhi, I will definitely come and have tea in your house.

Then Monimoy left. Almost immediately Satyawati entered the room. She was listening to our conversation from behind the curtains. She asked excitedly, "Show me what gift you got.

Byomkesh was trying to hide the ring, I too it off his hands and gave it to Satyawati. I said, "Take this. It doesn't suit Byomkesh's talent, and I guess he will not take it. So, it's yours.

Byomkesh said, "Hey, hey, what is this! Seeing the ring, Satyawati's eyes widened with joy, "O god, a diamond ring, a very expensive ring! The price of the diamond itself is a few thousand."
Satyawati put the ring on her finger and asked, tell me how it fits?

Satyawati suddenly erupted saying, Oh God, I was frying fish in the kitchen, I almost forgot about it because of this beautiful diamond ring. She wore the ring and hurried towards the kitchen.
Byomkesh lay down on the bed and took a deep breath, said, "A beautiful diamond ring can only increase the radiance of a lovely girl."

Adrishya Trikon

(The Invisible Triangle)

We had heard the story from Police Inspector Ramani Mohan Sanyal. Byomkesh and I had met Ramani babu when we went to a large city in western India on some secret government work. Due to red tape in government work, our work was getting delayed hence we were sitting doing nothing in the Dak bungalow. Ramani Babu used to come to our bungalow almost every evening, and we used to have a good chat. His face was very sweet and charming. But that is his disguise. In fact, he is a very clever and intelligent policeman. His age was less than ours, not more than forty years. But our conversations were very interesting and lively cause we belonged to the same field of catching criminals.

It occurred to us that his frequent visits to us could not be of unselfish kindness; I was waiting in the hope that his purpose of frequent visit would be revealed in due time. Then one day he told us a story. Not exactly a story but a series of events related to a murder.

After finishing his story, Ramani Babu said, " Byomkesh Babu, I know who the killer is, I know why he killed; But still, I can't hang the man on the gallows. I don't have any evidence. The only way is confession if the accused admits the crime himself. You have a lot of tricks in your head, can't you come up with a plan to trap the guy?
Byomkesh smiled and said, "I'll think about it.

"The story attracted me; It seems that Byomkesh's mind will also be drawn towards it. After Ramani babu left that night, Byomkesh said, 'Can't you write a story from the series of events that Ramani babu told us?
I said, "I can. The series of events are interesting. Only I have to understand the psychology of the characters and twine them together."
Byomkesh said, "Then write. But there is one condition: Please don't distort the facts to make the story interesting."
I said, "you don't have to remind me of that."

It took me two days to write the story. After finishing the draft, I gave it to Byomkesh, who read it and said "It seems to be correct. Let's read it to Ramani babu and see what he says.

"When Ramani Babu came at night, I let him read the story. After reading the draft he looked at me with joy and said, "this is it! This is exactly how the events happened and you have done a great job in intertwining the events together in form of a story.

Below is the story.

Shiv Prasad Sarkar was a rich man in this city who was made it big from his liquor business. His was a workaholic and had accumulated a lot of money, besides a huge house, and expensive cars. People called him a miser, he called himself a wise spender. The line between these two attitudes is very thin and we will not try to define it.

But it is in nature of the universe to create an equilibrium. Shiva Prasad Sarkar's only motherless son grew up, his character turned out to be the exact opposite of his father's: he was a spendthrift having no control on his finances, he has no affection for money. He had a deep affection for any legitimate and illegitimate goods that can be obtained using money. He started squandering all the money which his father had accumulated.

His father Shiva Prasad was not blindly in love with his son, but he cared for him a lot. Observing his son's erratic behavior, he married him to a beautiful girl. But that did not change his character. Sunil remained attached to his wife for some time, then got back to his old lifestyle.

The bride's name is Reba; She is beautiful but intelligent, she knew how to hold a family together. Above all, she is educated of modern thinking. She ignored her husband's tyranny and devoted herself to the service of her old father-in-law. Siva Prasad himself looked after the affairs of his business till old age; because the son was incompetent, and Shiva Prasad could not trust any of his employees with his business affairs. Reba used to drive her father-in-law to office, help him with daily business affairs and drive him back home. Thus, Reba took the place of Shiva Prasad's son.

Then, four years after the marriage of Sunil and Reba Shiva Prasad passed away. Upon his death it was revealed that he had bequeathed all the property to his daughter-in-law.

After inheriting all the property, Reba first sold of seventy five percent of the liquor business. She sold of the big house and bought a nice little house in a secluded part of town; she replaced the big car with a small Fiat car. She told the husband, "You will get three hundred rupees per month as monthly allowances. If you borrow any amount from anyone, I will not be responsible for it. I have printed this notice in the newspaper. "Then they moved to the small house and started living there. They did not have any children.

This is the introduction of the story.

Sunil is about thirty years old, has a stalky fat body, a round and flat face resembling an owl. His face seems to portray that he is not intelligent. People who squander away their parents hard earned money, are rarely intelligent but their instincts make up for their lack of intelligence. This is a universal truth which requires no proof. Everyone used to believe that Sunil was a fool having no knowledge of world affairs.

But Sunil was not an idiot. He may not have seemed intelligent, but he was wise. After his father's death, when he saw that the property was gone, he didn't quarrel with his wife, he didn't fight for the money, he went into hibernation. As long as Shiva Prasad was alive, he used to pay Sunil's market debt. But Reba printed an advertisement in the newspaper that she is not liable for his debt, hence no one was willing to loan Sunil money. How much enjoyment can be done on a daily allowance of 10 rupees? So, Sunil started staying at home like a saint. Once or twice a week he used to go out in the evenings. He spent his majority time at home reading thriller novels. His relationship with Reba was purely a practical one; They stayed in the same house but there were huge differences among them. Their sleeping arrangements are also in separate rooms.

Reba drives down to her office in the morning. She owns twenty percent stake in in the liquor business, she checks the accounts herself every day. She returns home in the afternoon for lunch and in evening she goes out again. But this time it is not business; There is a small club of girls, she goes there to meet friends and gossip, sometimes she goes to the theater; Then comes back home. Sunil stays at home all day. There is an old woman, her name is Anna; she does all the housework and cooking, there is no other servant. Reba has reduced costs in all aspects.

One evening, Sunil was reading a mystery novel in in the living room. Reba returned home at eight in the night. She parked the car in the garage, changed his clothes, took a Bengali book in her hand and sat on a sofa in the living room. There was no conversation between husband and wife. There was still time for dinner. Reba opened the book and started reading. The name of the book was "The adventures of Byomkesh Bakshi."

Sunil's blunt face was expressionless. He raised his eyes once and looked at Reba, then fixed his eyes again on the book, then he cleared his throat a little and said, Reba.
Reba raised her eyebrows and looked towards Sunil.

Sunil hesitated a bit and said, "Reba have you ever seen someone lurking around our house at night?"
Reba closed the book and looked at Sunil for a while, and finally said, "No. Why?"
Sunil said slowly, "I have been noticing for a few days, a man keeps lurking around our house after evening. He walks along the road looking towards our house, he seems to be keeping a watch on our house.
Reba thought for a while and said, "What does the man look like?"
Sunil said, "Looks like goon. A black unkept strong young man with turban on his head.

There was pin drop silence for a while; then Reba made up her mind and said, "Tomorrow morning you go to the police station and report this matter. We live in a secluded place, if that person is a thief or goon then we might need their help.

Sunil hesitated for a while, and finally said in a low voice, "You are the owner of the house, it would have been better if you had informed the police."
Reba said, "but I did not see that man. Let us go together and report this matter."

The next morning, they went to the police station; instead of going to the small police station in their area, they went to the Main police station of the town. There the senior constable, Ramani Babu is a Bengali, with whom they had a little acquaintance.

Ramani Babu sat them down and welcomed them. Sunil's manner of speaking was a little slow and random, hence Reba narrated the incident. After the report was registered, Ramani babu said, "Your house is in a secluded part of the city. However, don't be afraid. I am making necessary arrangements; we have a have a patrolling team they will keep an eye on the house at night.

Reba went to work from the police station and Sunil walked back home. That evening, Reba said, "I won't go out today, I am not feeling great." Sunil kept the book aside and said, "Then I will go out for a bit. Dissatisfaction appeared on Reba's face, "You will go out! But don't be late, come back early. Better still you take the car." Sunil said, "No need, I will walk, walking is good for health.
Reba's mind became a little happy in spite of the fear, she loves her little car,cares for it with his own hands; she did not want to leave the car in Sunil's hands.
Sunil wrapped a grey shawl around him and went out. Winter was setting in, by five o'clock it starts getting dark.
By the time Sunil reached the alleys in the center of the city, it was pitch dark. He knocked on the door of a dilapidated house; A dark young man came out. Sunil said in a low voice, "Hukum Singh, I have some work for you?

Hukum Singh saluted Sunil. Mukund Singh and Hukum Singh are two brothers, there are famous wrestlers and goons of the city; They have known Sunil for a long time. Sunil gave some orders to Hukum Singh in a dutiful voice, then handed some money to him hurried out of the lane. In the dim evening light, no one noticed the man in the gray shawl; even if they noticed no one could recognise Sunil Sarkar. There was hardly a possibility that someone from the slum would be acquainted with him.

When Sunil returned home, Reba said, "You have come. What took you so late?" She was relieved to see Sunil back in the house. Reba has no love for Sunil, she has no compulsion to love her husband. She is very practical and independent. But no matter how independent women are, they feel safe when a man is around them.

Sunil looked at the clock and said, "I was gone for not even an hour. I wandered around a bit, but nothing happened.
No further words were spoken. After drinking tea, both sat down reading books.

But Reba could not settle down. The front door was closed, she occasionally got up and looked out the window towards the street. The road in front of their house comes from the city and after passing Reba's house, it disappears into fields and bushes. The last lamppost of the road stands almost in front of the house and shines dimly.

Reba sat on the sofa after peeking out of the window and, opened the book in her hand and kept staring at it. Then she asked, "When does the police patrol come at night?
"Sunil raised his stupid face from the book and looked for a while, finally said, "I don't know. I think it maybe ten or eleven at night.
"Reba made a disgusted face, and but said nothing. Both of them got back to their books.

It was exactly eight o'clock in the night. Reba looked up startled. A sound came from the street. Reba got up, drew the window curtain again, and looked outside. A man was coming from the direction of the city. She could hardly see the man properly in the dull light of the street, he was a strong able bodied dark man with a turban on his head and a long staff in his hand. His turban was shading his face so she was not sure that she could recognise him elsewhere. The man walked towards the house waited for a while and walked away.

Reba started breathing heavily. Sunil turned to Reba and saw that her face was full of fear, she silently asked Sunil to come by the window. Sunil got up and stood by Reba's side next to the window. Reba whispered, "That must be the man you saw the other day." Sunil nodded his head.

Both stood near the window. After some time, the sound of shoes was heard again; the man was coming back. Reba held her breath. The man came and stared at their house and slowly walked back to where he had come from. After his footsteps faded away, Reba looked at Sunil with questioning eyes. Sunil's heart was filled with satisfaction, but he kept a fearful expression on his face and said, "That guy seems to be the one.

"Both of them came back and sat down. Reba's face was full of fear. Sunil opened the book with a furtive glance at her. The maid came and asked if dinner should be served. Then both of them went for dinner. While eating, Sunil said, "It seems like there is nothing to be scared about. The police have said they would keep a watch on our house.

Reba's heart was still pounding hard, she said "The police will not stand guard in front of the house all night, they will come on patrol sometimes. If five robbers break the door and enter the house, then what will we do?

Sunil lowered his head, kept on eating and finally said, "do we have any sticks or iron rod in the house?" Reba looked at her husband with deep annoyance, she did not feel the need to answer this childish question. She said, even if we have who will wield the sticks or iron rod.

Reba bolted the door of her bedroom and went to bed. There was no need for so much caution, Ramani Babu had made good security arrangements and the police was patrolling every few hours. But Reba's anxiety did not go away; she lay awake in bed for a long time.

She thought she should not have bought the house in the outskirts of the city, but who knew then? Now if they leave the house for the fear of burglars, she will lose face in society. The husband is also a worthless idiot. What can be done? What about keeping two strong-armed servants? But can the servants be trusted? The keeper can become the eater. If the robbers subdue the servants by bribing them, they will open the door at night for the robbers to burgle the house. Old Anna is good enough, she is a trustworthy lady who has been working for them for a long time. There are precious jewels in the iron chest in the bedroom, but not a weapon for self-defense.

Reba sat up on the bed excitedly as she suddenly remembered something. Her father-in-law had a pistol. When he died six months ago, the pistol was handed over to the police station. She decided that next morning she will go to the police station and ask Ramani babu to return the pistol. With a weapon in the house there will no more worries of a break in. Reba fell asleep after the thought of getting the pistol back.

The next morning, Reba took Sunil to the police station again. On the way, in response to Sunil's unspoken question, Reba said, "Father's pistol is deposited in the police station, isn't it better to take it back?" Sunil thought for a while with wide open eyes, as if these thoughts did not come to his mind, then shook his neck and said, "It will be good indeed."

At the police station, Ramani Babu heard the proposal and said, "That's fine, just submit an application, and it will be done." The license will be issued in whose name?
Reba had not thought about this. She is a woman, has never fired a pistol before; she was scared of firearms, but she didn't want to reveal it. Reba said, 'Why, in his name?

Ramani babu said," So be it. Please submit your application now; I will visit your house tomorrow as it is a standard procedure. You will get the pistol tomorrow." Reba wrote the application, Sunil signed it. Ramani babu asked, "Sunil babu, have you ever fired a gun before?"
Sunil hesitantly said, "no. Actually yes, long ago I secretly took my father's pistol and had fired it a few times. I was young and imbecile then.
Ramani babu smiled and said, 'It was illegal. One can only fire a gun if they have a license, except special circumstances like when someone is in grave danger of being harmed.
That evening, Ramani Babu came for routine enquiry and after having tea and snacks left after an hour. After spending time with them he formed an opinion about the couple. He thought that Sunil is a dumb and spineless man who is a puppet in the hands of Reba. He thought that dumb people like Sunil go berserk after getting money but now he has recovered. He was still not aware about Sunil's true nature.

The next day, Sunil went to the police station to get the license and the pistol. While returning home he also bought a box of cartridges from the gun shop. When Reba returned home in the afternoon, Sunil placed the pistol and cartridge box on the table in front of her and said, "Here you go."

Reba examined the firearm with a wary look and said, "What should I do?" You keep it, you will use it if needed.
Sunil had expected this, he took the pistol and cartridges and kept them in his room.

Two days later, the turbaned goon was once again seen loitering in the street looking at their house. Then he was not visible for a week.

After a week passed peacefully, Reba breathed a sigh of relief and said, "I think they found out there was a gun in the house, so they gave up on their plans."
Sunil shook his head like a wise man and said, "Yes"

Then as the days passed, Reba's mind became free of fear. She went back to her normal lifestyle. Reba started going to work in the morning and to the ladies' club in the evening. Sunil spent his time at home and read mystery-thrillers; rarely did he leave the house during daytime. However, every evening he went for a walk for an hour. He had no friends; he sometimes went to the railway station to buy books from the book stall; Sometimes he met Hukum Singh in the slums of the city. His work with Hukum Singh was not over yet.

In this way two months passed, winter came to an end, and the thought of getting burgled was completely erased from Reba's mind.

One evening Reba's two friends came home; Reba was busy chatting and entertaining them. When Reba's friends come home, they completely ignore Sunil, he doesn't even get an iota of respect from them. So, when they come, Sunil either stays in his room or goes for a walk. Even today, he went to his room, then quietly left the house through the back door. He was waiting for this opportunity for long.

Sunil went to town and met Hukum Singh in the slums. After ten minutes of listening to Sunil's instructions he finally said, "I have heard that there is a pistol in the house?" Sunil took out the pistol from his pocket, opened the pistol and showed that there was no bullet in it. He said, "You can enter the house without fear."
Hukum Singh folded his hands and said, "My reward?"

Sunil had accumulated six hundred rupees in two months. He handed it to Hukum Singh and said, "Take this. I don't have more now. You finish the work and take the jewelry from her body. Then when I inherit the property, I will get ten thousand Rupees. I am going to the railway station now, will return home after eight o'clock."

Hukum Singh said, 'Very well."
"You will remember my instructions?"
Yes Sir! You stay calm, I'm getting dressed and going out right now.

Hukum Singh entered his house to change his appearance. Sunil did not go to the station but hurried back to his house.

It was already dark. After nearing his house Sunil saw that Reba's friends were still there. He was relieved and hid behind a big tree on the roadside. He stood there and pulled out the pistol from his pocket. From the other pocket he took out the bullets and loaded the pistol. He waited in the dark and prepared for action.

After some time, Reba's friends left, and Reba closed the front door from inside. At around seventy thirty in the evening Reba called Anna and asked, "Where is Sunil?" Anna said, "Sunil Babu has gone out." Your friends entered through the front door and at the same time Sunil babu went out through the rear door." "Well, you go now and prepare dinner."

Reba was not worried. She is no longer afraid of thieves and robbers. She let a sigh of relief at the thought of something else. If life continues like this, what else do I need.

Outside, Sunil was hiding behind a tree and Hukum Singh was seen coming towards his house. He was coming furtively like a blood hound. He came in front of the door, looked back, then knocked softly on the door.

Thinking that Sunil has come, Reba opened the door. Hukum Singh entered swiftly and jumped on Reba and started strangling her with his strong hands. A high-pitched scream escaped Reba's voice, then no more sound. Anna could hear her scream from the kitchen, she came out and saw a large dark man with two hands as black as a hawk, strangling Reba's throat. Anna stood frozen for some time then ran back to the kitchen and slammed the door shut. When Hukum Singh saw that Reba's body was lifeless, he laid her on the floor and took off her bangles, earrings, necklace and put them in his pocket, then went out the front door.

Sunil was waiting behind the tree for this moment. "Shouting who is it? who is it? He ran towards the front door. Hukum Singh stood there in shock, Sunil came running and drew his pistol from his pockets and emptied all the bullets Hukum Singh's chest. Hukum Singh fell there with his face down and dead in a matter of seconds.

Sunil then entered the house shouting, what happened? Ah Reba he said and started crying. Anna heard Sunil's voice from the kitchen and came out trembling. Sunil said in a low voice, "Anna, what happened? Reba is dead! A goon killed Reba. But I also killed the goon! He jumped up and said, the police! I am going to report this incidence to the police and ran out.

After some time, the police came from the local police station. Anna told the police what she had seen. Ramani Babu came after hearing the news. Sunil sipped his drink like a moron and said, "I was out for a walk, when I came back and reached near the house, I heard a scream. I rushed to see the man coming out of the house. My head was disoriented. I killed him with a pistol. Then I entered the house and saw his Reba's dead body lying here. He covered his face with both hands and started crying.

Ramani babu remained silent for a moment and asked, 'You went out for a walk with a pistol?"
Sunil shook his head and said, "yes. The pistol in my name, I always keep pistol with me."
Ramani babu said, give the pistol I confiscated it.
Sunil handed the pistol to Ramani babu without any hesitancy. He no longer needed the pistol.

Byomkesh said, "Sunil Sarkar might seem stupid, but is very intelligent."

Ramani babu said with a hearty laugh, "Byomkesh babu, I thought I was smart, but Sunil Sarkar made a fool of me. I didn't understand his intentions. There is no way I will catch him for murdering Hukum Singh. Apparently, Hukum Singh entered his house and killed his wife and was fleeing away her jewellery, so Sunil had the right to kill her. He killed two birds with one stone; recovered his ancestral property and killed the lone accomplice he had. After the death of his wife, he is now the heir to the property, as he is the next of kin. Reba made was no will so Sunil has inherited the property after the court orders.

Yes, said Byomkesh and plunged into deep thought.
Ramani babu said, "Please find a way, Byomkesh babu. It is unbearable for me to see how easily a criminal can use his intelligence to commit a crime and roam free unhindered. I know he is the mastermind still cannot nab him for I don't have substantial proof.

Byomkesh raised his head and said, 'Reba loved the books written by Ajith?
Ramani babu said, "Yes, Byomkesh babu. I searched their house minutely, I didn't find any useful information, but I saw that all of your exploits written by Ajit Babu were present there having Reba's name written on them. It seems Reba loved reading your exploits."

Byomkesh was again lost in thought. We light up cigarettes and waited for Byomkesh to come up with a solution to this problem. Ten minutes later, Byomkesh sat down. We eagerly looked towards him.
He said, "Ramani babu, can you get hold of a copy of Reba's handwriting?
Reba's handwriting? Ramani babu raised his brows.

Byomkesh said, "I need Reba's handwriting. You can check her account books or can get it from any old letters of her."
Ramani babu scratched his head for a while and finally said, But for what purpose?

Byomkesh said, "The purpose is that Reba loved to read my mystery stories, so it is quite possible for her to write to me for an autograph. Girls have a weakness of writing to famous people and celebrities requesting for an autograph. Now say for example, Reba wrote me a letter six months ago; asked for my autograph, then informed me that her husband was plotting to kill her, and that I should investigate if I heard of her accidental death.

Ramani Babu thought deeply and said, "I understand. Make a fake letter, then show that letter to Sunil and get a confession from him." Byomkesh said, "I will try to get the confession. If he gets scared and tells the truth that is the only way, he can be caught."
Ramani babu said, "I will get Reba's handwriting sample. Anything else?"
Byomkesh asked, "Did Reba have a Letterhead with her name printed on it?
Yes, there was. You will get that as well. Anything else?

Yes, a tape-recording machine. If Sunil confesses, then we have to record that for evidence.
"Fine. I will arrange everything and come again tomorrow morning." Saying that, Ramani Babu left excitedly.

The next morning, we had just woken up when Ramani Babu arrived with a leather satchel in hand. He laughed and said, "I have arranged everything."
Byomkesh gave him a cigarette and said, "What all items have you arranged?
Ramani Babu opened the satchel and took out a piece of paper and said, here you go, this is Reba's handwritten letter.

It was a sheet of paper torn from a letter. The letter was written in Bengali. On it was written, "If the husband has no duty towards the wife, why should the wife have any duty towards the husband? We are people of the modern age, there is no point in clinging to old-fashioned rules."

Byomkesh asked, "This is Reba's handwriting! I see no signature. Where did you get this?
Ramani Babu took a piece of white paper from the satchel and said, "Here is the blank letterhead with Reba's name printed on it. Last night I left here and went to Sunil's house; I told him directly, I will search your house one more time. He didn't object. Will these letters serve the purpose?

Byomkesh observed the piece of the torn letter and said, "Yes this will do. Copying Reba's handwriting will not be difficult. It is not difficult to imitate handwritings of those who write in Rabindriya verses. Have you arranged the tape-recorder?
Ramani babu said, "Got it. I will bring it whenever you say. So, when will you try to force a confession?"
Byomkesh thought for a while and said, "Let us do it today itself, the sooner the better. I will write a letter for Sunil, please arrange for the letter to be delivered to him.

Byomkesh started writing a letter to Sunil.

Dear Mr. Sunil Sarkar,
I was introduced to your wife through correspondence; She loved to read stories crime stories. I heard that she is dead. I am sorry for your loss. I have come here for a few days and am staying in the Dak bungalow. If you can come down this evening at seven in the dak bungalow, I can show you the last letter which I received from your wife. Please Note: This letter is very important for your wellbeing.

Warm Regards,

Byomkesh Bakshi.

Byomkesh stuffed the letter in an envelope and gave it to Ramani babu. He said, "Well, I will leave now. I will send the letter in such a way that Sunil does not know that you have anything to do with the police. I will bring the tape-recorder at noon."

After Ramani babu left, Byomkesh took Reba's handwritten letter and began to examine it. He inspected the letter from all angles, held it up to the light, observed the edges of the torn part. Then he lit up a cigarette and started thinking.
I asked, "what are you thinking about?"
Byomkesh exhaled smoke upwards and said, "The letter was intact, it was torn recently. I am wondering where the rest of the letter is."
I also thought for a while then said, "Reba may have written a letter to a friend of hers, Ramani babu has collected it from her. This friend maybe wants to keep her identity hidden."

Maybe, not impossible. Reba's friend may have given Ramani babu a condition that her name will not be revealed. So Ramani babu avoided my question. Let's get the forgery done. Ajit, give me paper and pen.

Then he took two hours to examine the handwriting of Reba. Finally, he gave me the original and the copy and said, "Let's see how it turned out. Of course, I had to guess the signature, it would have been nice to have a sample of her signature, but I guess this will be good enough.

I Kept Reba's letter and Byomkesh's draft side by side and saw that there was absolutely no difference in the style of writing. An ordinary person would not be able to distinguish if the handwriting in both the letters is different.

Byomkesh then started carefully writing the letter on Reba's letterhead. The letter went like this-

Dear Byomkesh babu,

I can't tell you how happy I am to receive your letter and autograph. You have many discerning readers like me, who must bother you for autographs. Still, thank you very much for writing back to me. Your autograph is treasure for me, and I will carefully keep it with me. Emboldened by your kindness, I am writing something about myself. My husband is dumb and does not have a good character, so at the time of my father-in-law's death he bequeathed all his property to me. The property is huge, and I will not let my husband touch it. I suspect that my husband is plotting to kill me; I think he has hired goons to murder me. I don't know what will happen. But if you get any news of my accidental death, then please look into the matter. You are the truth seeker and I believe you will never remain silent on the death of a helpless woman.

Regards,

Reba Sarkar.

Byomkesh folded the letter and stuffed it into an old envelope.

Ramani Babu came at three o'clock, along with a young policeman, who is a radio operator. In his hands he held a tape-recorder box, a microphone and some other equipment's.

Ramani Babu consulted with Byomkesh and said to radio operator, "Biren, please get down to work. Biren replied in the affirmative and started setting up the equipment.
The microphone was attached to the wire of electric light hanging over the table in the living room. The tape-recorder was placed in Byomkesh's bedroom. When the recorder is turned on, it creates a little noise, if the machine is in another room, the sound of the machine cannot be heard in the living room.

After all equipment was setup, Viren went into the next room and closed the door. We sat by the table and talked in our normal voice and then went into the next room. Viren rewinded the tape of the machine and started it again. We heard our own voices. Our voices were quite clearly audible, it was not difficult to recognize our individual voices. Byomkesh was satisfied and said, "The setup seems good." Have you sent the letter?
Ramani babu said, "Yes have sent it. He will surely come. After receiving such a letter, he will definitely come. He will want to know if you have something that will incriminate him and if you want to blackmail him. Well, we go now, I will come again after evening."

Ramani babu came with Biren at six o clock; the police car dropped them off. Ramani babu said, "I came a little earlier. What do I know, if Sunil comes before seven?"

Byomkesh said, "You did the right thing. At first you both will stay in the next room, so that Sunil does not suspect that I am connected with the police. I and Ajit will stay in the living room; after Sunil comes you will join us when the time is right.

Ramani babu took Biren to the next room and bolted the door. We both prepared for the action and waited in the living room.

Gradually it got dark. I switched on the lights and sat down smoking a cigarette. Byomkesh picked up the morning newspaper and smoked a cigarette while reading it. All my senses were heightened specially my ears. A few minutes before seven o'clock, we heard the sound of a car coming to a halt near the main gate of the Dak Bungalow; We exchanged glances. After two or three minutes, Sunil Sarkar came and stood in front of the door.

There is no particular discrepancy with the description given by Ramani Babu; In addition, I noticed that there was a gap in his teeth and his teeth were sharp and protruding like a crocodile. He had a flat face with short sharp protruding teeth. Altogether, his face was not pleasing to the eye and on top of that he was of evil character. Reba may not have been very affectionate towards her husband, but she cannot be blamed for that cause nor was Sunil good looking nor he had a good character.

Sunil stood like a halfwit near the door for a while, finally said in a broken voice,"Byomkesh babu? Byomkesh was sitting immersed in the newspaper, he turned his head and said, Sunil babu? Come in."

Sunil came and stood near the table with a facial expression of a clown. Who will say seeing him that he is far too clever than what meets the eye? Byomkesh scrutinized him from top to bottom and gave him a hard dry look and said, "You are indeed a good actor, but you are not a buffoon like you want people to presume. Please sit down.

Sunil sighed and sat down on the chair, inspected Byomkesh with his keen eyes and said in astonishment, 'What are you saying?
Byomkesh said, "Nothing. No point in discussing it when you are hell bent on acting stupid. Sunil Babu, you killed two people to get back your ancestral property; One, your wife; second, Hukum Singh. I came here and investigated the matter. You ordered Hukum Singh to kill your wife, then killed Hukum Singh with your own hands. Hukum Singh was an accomplice in your conspiracy, so he needed to be removed; If he was alive,he would have milked you for the rest of his life. You killed two birds with one stone.

Sunil shouted at Byomkesh, "What are you saying! I killed Reba! What are you saying? A goon named Hukum Singh strangled my wife. Anna saw, Anna saw with her own eyes Hukum Singh strangling Reba. Byomkesh said, "Hukum Singh is a mercenary for hire; you gave him money to kill Reba."
"No no, these are all lies. I did not kill Reba; She is my wife, I loved her."

"The proof of how much you loved Reba is in my pocket here said Byomkesh tapping his finger in his breast-pocket."
What? Reba's letter? Let's me see what letter Reba wrote to you." Byomkesh took out the letter and handed it to Sunil. "Don't tear the letter, we have a photostat copy.
Sunil didn't listen to his warning; he held the letter with both hands and started reading.

At this time, Ramani babu quietly opened the door and stood next to Byomkesh's chair. They exchanged glances; Byomkesh shook his head.

When Sunil finished reading the letter, he was the first to look up. His eyes fell on Ramani babu. The mask of stupidity fell from his face in the blink of an eye. He shouted Ohh, this is the matter! Police conspiracy! trying to frame me. Byomkesh babu, do you know who is responsible for Reba's death?Ramani Daroga, said he and pointed a finger at Ramani babu.

We were not prepared for the onslaught from Sunil's side. Byomkesh looked up in surprise and said, "Ramani babu is responsible! What do you mean?
Sunil said, "Don't you understand? Ramani Daroga was Reba's special friend, he was Reba's lover. That is the reason why Ramani Daroga has hatred for me.

The house was silent for a while. I looked at Ramani Babu's face. He was staring at Sunil. His face turned scarlet red with anger. I was afraid that now both men will have a fist fight.

Byomkesh said in a calm tone, "So this is why you killed your wife."
Sunil said, "I didn't kill her. You people thought that you would catch me with this fake letter." Sunil crumpled the letter in his fist and threw it on the table. Sunil Sarkar is not so easy to catch. I am leaving. Arrest me if you can?

We were sitting silent as Sunil slithered away from the room like a snake. In these few moments, Sunil's character real character was visible to us. His character is exactly like that of a snake. Venomous and brutal. He raises his hood like a snake, bites with his venomous fangs and disappears in his hole again.

Ramani babu took a long deep breath and sat on the chair. Byomkesh said to himself, "He slipped away."

Suddenly a muffled sound came from outside. We were all startled. Byomkesh got up first and walked to the door, we followed him. Sunil's car was standing in front of the bungalow and in front of the car on the ground lay Sunil. He was writhing in pain. A knife was protruding from his back. In agonizing pain Sunil tried to roll over; Byomkesh and I helped him roll over. Sunil opened his eyes once, it is not possible to say whether he could recognize us, but he said in a muted voice,"Mukund Singh." then he breathed his last.

I turned and looked everywhere but could not see anyone; the road was deserted. A question arose in my brain, who is Mukund Singh? The name seems familiar. Then remembered, Hukum Singh's brother's name is Mukund Singh. Mukund Singh has avenged the death of his brother.

By the time the body was dispatched, and the legal duties completed, it was already half past nine. We came back and sat down. Ramani Babu was also very tired, he came to and sat with us. Biren was still waiting with the machine in the next room. Ramani babu called him and said, "You go, keep the machine here. I will take it later."
Biren left.

The three of us smoked cigarettes for a while. Then Byomkesh said, "Sunil evaded the law but could not escape the hands of destiny. Was not expecting this turn of events."

Ramani babu said, "One problem is solved, but immediately another problem has arisen. Now Mukund Singh has to be caught. My work is not finished, Byomkesh babu.

After smoking a cigarette in silence for a while, Byomkesh said, "How true is Sunil's complaint?
Ramani babu let a deep sigh and said, "Yes. Me and Reba lived in the same town, in the same neighborhood. I knew her from childhood, but there was no love.

Then when Reba was married to Sunil, she moved to this town, and I met her again. Reba was not of bad character, but I don't know how our proximity grew. I never doubted that Sunil came to know about our proximity, then when Reba died Then I realized that Sunil was a venomous snake in the mask of a moron. Then I tried to trap him, finally you came, and I came to you for help.

Byomkesh said, "The torn part of the letter you gave me was written by Reba to you?
Ramani babu said, "Yes. We couldn't meet often hence Reba used to write letters to me, writing about her ordeals in life and her desires. She wrote many letters to me. But let's not talk more of Reba, tell me what to do with the tape recordings.

Byomkesh said, what else to be done, let's delete it. Come on.
We went to the next room and played the recorder. I heard the living voice of the recently deceased Sunil. Then we erased the recordings.

Chitrachor

(The Photo Thief)

Satyawati came and stood next to Byomkesh's chair with a glass of pomegranate juice. She said, "Come on, drink this."
I looked at the clock and saw that it was exactly four o'clock. Satyawati is as punctual as the clock. Byomkesh was sitting comfortably reading a book, he looked at the cup with sad eyes for a while, then said, "Why should I drink pomegranate juice every?"
Satyawati said, "Doctor's orders."
Byomkesh grimaced and said, "To hell with the doctor. I don't like to drink it. What good will it do?"

Satyawati said, "pomegranate juice will increase your blood count, come on be a good boy and drink it." be blood on the body.
"Byomkesh looked towards Satyawati, and asked, "What is there for dinner?"
Satyawati said, "Chicken broth and toast?"
Byomkesh grimaced and said, again chicken broth, and who will eat the chicken.
Satyawati smiled and said, "Who else but Ajit."
I quickly said, "Not only me, but your better half will also get a share."
Byomkesh glanced at me with anger, then swallowed the pomegranate juice and made a distorted face.

A few days ago, I took Byomkesh to a town in Santhal Pargana for a change of air. In Calcutta, Byomkesh was suddenly stricken with a serious illness and became bedridden; after two months of tug-of-war with death, we rescued him. While caring for the patient, Satyawati became as thin as a stick, my condition also deteriorated. Therefore, on the advice of the doctor, we went out in search of fresh air and water in the Santhal Pargana. Coming here, the results were visible soon. Satyawati and myself have regained our health and Byomkesh's health too has improved with rapid blood circulation and an insatiable hunger. After his long illness his disposition has become that of a child; all day long he craves for food. It is with great difficulty that we both keep him under control.

I have met only two gentlemen since coming here. One, Professor Adinath Som; We have rented the lower floor of his house. Second, the local doctor Ashwini Ghatak. We have brought a patient here alongside us, so I felt it was necessary to have acquaintance with a doctor. There are many other bengali's in the city, but I haven't had a chance to talk to anyone yet. I have not been able to go out of the house since coming here, the days have passed caring for byomkesh and unpacking stuff and settling down. Today is the first opportunity; A prominent bengali in the city has invited us for a tea party. Although we did not want to reveal our true identity still the news of Byomkesh's arrival has spread through the city like the aroma of jasmine and hence the invitation for a tea party.

We didn't want to take Byomkesh to the tea party so soon; but being locked up in the house for a long time, he is fed up; The doctor has also given permission, so we decided to go to the tea party.

Byomkesh sat comfortably reading a book and kept glancing at the clock. I was standing by the window lazily smoking a cigarette; The beautiful scenery of the Santhal Parganas caught my attention. Here there is a close union of lushness with dryness, emptiness with abundance; Human presence is yet to turn this beautiful paradise into shambles.

Byomkesh suddenly asked, "When did you ask the rickshaw to come?"
I said, "Half past four."
Byomkesh looked at the clock once more and lowered his gaze into the book. The feeble sound of the seconds hand has made him impatient. I laughed and said, Have some patience my dear friend.

Byomkesh snarled at me, "Aren't you ashamed! You are smoking a cigarette right in front of me.
I threw the half-smoked cigarette through the window. Byomkesh is yet to receive permission from Satyawati to smoke; Satyawati has sworn him to not smoke without getting her permission. She had said, "If you smoke without my permission, you will find me dead." I also avoided smoking in front of Byomkesh, because there is no more sin than

showing greed to a vowed drug addict. But sometimes mistakes do happen.

Exactly at half past four two rickshaws arrived at our main door. We were already dressed up and ready to leave. We went out as soon as the rickshaws arrived.

There was no connection of the ground floor to the first floor, the stairs to the first floor were located on the eastern side of the open balcony. There was a little open space infront of the house, then the main gate. I came out of the house and saw our landlord Professor Som standing near the gate with an annoyed face.

I think Professor Som is around forty years old, but he does not appear to be more than thirty; his behavior shows no sign of maturity and he is very active and athletic. But there is one thorn in his life, his wife! He does not have a happy married life.

Professor Som was standing outside well dressed for attending the tea party. I knew he was invited to the tea part, so I asked,"You are standing here alone! Wont you be going to the party?"
Professor Som once looked at the first floor of his house and said, "We will go. But my wife is yet to get dressed. You guys carry on. Will join you later."

We sat on the rickshaw. Byomkesh and Satyawati sat in one, and I sat alone in the other. I saw a smile flash on Byomkesh's face. Satyawati tied a shawl around him, and she didn't want him to catch a cold.
The rickshaw started moving on the gravel road and I enjoyed the surroundings. The place was not crowded with houses, but few houses were scattered here and there along the road. The place was serene and calm and devoid of pollution with few houses spread out on the uneven hillside. Though the city is large, but it is scarcely populated and there is prosperity here. A few nearby mica mines are the main source of prosperity here. This city has courts, banks etc. and majority of the prominent residents here are Bengalis.

The person who invited us is Mahidhar Chowdhury. I have heard from Professor Som that this gentleman is very generous; Even though he is old, he is always indulged in various types of activities. He is a spendthrift and finds ways to spend his money by arranging hunting sessions, throwing picnics and parties etc.

We arrived in front of his residence within fifteen minutes. Around ten bighas of land is surrounded by a stone wall, the place resembles a fort. The place is full of greenery containing several trees, seasonal flower gardens. The uneven, rocky land contains a fishpond full of exotic fishes and other expensive marble statues. By looking at his garden, it is not difficult to understand that Mahidhar Babu is super rich.

In front of the house there is a flat tennis court with trimmed grass, tables and chairs have been arranged on it for the guests to sit, the evening winter sun has kept the place warm. The beautiful two-storied house seems to have composed the background of this scene. When we arrived, Mahidhar Babu welcomed us. The man is of huge built, fair body, short trimmed white hair, a clean shaved round face and a smile between his cheeks. His face suggests that he is innocent and simple natured person.

He introduced us with his daughter Rajani. Rajani is about twenty or twenty-one years old; she is a beautiful girl of fair skin and a jovial nature. Her eyes portray her intelligence and witty nature. Mahidhar Babu is a widower, and this girl is his only relative and heir.

Rajani instantly made friends with Satyawati and took her to a distant sofa and started gossiping. We also sat down. All the invited guests are yet to arrive, only Dr. Ashwini Ghatak and another gentleman have arrived. Doctor Ghatak was already known to us; we started a conversation with the other gentleman. His name is Nakulesh Sarkar; A middle-class businessman who also is a photographer and owns a photography studio. Photography is his hobby; he earns a good amount from photography and is the only photographer in town.

The conversation began in general. Mahidhar babu once pointed at Doctor Ghatak and said, "Oh Ghatak, you can't make Byomkesh babu strong even after so long! Are you a general physician or veterinary doctor, like your name suggests? ha-ha." He started laughing.

Nakulesh babu burst out and said, "Is there a way without becoming a horse doctor? It's Ashwini and then Ghatak, both him first name and family name are synonyms of horse."

The doctor is much younger than us hence he didn't mind the joyful banter. I saw that many people tease Doctor Ghatak, but all revere his medical practice. There are a few other senior doctors in the city, but this young chap has made a good name for himself in the last three years.

Gradually, the other guests started arriving. First came Ushanath Ghosh along with his wife and son. He is a deputy, in-charge of the government depot here. He has a tall and broad face, dark complexion, dark glasses. Aged about thirty-five, he is of serious nature and pauses while he speaks and has a poker face smile. His wife is frail and thin with a face full of eagerness and always anxiously looking at her husband from time to time. The son is five years old; he seems to be shrinking in fear all the time. Ushanath Babu probably keeps his family members in strict control and has complete authority over his wife and child.

Mahidhar babu introduced him to us, he uttered two or four words in a low voice with a serious face. It seemed like a mundane greeting, but we could not hear anything. His eyes remained invisible behind two black glasses. I started to feel a little uncomfortable,there is no happiness in talking to people whose eyes are not visible to you.

Then came the DSP of police, Mr. Purandar Pandey. He is not a Bengali but speaks crisp Bengali; He also likes to socialize with Bengalis. The man looks handsome dressed in a police uniform. He held Byomkesh's hand and said with a soft smile, "You have come, but it is our misfortune not to welcome you with a complex mystery. There is a complete lack of mystery in our area. It is not that there is no theft, but there is no room for using grey matter in these cases."

Byomkesh also laughed and said, "That is good for me. I am supposed to be deprived of complex mysteries and many other tempting things. Doctor's advice you see.
At this time another guest appeared. This is Amresh Raha, the manager of the local bank. He is thin and has a very normal frame, his face lacks any special characteristics apart from a french beard. I think he is trying

to give his face some character by sporting a french beard. His age is hard to determine, somewhere between late adolescence and middle adulthood.

Mahidhar babu said, 'Amresh babu, you were too eager to meet Byomkesh babu. Here you go."
Amresh babu bowed and said cheerfully, "Who doesn't want to meet a distinguished man? You were equally eager to meet him, why blame me only?"

Mahidhar babu said, "But you are too late to come today. Everyone has come, only Professor Som is left. He still has a valid excuse; Girls take a long time to dress up. You don't have that excuse either. The bank closes at half past three, what took you so long?

Amresh Raha said, "I thought I would come in early, but Christmas is almost here, hence the work pressure is a bit more. The year is also coming to an end, people will start withdrawing money from the bank as soon as the new year comes. It must be arranged, hence the delay in coming here."

In the meanwhile, some servers had already started bringing various food and drinks from inside the house in big trays and placing them on the tables. Tea, cakes, Sandesh, poppadum's, Dalmut etc.
Rajani got up and started serving the food. Some people went and picked up the plates by themselves. Soon the place was filled with laughter and jovial conversations.

Rajani took a plate of sweets, stood in front of Byomkesh and smilingly said," Byomkesh babu, have few sweets?
Byomkesh had a glance at Satyawati, he saw that Satyawati was keeping an eye on him. Byomkesh scratched his neck and said, "You have to excuse me, I am not allowed to eat these things.
Mahidhar babu looked at Byomkesh and said, you aren't allowed to have anything? Please have a few. Hey, doctor, isn't your patient allowed to eat anything? The doctor stood near the table and chewed a handful of Dalmut in his mouth, saying, "It is advised not to eat these snacks."

Byomkesh smiled and said, you heard it from the doctor, just give me a cup of tea. Do not be disheartened, we will come again; today's visit is just a prelude.

Mahidhar Babu was happy and said, "Every evening someone or the other comes at my house. It would be good if you also come in the evening's, we will have great discussions.

Finally, Professor Som came along with his wife to the party. Professor Som seemed a tad shy. I am yet to give the description of Malati Devi i.e., Professor Som's wife. Malati Devi is almost equal to her husband in age; she has a dark fat loose body; it is unlikely that anyone will be impressed by her looks.

Moreover, she likes to put on a lot of makeup and dresses loudly. The way she has dressed up today for a tea party would even bring shame to celebrities. She is wearing a scarlet red Madrasi silk saree, and her entire body covered with gold and diamond jewelry. Professor Som was dressed simply, and the couple bore a stark difference in their appearance.

Rajani hurried to meet and greet them, but Malati Devi's face bore no happiness. She glanced from Rajani's face to her husband's face with crooked eyes and sat down on the chair.

The party was in full flow with everyone gossiping among themselves. Byomkesh's face bore the expression like that of a martyr, he sat silently sipping on tea. I took a drink and started chatting with Nakulesh Babu; Ushanath Babu was listening to Purandar Pande with a serious face and shaking his neck in unison; His son sneaked up to the dining table and came back with a sad face; His mother held a plate of food and looked worriedly at her son and then towards her husband seeking permission.

At this time, among the clatter of conversation was heard Mahidhar Babu's high-pitched voice, he said, "Mr. Pandey weren't you saying a while ago that there is a complete lack of complex mysteries in our area. You all judge how far this is true. A thief entered my house last night."

The murmur was silenced; suddenly all eyes fell on Mahidhar Babu. He was standing with a smile on his face, as if the news was very funny.

Mr. Amresh babu asked, "Has something been stolen or not?"
Mahidhar Babu said, "That is a complex mystery. A framed photograph was stolen from the drawing room wall. I did not hear anything at night, in the morning I saw that the photograph was missing, and a window was open.
Purandar Pandey came and stood next to him, said, "Picture! Which picture?"

A group-photograph. A month ago, we all went for a picnic, that time Nakulesh babu had clicked the photo.
Pandey said, "Ok. Was anything else stolen? Were there any valuable things in the house?"
Mahidhar Babu said, "There were a few flower vases; apart from that, there were many silver wares in the next room. The thief escaped with nothing but a photograph. Tell me isn't this a complex mystery?
Mr. Pandey gave a wry smile and said, "If you want to believe it is a complex mystery, then you can." I am of the opinion that a tribal santhal saw your window open, entered inside and was attracted to the golden frame of the photograph. He might have thought that the frame is made of gold."

Mahidhar Babu turned to Byomkesh and said, "Byomkesh babu, what do you think?"
Byomkesh had been listening to their questions and answers for long, but his eyes were wandering lazily around, he now became a little conscious and said, "Mr. Pandey seems to have got it right. Nakulesh babu, you clicked the picture?"

Nakulesh babu said, " Yes. The photo turned out very good. I printed three copies. Mahidhar babu took one copy."
Ushanath Babu cleared his throat and said, "I bought one too."
Byomkesh asked, "Is your copy intact?
Ushanath babu said, "I don't know. I put it in the album, then I didn't see it again. It should be there."
"And who took the third picture, Nakulesh babu?"
"Professor Som."

We all looked at Professor Som. He was sitting lifelessly next to his wife. He became startled at the utterance of his name and his face turned red gradually. But Malati Devi's face showed no emotion; she remained as steadfast as a rock.

Byomkesh said, "Your photograph is intact, right?
Professor Som said with an annoyed face, "umm...umm...maybe, I am not sure.
I was a little surprised to see his expression. It was not a serious matter, why did he become so restless?

Amresh Babu rescued him from this situation. He smiled and said, "Let it be. If it is not there, then order a new copy." Nakulesh babu, I want one too. I was in the group too."
Nakulesh babu scratched his head. Said, "That photo will not be available anymore! Can't find the negative.
"What! Where has the negative gone?"

I saw Byomkesh was looking intently at Nakulesh babu. He said,"It was in my studio with other negatives. I went to Calcutta for a couple of days, the studio was closed; when I came back, I couldn't find it."
Mr. Pandey said, "You will find it for sure, do a thorough search. It should be there, where else can it go?

There was no further discussion on this subject. Meanwhile, the shadows of the evening were slowly drawing in. We decided return to our home, as it is not safe to keep Byomkesh outside after sunset.

Then suddendly I saw a ghostly man come and stand beside Mahidhar babu. It could be guessed from his attire that he was not an invited guest. His long skeleton thin body was wrapped in a half-dirty dhoti and cotton shirt, his eyes had sunk in, and he looked like he hadn't had food for several days.

Mahidhar babu was sitting not far from me, so I overheard their conversation. Mahidhar babu said in a slightly unhappy tone, "What do you want again? I gave you the money day before only."
"Sir, I don't want money," said the man in a low voice. I have drawn a picture of you, so I brought it to show you."
"My picture!"

The man had a folded paper in his hand, he opened it and held it in front of Mahidhar babu's eyes. Mahidhar Babu looked at the photo in amazement. I was also curious, got up and stood behind Mahidhar babu's chair. I was surprised to see the picture. Crayon drawing on white paper, a bust portrait of Mahidhar Babu; the photo was an exact representation of Mahidhar babu's face.

Seeing me, Rajani also got up and stood behind Mahidhar babu's chair, she exclaimed "wow! What a beautiful picture."
Then some others came and joined in. The photo was passed from one hand to another and everyone were full of applause for the artist. The starving artist stood nearby and rubbed both his hands.

Mahidhar Babu said to him, "You can draw beautiful pictures. What is your name?"
The painter said, "my name is Falguni Pal."
Mahidhar Babu took out a ten-rupee note from his pocket and said in a happy voice, "Very well. I will take the picture. Here's your reward."
Falguni raised her hand like a crab and immediately pocketed the note.

Purandar Pandey was looking at the picture with his brow furrowed, he suddenly raised his face and asked Falguni, "How did you draw his picture? From a photograph?
Falguni said, "Oh, no. I saw him once the day before."
"So, you saw him only once and you drew his picture?"

Falguni said excitedly, "I can, I can. If you allow me, I can draw your picture as well."
Pandey remained silent for a while and said, "Okay, well. If you can draw my picture, I will also give you ten rupees as a reward."
Falguni bowed to everyone and went away. Pandey looked at Byomkesh and said, "Let's see." I wasn't in that picnic group."
Byomkesh nodded with his approval.

Then the party came to an end. Mahidhar babu's drove us back home in his car alongside Professor Som and Malati devi. At around eight o' clock in the night, the three of us were sitting in the living room with the doors closed. There was still time for dinner, Byomkesh was sitting comfortably sipping the strong medicine; Satyawati was sitting next to him on a chair wrapped in a shawl. I sat in front and occasionally taking out a cigarette pack from my pocket and putting it back inside. I had no desire to face the ire of Byomkesh for smoking Infront of him. We were discussing the events that occurred in the tea party.

I said, "How much we love art and literature. Falguni Pal is a shining example."The man is truly virtuous, but he is begging to feed his stomach.
Byomkesh was a little indifferent, he said, "He is begging to feed his stomach. How do you know?"
I said, "It is not difficult to guess his famished condition by looking at his face and clothes."
Byomkesh smiled a little, "You guessed wrong because it is not difficult. You are a writer, your sympathy towards an artist is natural. But lack of food is not the reason for the physical deterioration of Falguni Pal. In fact, he is more attracted to drinks than food."

You mean to say he is an alcoholic? How did you know?
First, by looking at his lips. If you notice the lips of a drunkard, you will see notice some defining characteristics, A little wet, a little dry. I can't explain it exactly, but I can understand it when I see it. Secondly, if Falguni was hungry, he would have looked greedily at the food items, there was still plenty of food on the table. But Falguni never looked at the food. Thirdly, I smelled alcohol on him when he passed me. Not very clear, but a faint smell of alcohol. Saying that, Byomkesh picked up his medicine cup and took a sip.

Satyawati said, "Lets it be, I don't like to listen to about drunkards. But what is the matter of photo theft? I did not understand anything. Why would someone steal a photograph?"

Byomkesh said to himself, "Maybe Pandey Saheb is right. But if not, then it is a matter of concern. It a group photograph which was taken at the picnic. Those who were invited at the Tea party today were in the Picnic except Pandey Saheb. Three copies were printed; One of them has been stolen, it is not known whether the other two are intact and the negative is also missing. After being silent for a while, he suddenly pointed his finger towards the ceiling and said, "I don't understand why he was so nervous when I asked him if his copy was intact?

After a moment of silence I said, "If someone has stolen that photograph with a special purpose, what could that purpose be?"

Byomkesh said, "There can be various motives?" Is it so easy to find out what is the motive, we have to look at different variables to come to a solution. I saw in an American newspaper that day, there is a monkey couple in their zoo. The male monkey is so ferocious that he drags the female away and hides her when a male visitor approaches the cage."

Satyawati giggled and said, "You have so many bogus stories. Can monkeys be so intelligent?
Byomkesh said, "It is not intelligence, but passion, Sexual jealousy in simple terms. Humans too possess that; Hope you will not deny that? Males have it, females have it more. if I get very friendly with Mahidhar babu's daughter Rajini, won't you be jealous?

Satyawati held one end of the shawl to her lips and remained silent with downcast eyes. I said, "But what is the connection between sexual jealousy and the stealing of pictures?"

Where there is free interaction of men and women, such jealousy can exist" said Byomkesh, while looking upwards at the ceiling.
"This motive does not seem very strong. But can't there be any other motive?"

"Maybe. Painter Falguni Pal may have stolen it. His claim that he can draw a picture by looking at a person is probably false. Pictures can be easily drawn by looking at photos. Falguni is trying to earn more money by impressing everyone, who knows!"
"Hmm...Anything else."

Byomkesh said with a laugh, "Photographer Nakulesh babu may have stolen the picture himself."
"What is Nakulesh babu's interest? "
"His picture will sell more." Byomkesh said with a small smile."
Do you think it's possible?" "Nothing is impossible in business. In America, crops are burned to raise the price of crops.

"Well. Anyone else?"

There may be someone among this group who wants to obliterate their existence.
"You mean a hardcore criminal?"

This time there was a soft tap on the door. I went and opened the door. Professor Som stood in a warm dressing-gown, I welcomed him. He came down about this time almost every day since we arrived. We used to gossip for a while; then he used to leave when it was time for dinner. His wife had come down a couple of times during the day she did not show any particular interest in us. Satyawati too was not keen in interacting with her.

Professor Som came and sat down. I gave him a cigarette and lit one myself. This is an opportunity to smoke in the presence of Byomkesh; he cannot say anything to me.
Professor Som asked, "How was the party today?
Byomkesh said, "It was nice. Everyone seemed to be quite charming gentlemen."

Professor Som took a drag on his cigarette and said, "It usually looks that way from the outside. But who knows it better than you? Mrs. Bakshi, tell me who you liked the most among the people you talked to today."

Satyawati said without hesitation, "Rajani. She has a beautiful nature, I liked her very much. Som's face lit up a little. Satyawati did not notice it and continued saying, "Sweet looks as well as sweet words, and great intelligence. Well, why is Mahidhar Babu not getting her girl married yet? He has no shortage of money."

We were startled to hear a sharp voice from near the door.
"Widow! Widow! Which Hindu son will marry a widow? We did not realise when Malati Devi came and stood at the door. As unexpected was the news was, so was the appearance of Malati Devi. I stared in astonishment. Malati Devi looked at us one by one with jealous eyes and said again, "You don't believe me? Ask him he knows. Everyone here knows. A widow doesn't dress up like a young girl. But she has no shame because she uses her beauty to trap men."

Malati Devi left as suddenly as she had arrived. We heard her steps on the stairs.

Professor Som was the most shocked of all of us. He could not rise his head in shame. A moment passed in silence. At last, he raised his face and said, "Please forgive me. Sometimes I want to runaway somewhere far from here, his voice trailed off.

Byomkesh asked in a low voice, "Rajani is really a widow?"
Som said slowly, "yes. She became a widow at the age of fourteen. Mahidhar Babu had married her off to a meritorious university student. Two days after the wedding, he boarded a plane and left for a foreign university to study. Mahidhar Babu sent his son-in-law to foreign to study. But he did not reach the country; he died in a plane crash on the way. Rajini can be called a virgin.

Everyone was silent for a while. I gave Professor Som another cigarette and held the lighted matchstick for him. After lighting up the cigarette Professor Som said, you are aware about my marital life. My life history is also like that of Mahidhar babu's son-in-law. I was the son of a poor man but a good student. I got married and went to attend foreign university with my father-in-law's money. But alas, my life took a different turn. I returned after studying and became a college professor. But I could not last long. I have been living here for seven years now after leaving work. There is no shortage of fooding or clothing; My wife has a lot of money."

I could feel the bitterness in his heart came out in his words. I hesitated a little and asked,"Why did you leave work?
Professor Som stood up and said, "in shame. In the era of women freedom, a wife cannot be locked in the house but what about us men. Sometimes I think, if the plane crash had happened to me instead of Rajini's husband, everyone would have been happy."

Professor Som moved towards the door. Byomkesh said from behind, "Professor Som, if you don't mind, let me ask you a question. Where is the group picture you bought?"
He said, my wife tore the photograph to tiny pieces because Rajani and I were standing side by side in the photograph.
Professor Som slowly left our room.

We did not have much conversation during dinner. Satyawati said, " Whatever one says, Rajani is a very good girl. She became a widow at a young age, what's wrong in it, if a father wants to dress her little girl up?"

Byomkesh took one look at Satyawati, then said casually, "I noticed a little incident at the party today, I guess you didn't see it. Mahidhar babu was narrating the story of the stolen picture, all eyes were on him. I saw Doctor Ghatak standing a little far away, Rajani silently went up to him and slipped a folded paper into his pocket. A startled exchange happened between the two. Then Rajani moved away. I think no one noticed the scene except me. Not even Malati Devi."

Five or six days have passed by. Byomkesh's health has improved in these few days and his appetite has increased exponentially. Satyawati has allowed him to smoke two cigarettes a day. I too have grown fat like a turkey due to the delicious meals served daily, even Satyawati's health has improved a lot. Daily In the evening we took Byomkesh for a walk on the streets, for breathing fresh air and because it is essential for quick recovery. Everyone among us was happy.

One day we were out for a walk when Professor Som came and joined us, saying, "Let's go, I am your fellow traveler today."
Satyawati asked, " and Mrs. Som, is she joining us?"
Som said cheerfully, "No. She has a cold. She is lying down."

Som is a sociable man, who becomes a little private when he is only with his wife. We wandered around the streets discussing various topics and the topic of the photo theft arose naturally.

Byomkesh said, "Well, tell me, was there any proposal to print this photo in a newspaper or magazine?" Som looked at Byomkesh with surprise for once, then said, "I never heard of anything like that. But Nakulesh babu has been to Calcutta in the meantime. Will he print the picture in a magazine or newspaper without informing us? I don't think so. Especially if Deputy Ushanath babu finds out he will be very upset."

"Why would Ushanath Babu be upset?"

"He is a bit of a strange person. He is quite a serious and arrogant on the outside but is of timid nature on the inside. He is especially afraid of the English masters. Maybe the Saheb's don't seem to want a Hakim to be photographed with ordinary people, so it is difficult to take photographs of Ushanath Babu. I remember, during the picnic, he did not want to be part of the first photo. He had to be persuaded by all of us. If this photo is printed in the paper, then Ushanath Babu will not spare Nakulesh babu.

I could tell by Byomkesh's face that he was getting excited. He asked, "Does Ushanath babu always wear those dark glasses."
Som said, "Yes. He has been transferred here a year and a half ago, and I have never seen him without those glasses. Maybe he has weak eyesight; cannot stand the light?

Byomkesh did not ask any more questions about Ushanath babu. Suddenly he asked, "what kind of a person is photographer Nakulesh Sarkar."
He is a shrewd and intelligent businessman, he always butters Mahidhar Babu, I have heard he has borrowed money from him."
"Is that so! how much money?"
"I don't know exactly but a large sum."

At this time, I heard the distant sound of a motorbike and saw a motorbike coming towards us. As we moved closer, I recognized the rider, DSP Purandar Pandey. He also recognized us, stopped the motorbike and greeted us cheerfully.

After exchanging pleasantries, Byomkesh asked, "Has Falguni Pal drawn your picture?"
Pandey's eyes widened and said, "It's amazing sir, he showed up with the picture the very next day. He drew the exact picture. But there's no chance of my photo getting into his hands. Truly a good artist I had to give him ten rupees as promised.

Byomkesh asked inquisitively, "Where does he live?"
"What to say, such a talented guy but leads a miserable life. He is a seasoned Drug addict--alcohol, marijuana, cocaine, he is a hardcore drug addict. Been here for a month. He sleeps wherever he finds suitable, sometimes on someone's balcony, sometimes on someone's

haystack. Mahidhar Babu allowed him to stay in his garden. In a corner of Mahidhar babu's garden compound there is a small hut, he has been staying there since the last couple of days."

His fate is similar to the fate of miserable and characterless artist. But I was reassured to know that he had found a shelter.

When Pandey started the motorbike, Som said, "Where are you going?" Pandey said, "I am going to Mahidhar babu's house. I heard from Nakulesh babu that he has suddenly fallen ill. So, on my way home I will take an update on his health."
"What ailment?"
"A little cold. But he is an asthma patient as well."
Som said, "I should go see him too. Mahidhar babu loves me very much."
Pandey said, "Well, jump on the back seat, let's go together. I'll drop you off at home when I get back." "That would be great," said Som, sitting on the rear seat of the motorbike behind DSP Pandey.
Byomkesh said, 'Well, tell Mahidhar babu we will go tomorrow afternoon."
"Ok Sure. Namaskar."

The motorbike drove off. We also turned towards our house. I noticed Byomkesh smiling to himself. I went back home and sat down to drink tea. Byomkesh remained a little absent minded. The door was open; heavy footsteps were heard on the stairs. Byomkesh was startled and said in a low voice, "If you need to answer the question of where Som has gone, say that he has gone to Mr. Pandey's house."

Before Byomkesh's advice could sink in, the need to answer the question appeared. Malati Devi came and stood near the door. Due to cold her face grew heavier and eyes ragged; she cast an inquisitive glance around the room. Satyawati stood up and said, "Come in, Mrs. Som." Malati Devi said hoarsely, 'No, my health is not good, Mr. Som went along with you, where did he go?

Byomkesh stood beside the door and said, "we met Mr. Pandey on the road, he took Professor Som to his house."
Malati Devi said in fear, "DSP Pandey? What does he need with him?"

Byomkesh said simply, "I did not hear anything about that. Pandey said, let's have tea at my house. Maybe they went to discuss some work." Malati Devi took a good look at the faces of the three of us, took a deep breath, then went upstairs without uttering another word. We came back and sat down.

Byomkesh looked at with embarrassment and said, "I had to lie through my teeth. What else could I do? I didn't want them to have a marital discord."
Satyawati said in a crooked tone, "Your sympathy is only towards men. Mrs. Som must have her reasons to suspect Mr. Som."

Byomkesh's voice got strong, he said, "and your sympathy is only towards women. If you people don't get your husband's love, you all become jealous, but you don't know how to keep your husband's love. Listen, Ajit, you have to be on guard on the outside balcony. Professor Som needs to be warned when he returns, if he is caught lying, then Professor Som will face trouble and we will also be in dire straits.
I had no objection. There was a chair lying on the outside balcony, I sat on the chair and smoked a cigarette with happiness. It's a bit cold outside, but it doesn't feel cold if you wear a sweater.
Professor Som returned after about an hour. The sound of motorbike could be heard. It stopped just outside the gate. Mr. Pandey dropped Professor Som and left. When he got on the balcony, I said, "Listen. Need to tell you something."

Byomkesh was sitting alone in the drawing room. I saw Som's face was serious with a hard look. Byomkesh said, "How is Mahidhar Babu?
Som said briefly, "Good."
"Was anyone else present there?"
"Only Doctor Ghatak."
Byomkesh then narrated the Malati Devi incident, and a tender smile appeared on Professor Som's serious face. He smiled and said,"Thank you."

The next morning, during breakfast, I noticed that the marital discord was not confined to the upper floor of the house but had trickled down to the lower floor. Satyawati's face was heavy, Byomkesh's face had an unfathomable hardness. Marital discord seems to be like a contagious disease like a cold.

How marital discord arises, how it ends, I am not aware of this fact. But these things are not new, I have seen it before. These discords arise like threatening dark black clouds of a rainy day and eventually melt into nothingness.

After finishing the meal, Byomkesh said, "Ajit, let's go out for a walk this morning."
I said, "Okay, let's go. Let Satyawati get ready."
Satyawati said in an irate tone, "I have work at home. I cannot afford to roam around all day long along with you guys.

Byomkesh got up and wrapped a shawl around himself and said, "I proposed that we both go. Come on, it's no use sitting at home.
Satyawati took a look at Byomkesh's feet and said sharply, "Whoever has a weak body should go out with his socks on" and left the room hurriedly.
I couldn't stop laughing and went to the balcony. After a few minutes, Byomkesh came out with deep lines on his forehead, but socks on my feet.

We went out on the road. I didn't understand if Byomkesh had any special destination in mind. I thought that he wants to go for a walk to get some fresh air. But after some distance he saw an empty rickshaw and hopped on it. I too joined him. Byomkesh said, "Take us to Deputy Ushanath babu's house."

As the rickshaw started moving, I said, "Suddenly Ushanath babu's house?"
Byomkesh said, "Today is Sunday, he will be at home. I have a couple of questions to ask him."
After riding for half a mile, I said, "Byomkesh, you seem to be worrying about the theft of the picture. Is there really anything serious about it."
He said, "I am trying to find that out."

After riding for another half mile, we reached Ushanath Babu's house. The house has a huge fence around it and is situated in Hakim Para. We asked the rickshaw puller to wait for us and entered the house.

We were startled to see few policemen at his door. Then we saw DSP Purandar Pandey's motorbike. Ushanath and DSP Pandey were in the main verandah. Seeing us, Pandey said in surprise, "You guys here, what a surprise!"

Byomkesh said, "Today is Sunday, so I came for a visit. Ushanath said with a cold smile, "Come in, our house was burgled last night."

"Is it so, what has been stolen?"

Pandey said, "It is not yet known." At night they sleep on the second floor, no one lives down below. The house is closed. Last night, a thief entered the house and tried to open the Almirah. He inserted a key in the lock but could not get it out."

"Ok. What was there in the Almirah?"

Ushanath babu said, "There were few government documents, and my wife's jewellery box. It is a steelcupboard. you say an iron chest."

Ushanath babu's eyes are covered with black glasses, his eyes are not visible. But even then, looking at his face, it seems that he is scared. Byomkesh said, "Then the thief could not take anything?"

Pandey said, "It is not clear until the cupboard is opened. A key maker has been called for."

"Good."

How did the thief enter the house?"

He broke a glass of the glass window then put his hand in and opened the bolt." Come will show you. We entered Ushanath babu's office room. A medium-sized room, a table, a few chairs, a steel cupboard and a picture of the Emperor of India on the wall, nothing else. Byomkesh examined the broken glass; Tried to turn the key to the cupboard, but the key did not turn. Apart from this key, the thief left no other sign of his arrival. Next to the office room was the drawing room, we went and sat there. Until the cupboard is opened, it will not be known whether something has been stolen or not. Ushanath Babu offered us tea, we shook our heads and refused.

The drawing room is modestly decorated. Here too, the picture of the emperor of India is on the wall. A radio set in one corner. Small low tables next to the chairs; on some were placed brass vases and on some photo albums. Nothing expensive is visible.

Byomkesh said, "It seems that the thief has not entered this room." Ushanath Babu said, "There is nothing to steal in this room." Suddenly he jumped up. He raised his black glasses for a moment and looked at the radio-device in the corner, then lowered his glasses and said, "My angel! Where did the angel go?" We said in unison, "angel!"

Ushanath Babu went to the radio and looked around and said, "A silver plated angel, the Magistrate's wife gave me as a gift. It was seated on the radio. It must have been taken by the thief. We also got up and saw the radio. There was a break in the dust line on the radio which suggests a small showpiece used to sit there.

Byomkesh said, "The thief may not have taken it. Your son may have taken it to play. Why don't you check it out once?
Ushanath Babu frowned and said, "Khoka is a civilized boy, he never touches anything. "Anyway, I'm looking into it."
He went upstairs. Byomkesh asked Pandey, "Do you suspect anyone?"

Pandey said, "Suspicion, no, nothing like that. But a Servant says, last night around 7:30 a destitute came to meet Deputy Babu. Deputy Babu did not meet him, the servant yelled at him from outside and drove him away. The way the servant gave the description of the man, it seems it was -"Falguni Pal?"
Yes. I have sent a sub-inspector to find out."

Ushanath babu came down from upstairs and said that nor his son nor his wife have removed the silver-plated angel. Surely the burglar could not find anything valuable hence stole the angel.

Byomkesh raised his face and said, "Good, did you search for the photograph?"
"Which photograph?"
"That group-photo that was talked about at Mahidhar babu's house."
"Oh, no, I didn't search for it. There is an album next to you, you shall find it there."
Byomkesh took the album and started to turn the pages. It has pictures of Ushanath babu's parents, brothers, sisters, wife and sons, even Mahidhar babu and Rajani's pictures, only the intended group photos are not there!

Byomkesh said, "The photograph is not there."
"What it is not there?" Ushanath Babu got up and looked at the album himself, but the photo was not found. He then said, "I don't know where it went. But it's not something expensive. If documents or jewelry from the cupboard is stolen, then I need to worry."

Byomkesh said, "you do not need to worry, the thief couldn't steal anything. The jewelry box is safe, even your angel would be found with a little searching. Now we will take your leave, Mr. Pandey, don't deprive me if you find the thief?"

Panda smiled and shook his head. We came out; Ushanath Babu also came along with us. Byomkesh beckoned Ushanath babu, took him to a corner of the balcony and spoke to him quietly. Byomkesh talked for a while then he came back and said, let's go Ajit.

The rickshaw puller was waiting, we went back. Byomkesh remained pensive for a while, then said, "Ajit, Ushanath Babu once lifted his eyeglasses, did you notice anything then?"
"Why no. Was there anything to be noticed?"
"Ushanath babu's left eye is made of stone."
"Is that so? This is the reason for the dark black glasses."
"Yes."
"Three years ago, he developed an abscess inside the eye, and the eye had to be surgically removed. He always fears that he will lose his job if his seniors find out."
"Well, he is a cowardly person! This is what you were inquiring of him?"
"Yes."

I could not determine the importance of this information. If Ushanath Babu is partially blind, then what damage will it do to the world?
The rickshaw gradually started to approach our house. Suddenly Byomkesh said, "Ajit, while we were leaving, you had asked if the matter of photo theft was serious or not. That question can be answered now. The matter is serious."
"Is it true? How did you fathom that?"
Byomkesh did not answer, just smiled at me.
In the evening we got ready to go visit Mahidhar babu. Satyawati said, "Ajit, please take the torch. It will be night when you return." I put the torch in my pocket and said, "You are not going out then?" Satyawati

said, "No. There is a person upstairs who is sick, she needs someone to talk to. Even if I sit near her and talk to her, her mind will be in good state."

I said, "Your sympathy for Malati Devi is increasing gradually."
"Why won't it increase? Surely it will increase."
"And I feel your sympathy towards Rajani is decreasing in that proportion."
"Not at all, it has not decreased even a bit. What is Rajani's fault? Patriarchy is the root of all problems." I said in a serious tone, "Don't always blame patriarchy for every issue."
Satyawati left for the kitchen in disdain.

When we reached Mahidhar babu's house, it was not dawn yet. There were no guards at the open gate. I think the gate is open at night, the fence is there just to restrict the movement of cows and goats. Humans can enter his house unhindered.

The front door of the house was open; but it did not seem that there was anyone in the house. After knocking for two or three times, an old servant came out. He said, "Mahidhar babu is sleeping upstairs. Rajani Devi is taking a stroll in the garden. You people please sit down. I will summon them."

Byomkesh said, "No need for that. We will have a look around ourselves." Byomkesh walked to the garden and started walking towards a specific direction. Due to the large trees and the bushes the visibility in the garden is low. I understood that Byomkesh is searching for the house of Falguni Pal.

We reached a corner of the garden and found a mud house, roofed with tiles; probably a place for storing garden materials and tools. Next to it was a large well.

The door of the house was open, but it was dark inside. I shone a torch in. Someone was lying on a bed of straw in the darkness, as soon as the light shone on him, he got up and came out. We saw Falguni Pal.

Today, Falguni seemed sad, his voice was full of pride. He saw us and said,"are you policemen, have you come to search my house? Please search with all your heart. You will not find anything." I may be poor, but not a thief."

Byomkesh said, "We have not come to ransack. I just want to ask you one thing. Why did you go to Ushanath babu's house last night?
Falguni said in a bitter tone, "I drew a picture of him, so I went to show it. The doorman did not let me see him but drove me away. I don't have an issue with that but what is the need to call the police for such insignificant matter?"
Byomkesh said, " It is injustice on their part. I will tell the police; they will not trouble you again."
"Thank you," said Falguni, and re-entered his hut. We also returned.

Dusk had set in and hardly anything was visible in the garden. We strolled aimlessly in the garden but did not see Rajani.

At the other end of the garden was a tall rock structure formed by large stone blocks. It was surroundedby a band of green moss. The rock was square in shape, almost like a pyramid. We were passing by it and suddenly stopped as we heard someone speak. A feeble voice could be heard from the other side of the pyramid. "Pictures, pictures, pictures. I don't need the pictures, what about the pictures?"
"Quiet! Someone will hear."

The two voices were familiar; the first is Doctor Ghatak's, the second is Rajini's. We thought of Doctor Ghatak as a simple and polite man and didn't expect such fierceness in his voice. Rajini's voice was also firm but nothing unusual.

When Doctor Ghatak spoke again, his voice had softened, but the frenzy of emotion had not abated. He said, "I want you, you! A man cannot survive by drinking milk instead of water."
Rajani said, "and me! don't I want that too? but there is no way."
The doctor said, "There is a way, Listen, I tell you."
Rajani said, "But my father?"
Doctor Ghatak said, "You are not a minor." Your father cannot stop you.
Rajani said, "I know that! But listen dear, father's health is getting worse, let him recover, then we can work something out."
The doctor said, "No. Today I want to know whether you agree to my proposal or not."

A little silence. Then Rajini said, "Well, I will tell you today, but not now. Give me some time, you come tonight at half past ten, I will be here; then we will talk. Now maybe someone has come home, if they don't see me- "

Byomkesh silently grabbed my hand and pulled me. Both of them were coming back, suddenly we saw another person from the other side of the pyramid walking away. For once I thought it was the doctor; But before I knew it, the man disappeared into the darkness. Byomkesh said, "Come on, let's go home. There's no more work to do today. We came out into the street. It was dark, there was no moon in the sky, and kerosene lamps flickered far and wide along the road. I switched on the torch to determine our path.

Byomkesh was absorbed in thought. I think he was thinking about Doctor Ghatak and Rajani and what they are up to. I did not try to break his line of thought. As we were about to reach home Byomkesh asked, "Did you recognise the unknown person?"
"No. Who was he?"
Byomkesh said, "He is our landlord professor Adinath Som."

"Was that him?" Byomkesh, the matter has become somewhat complicated for me. Picture theft, angeltheft, drug addict painter, blind deputy, illegal love, snooping professor. I can't understand anything."
"It is not that easy to understand, even I am having a hard time decoding everything."

"Well, in the matter of the doctor and Rajani, shouldn't we do something about it?"
Byomkesh said firmly, "Nothing. We are the spectators of the cricket game, we can clap or pray, but it is not for us to come down to the playing field and disturb the game.

Returning home, I saw Satyawati alone weaving a woolen sleeve. I said, "How is your patient? Satyawati did not answer, she bent over the needlework and began to spin the needle quickly. I asked, "What, why are you silent? You went to see Malati Devi, right?"
"I went" said Satyawati without raising her face, but her face gradually reddened.

Byomkesh stood watching from far, then suddenly rushed into his bedroom with a giggle. Satyawati was startled, she cast an angry glance at the bedroom door, then went back to her work.
I was sitting next to her and asked, "Tell me what's going on?"
"Nothing. You want to drink tea right; I will bring you tea. Saying so she started to get up. "I interrupted and said, "Oh, tell me what happened first! Tea we can have later."

Satyawati replied in an angry tone. "Nothing has happened, it was wrong for me to go to her. Such a rotten and dirty mind she has. She has such a dirty and polluted mind, my god! She said to me...Let it be I cannot even bring such words or thoughts to my mind. I wished if I could just break her jaw."

Another sound of mocking laughter came from the bedroom. Satyawati went away. I could guess what Malati Devi might have said to Satyawati and my face became red with anger. Few women are indeed highly suspicious of others, but any woman who accuses Satyawati of such a despicable act should be shot dead. Byomkesh was laughing but my entire body swelled in anger.

I went to bed at night but couldn't sleep. My mind was plagued with thoughts. I got up from bed and saw it was already ten o'clock; ten o'clock in December is late night here. Byomkesh and Satyawati were fast asleep.

I have a habit of smoking a cigarette when I am restless and cannot sleep. Hence, I got up from my bed, wrapped a shawl and lit a cigarette. But the air in the room will become polluted with smoke; hence I opened a window and stood in front of it and started smoking the cigarette.

The window was road facing. I could see the main gate in front, the road beyond it, and the municipality streetlight; The streetlight was dimly lit maybe the lamp was running out of oil. Standing near the window for two or three minutes, I was startled by a faint rustling sound outside. Who is coming down from the balcony? Through the gap in the window, I saw a shadowy figure pass through the gate and go out. When the shadowy figure passed by the streetlight, I recognised him, it was Professor Som dressed in a black coat and pant.

Like lightning speed, it hit me, I understood where Professor Som was going all night. At 10:30 tonight Dr. Ghatak and Rajni are supposed to meet in Mahidhar babu's garden. But Professor Som also will be present there! But why? What is his intention?

I was amazed to think of the situation, then something happened which immediately caused more amazement. Again, I heard a rustling sound, now Malati Devi came out. It was not difficult to recognize her. With a strained cough she disappeared in the same way that Som had gone. The situation was clearly understood. The husband is going on a clandestine mission, and the suspecting wife has followed him in this cold night with a weary and sick body. Malati Devi wants to catch her husband in the act. What a miserable life! How terrible is the married life of a loveless husband and a faithless wife, divorce is better than this.

I started wondering if I should do something in the present case, shall I wake up Byomkesh and give him the news? No, there is no need, let him sleep. Rather, as my sleep has vanished, it doesn't seem that I will sleep in the next two hours. So, I'll sit by the window and watch. Let's see how this mystery unfolds.

I lit a cigarette again and was staring at the road ahead. After ten minutes the streetlight died due to lack of oil. Just then a shadowy figure entered through the gate. I recognised in the starlight night that the shadowy figure was none other than Malati Devi. She did not try to mute her footsteps. I heard a subtle sound of her voice; I could not make out whether it was a suppressed cough or a suppressed cry. She went upstairs.

Malati Devi returned so soon, but there was no trace of Professor Som. It seems that Malati Devi could not follow her husband for long and she must have lost track of him in the dark. Professor Som returned at half past eleven, he sneaked in the house silently as a bat.

In the morning, I told Byomkesh about the incident of last night. He listened in silence, making no comment.
A constable handed us a letter from DSP Pandey, dated the previous day.

Dear Byomkesh babu,
Deputy Saheb's cupboard was opened, and nothing was found stolen. You said the angel figurine would be found, but the figurine is still missing. No trace of the thief was found. I am writing to you because you wanted to know the progress in this case.

Regards,
Purandar Pandey.

Byomkesh put the letter in his pocket and said, "DSP Pandey is a true gentleman."

Suddenly photographer Nakulesh Sarkar appeared before us. After Mahidhar Babu's party, we had met Nakulesh Babu once or twice on the street. He said very excitedly, "I was passing this way, I thought I would pass on the news. Surely you haven't heard. Falguni Pal, the one who used to draw images, has drowned in a well in Mahidhar babu's garden. I was stunned for a while. Then Byomkesh said, "When did this happen?

Nakulesh said, "I think it was last night, I don't know exactly. The drunken man, unable to cope in the dark, fell into the well. This morning I went to check on Mahidhar babu's health, there I saw the gardeners pulling Falguni's dead body from the well."

We stared at other's face in silence. Last night lot of strange things have happened in Mahidhar babu's garden.

Well, I'll leave now, I'll have to go back with the camera again." Saying so Nakulesh babu started to get up. "Sit down, have tea."

Nakulesh could not ignore the invitation for tea, he sat down. The tea came instantly and after a few words, Byomkesh asked, "Did you find the negative of the group photograph?"
"Which negative? O yes, I remember, I have searched for it, but I couldn't find it. It is a huge loss for me; if I had it, I would have sold five more copies."
"Well, tell me who was in that photo?"
"Who were there! Me, Mahidhar Babu, his daughter Rajani, Doctor Ghatak, Professor Som and his wife, Deputy Ushanath Babu and Bank manager Amresh Raha went to the picnic. Everyone was in the photo.

The photo came out good, rarely do group photographs come out so good. Well, I will leave now, will definitely come some other day."

Nakulesh babu left. We both sat for a while. My heart became heavy thinking about Falguni. He was a drunkard and drug addict, but God had given him talent. If he was meant to die in such a way then, why was he given such talent?

Then Byomkesh took a deep breath and stood up; said, "This possibility did not occur to me. Come, let us go out."
"Where will we go?
"We need to visit the bank, need to withdraw some money."

After coming here, we had deposited some money in the local bank, which was withdrawn according to the needs of our family.

We went out to the balcony and saw Professor Som coming down from the first floor wearing a dressing gown. He had an anxious look on his face, Byomkesh greeted, "How are you doing?"
Professor Som said, "The news is not good. Wife's illness has worsened. Pneumonia, probably. Fever has increased; she seems to be not talking sense."

"No wonder. She caught a cold last night after spying in the cold bitter night on her husband. But Som doesn't seem to know it. Byomkesh said, "Have you informed Dr. Ghatak?

Professor Som's face darkened at the name of Doctor Ghatak He said, "I will not call Ghatak. I have sent for another doctor."

Byomkesh observed him with sharp eyes and said, "Why? Don't you have faith on Doctor Ghatak? But you recommended Doctor Ghatak when I first came here."
Professor Som kept his mouth firmly shut. Byomkesh then said, "Let it go, just got the news that Falguni Pal drowned in Mahidhar babu's well last night."
Professor Som didn't show much interest, saying, "Alright, maybe he committed suicide. These artistic people always seem unsatisfied with life.

Byomkesh asked like a gunshot, "Professor Som, where were you last night at eleven?"
Som startled up; his face went pale. He said in a smug voice,"I, I! Who said I went somewhere? I didn't...

Byomkesh raised his hand and said, "There's no point in lying Professor Som, you are responsible for your wife's deteriorated health. She. followed you out into the street last night. If she dies, then it's on you."

Som said with fear-filled eyes, "My wife Byomkesh babu? believe me, I don't know.
Byomkesh raised his forefinger and said in a serious tone, "But we know. I am your well-wisher, so I warn you. You will be careful. Come Ajit."

Professor Som stood like a statue; we came down on the road. We walked for a while when Byomkesh said, "I have scared Som very much." Then he looked at his watch and said, "There is still time for the bank to open, come, let's go to Ghatak's dispensary."

The doctor's dispensary is towards the bazaar. We were about to enter the doctor's room when we heard the doctor say to his patient, "Look, your son has typhoid; It will be a long case, he will take a long time to recover. I'm not accepting long cases now! I won't be able to handle this case. You better go to Sridhar babu instead, he is the senior doctor."

We entered; the other man left. The doctor happily welcomed us, he said, "Please come in. When the patient physically comes to the doctor's house, it should be understood that the disease is cured. Mahidhar Babu called me a horse doctor that day. Now you tell me, I am a human doctor or are you a horse?" he laughed loudly. The doctor's mind seems very cheerful today and his eyes are lit with joy.

Byomkesh said with a smile, "I have to admit that you are the doctor of humans rather than horses, having a doctor like you is an honour. How is Mahidhar Babu?" The doctor said, "Very well. Almost recovered."

Byomkesh said, "Did you hear that Falguni Pal died?"
The doctor was shocked and said, "That painter! What happened to him?"

"Nothing, he drowned in the water last night. In brief Byomkesh told him whatever he knew.
The Doctor remained puzzled for a while, then said, "I should go. Mahidhar babu's body is very weak. I should go and do a quick checkup." The doctor stood up to leave.

Byomkesh suddenly asked, 'When are you going to Calcutta?" The doctor's expression suddenly changed; he looked steadily into Byomkesh's eyes for a moment and said, "Who told you that I was going to Calcutta?"

Byomkesh only smiled softly. The doctor then said, "Yes, I want to go sometime soon. Well, I will leave now, will visit your house if I get time."

The doctor left and we walked towards the bank. On the way I asked, "How did you know that the doctor is going to Kolkata?" Have you become an astrologer these days? "

Byomkesh said, 'No. But when a doctor says that he will not take up a long case, go to another doctor, then it can be assumed that he will go out on a long holiday," "But what is the guarantee that he will go to Calcutta?" "I guessed it from the doctor's expression."

The bank was at a stone throw distance from the Doctor's chamber. We went and saw that the bank had opened, and the main gate was guarded by two-gun wielding guards.

A large room was divided into two sections by wooden panels and in the panels were present a Rows of windows at equal intervals. Through these windows the bank employees transact with the public.

Byomkesh was standing outside a window and writing checks, I saw the manager Amresh Raha standing inside the partition and talking to a clerk. Amresh babu also saw us, he came out with a smile on his face and said Namaskar. I was lucky to see you or else you would have left without having any word with me.

We had not seen Amresh babu after the tea party. He was ashamed of that; he stroked his hand through his French-cut beard and said, "Every day I think of going to your house, but one thing or another disrupts the plan. Working in a bank is like a twenty-four seven job."

Byomkesh said, "There is happiness in such servitude. You are surrounded with money all the time." Amresh babu made a pitiful expression and said, "What happiness, Byomkesh babu. It's like a donkey carrying a load of sugar, but at the end of the day the donkey gets to eat only grass.

Byomkesh uncashed the cheque then Amresh Babu said, "I won't let you go easily today, let us have some tea in our office room. I have read about your investigative talents from Ajit Babu's writings. I don't want to miss this opportunity to interact with you. In our country, there is a huge dearth of talented people.

The gentleman is not only respectful of Byomkesh, but also a lover of literature. I regretted not having interacted more with him that day. He showed us in. He has his own personal cabin, he went up to his cabin door and said, "No, not here. Come Lets, go upstairs. Here there is a lot of hustle bustle and work rush, it will be quite quiet upstairs.

The door of the office room was open; I looked in and saw nothing save a simple table,chairs, books, and a few large iron chests. The stairs were right next to the office door. We took the stairs to the first floor and Byomkesh asked as we climbed up, "Upstairs is your quarters?
"Yes. It's easy for me and bank both."
"Your family stays along with you here?"
"I don't have a family, Byomkesh babu, God gave me good wisdom, hence I did not marry. I am a Single person hence have no expenditures; it would have been hard for me to sustain a family with such a paltry salary.

The upstairs room seemed quite spacious for one person. Three or four rooms in total and an open roof in front. Amresh babu took us to the living room and made us sit. The house was Immaculately clean, no pictures on the walls, no carpet on the floor. On one side, there was a dewan, two-three reclining chairs, a bookcase. The room didn't have much furniture but was immaculately clean and organized. It can be understood that the householder is a tidy person."
"Please Sit down, I will order tea for everyone." He said and left.

The bookcase attracted me, I got up and looked at the books. Most of the books were novels, cartoons, story books etc. Along with this collection was Byomkesh's novels written by me, I was thrilled to see my books in his bookcase.

Byomkesh joined me, he pulled out a book and surfed through the pages. I saw that the book is not in Bengali language, but the script of some other province of India, much like Hindi, but not exactly Hindi.

At this time Amresh babu came back. Byomkesh asked, "You also know Gujarati language?"
Amresh babu giggled and said, "Not quite. Once I tried to learn Gujarati but was not able to. For a bengali boy it is tough to deal with his mother tongue on top of that we have to learn English. if you have to learn a third language, then a common bengali is out of his wits. But if I could have learnt it, it would have been beneficial for me. Knowing Gujarati is very beneficial for bank jobs."

We sat down again. After a few words, Byomkesh said, "Have you heard, Falguni Pal is dead?"
Amresh babu jumped up from his chair, "what, Falguni Pal is dead! When, where and how did he die?"
Byomkesh explained how he was found dead. Amresh babu sadly shook his head and said, "Oh poor man! He was in dire straits. He came to me yesterday."

Now it's our turn to be surprised Byomkesh said, "He came to you tomorrow? when?
Amresh babu said, "In the morning." Yesterday was Sunday, the bank was closed; I was having a cup of tea when Falguni appeared, he had drawn my picture, so she came to show me.

The servant served us three cups of tea. Seeing his dress, I understood that he was an employee of the bank, maybe a peon who also does Amresh babu's housework in his spare time. Seeing his ways, Amresh babu seemed to be a spendthrift.

Byomkesh swirled the spoon in the cup of tea and said, "Did you buy the picture or not?"

Amresh babu said with an angry face, "I had to buy it." I went to pay him five rupees, but he did not take it, he demanded ten rupees and finally had it his way.

Byomkesh took a sip of tea and said, "I want to see the last picture of the dead painter."
"Please have a look. It seems to be well drawn. Although I do not understand anything about art?"
He brought a thick rectangular piece of paper from the bottom shelf of the bookcase and held it in front of us.

Falguni has painted a good picture; Amresh babu's uncharacteristic facial appearance has been aptly highlighted in the picture. Byomkesh has immense knowledge of paintings and art; he squinted and examined the picture.

Amresh babu was previously very cheerful, but after hearing the news of Falguni's death, he seems to have become depressed. After finishing his tea in complete silence, Amresh babu said, "on hearing Falguni's death I remembered, that day at the tea party we were discussing about the stolen photograph of Mahidhar babu. Do you remember? Have you found any trace of the photograph or the thief?"

Byomkesh was engrossed in looking at the picture, hence did not answer. I too could not understand whether I should say anything, so I kept looking at Amresh babu like a moron. Amresh babu then said to himself, "It's a small matter, so I think no one is concerned about the theft."

Byomkesh put the picture down and took a deep breath, "Great picture. If the man was alive, I would have asked him to paint me. Amresh babu please store this picture carefully, today no one knows Falguni Pal's name, but one day his paintings will sell for millions."

Amresh babu said cheerfully, "Is that so! Then the ten rupees did not go to waste. Will it be good if I frame this picture and hang it on my wall?"
"For sure."
Then we stood up to leave. Amresh babu said, "See you again. The year is about to end, I have to visit Calcutta during New Year's and discuss business with the owners. We have two days off this New Year."

Why two days off?

This year 31st December falls on a Sunday. If you consider Saturday as half off day, then you will get two and a half days off. You guys would be here till then, right?
"We would be here till the 2nd of January I Guess."
"Namaskar."

We came out. We didn't have to go down from inside the bank, there was rear entry to the building. We took the stairs at the back of the house. While walking through the market, I suddenly remembered that I had run out of cigarettes. I said, "Come, I need to buy a tin of cigarette." Byomkesh was startled, he was absent minded. He Said, "yes yes! I also have a few things to buy.

We entered a large store. I went one way to buy the cigarette's whereas he went in the opposite direction. While buying the tin of cigarette's I noticed that Byomkesh bought a bottle of expensive essence and put it in his pockets. I smiled to myself. I don't understand why they quarrel and why they patch up. Married life is a ridiculous puzzle to me.

That day, after lunch, I lay down in bed to rest and when I woke up, it was already half past three in the afternoon. From the room of Byomkesh came giggling sounds; I saw that Byomkesh was sitting in the chair and Satyawati was standing behind him with her hands around his neck and talking to him. Smiles were evident on both faces. I moved aside and said in a loud voice, "O love birds, if you guys are busy then shall I arrange tea?"

Satyawati shyly came out while covering her face with her sari and went towards the kitchen. After a while Byomkesh came out puffing smoke from a lit cigarette. I was surprised and said, "What's the matter! You are smoking like an engine." Byomkesh said with a cheeky smile, "I got permission to smoke from today, as much as I want." I realized that marriage is not only about love, but it also needs intelligence.

After drinking tea, I went upstairs to take news of the patient. You have to fulfill your social duties.

Professor Som's face was thoughtful. Malati Devi's condition is very bad, but not worth giving up. Both her lungs were affected, and she was on oxygen. She had very high fever and was talking nonsense all the time. A nurse has been appointed for the service.
I had a brief talk with Professor Som and came back after sympathising.

Doctor Ghatak arrived shortly. Nowadays, the doctor's attitude is different, a little wary, a little suspicious, a little introspective. He was looking at Byomkesh from time to time as if he had some doubts regarding him. The conversation was normal. The doctor went to Mahidhar babu's house in the morning and said that he had seen Falguni Pal's dead body.
Byomkesh asked, "What did you see? Is the cause of death known?"
The doctor kept quiet for a while and said, "Nothing can be said for sure until the autopsy is complete."

Byomkesh said, "But you are a doctor, did you not understand anything?"
The doctors hesitated and said, "No?
Byomkesh then said, "Let that be." How is Mahidhar Babu? Yesterday afternoon we went to see him, but no one responded even after calling out, so we came back."
The doctor asked cautiously, "at what time did you visit him."
"At around five in the evening."

The doctor thought for a while and said, "I am not sure. I also went in the afternoon but returned before five. Mahidhar babu is doing fine. But he is in a shock for what happened today."
Byomkesh asked, "and Rajni Devi! How is she doing?"
The doctor face turned a bit red, but he slowly said, "Rajni Devi is fine. I did not hear that she was ill. Well, now I will take your leave."
The doctor got up. We also got up. Byomkesh came to the door and said, "So, you ready to go to Calcutta?"

The doctor stood back, his eyes blazing. He gritted his teeth and said, "Byomkesh babu, you have come here for healing, not for spying."Don't bother with what's outside your domain. Saying that, he went out.

We came back and sat down. Byomkesh lit a cigarette and said, "Dr. Ghatak is a very good man, but if you step on his tail, he becomes a very dangerous snake."

We heard the sound of a motorbike near our gate. Byomkesh jumped in excitement and said, Mr. Pandey has come. What a pleasure, please come in."

Pandey entered. He said with a tired smile, "Byomkesh babu, your words came true. We have found the angel."

Byomkesh gave him a chair and said, "Sit down." Where did you find the angel?"

From Mahidhar babu's well. After retrieving Falguni's dead body, I sent a diver down the well. The diver retrieved Ushanath babu's angel."

Byomkesh narrowed his eyes for a while and said, "Anything else?"
"Nothing else."
"Have you received the post-mortem report."
"Received. Falguni did not die due to drowning in water, he was thrown into the water after his death. "Hmm, which means someone killed him last night and then threw his body into the well. Not suicide."
"So, it seems. But who will benefit from killing a worthless person like Falguni Pal?"

"Indeed, someone must have benefitted from killing a worthless person like Falguni Pal. If Falguni Pal had come across any deadly secret, his survival would have become dangerous for the killer. Falguni Pal was penniless, but not stupid.

Pandey said bitterly, "Yes, that is true. But I wonder how the angel came into the well? Did Falguni steal the angel? Falguni had a fight with the murderer about the angel? Then the murderer pushed Falguni into the well? But the angel is not such aprecious thing?"

Byomkesh said, "Well, were any injury marks found on Falguni."
"No. But a lot of opium was found in his stomach. He had drunk alcohol spiked with opium."
Byomkesh said, "Hmm, look, how Falguni died is not the big deal, why he was killed is more important."
Pandey looked at him curiously and said, "Have you made any breakthroughs regarding this case?"Byomkesh said with a soft smile, "I

think I have untangled some of the knots. I have a lot to tell you. But do you have the time to listen to me?"

Pandey took Byomkesh's hand and pulled him towards the door. I will spare time for you, please come to my house and we will have a conversation, I will let you return only after serving you dinner?

Pandey took Byomkesh and left. I and Satyawati played cards till half past nine. When Byomkesh returned, I asked, "What has taken you so long?" Byomkesh said with a heavenly smile, "Ah, the chicken which was served by DSP Pandey was delicious!"

I said in a serious tone, "Don't digress from the topic. What conversation you had for five hours with DSP Pandey?"
Byomkesh bit his tongue, "I shall not reveal the secrets of the police to you. But nothing has been said that you are not aware of."
"Who is the murderer?"
"Panchkori Dey!" Saying so Byomkesh slipped into his bedroom.

Christmas has come and gone, and New Year's is almost here. People don't celebrate Christmas and New Year's with great pomp here, only the English Sahebs and Mame's drink whiskey and dance a little.

In these few days nothing significant has happened. Malati Devi's condition was improving. She was recovering well and found a young nurse in her room, again her suspicions and anger flared. She abused the nurse and chased her away. As a result, her situation again worsened, Professor Som was in a mess.

On Saturday 30th December morning Byomkesh said, "Come on, let's go out in the sun for a bit today.
We hailed a rickshaw and went out.

First, we went to Nakulesh babu's photography shop. Downstairs is the shop, upstairs is Nakulesh babu's residence. He was upstairs, he looked a little uncomfortable seeing us. It seemed he was packing something. He gave a wry smile and said, "Please come in, do you want to get a photograph clicked?"

Byomkesh said, "Not now. We were passing by; thought we would check out your shop."
Nakulesh babu said, "Very well. But I take click good pictures. Everyone here gets their pictures clicked from me. Have a look at these pictures."

Many pictures were hanging on the walls of his room; among these were pictures of Mahidhar Babu and Professor Som. Byomkesh saw it and said, "Wow, it's quite a good picture. You are a true artist."
Nakulesh babu smiled happily and said, "Yes yes. Hey Lalu, get two cups of tea from the shop next door."
"We don't need tea, we just had tea a while back. You seem to be going somewhere?"

Nakulesh babu said, "Yes, I will go to Calcutta for two days." My son and wife are in Calcutta, I am going to bring them back here."
"Well, then you carry on with your packing."

Byomkesh got into the rickshaw and said, "Take us to the railway station."
I asked, "what is the matter everyone is going to Kolkata?
Byomkesh said, "Kolkata has a certain charm at this time of the year.

We arrived at the railway station. This is the terminal station of the branch line, not too big a station. From here the big junction station is about twenty-five miles away, you have to get down there and catch the main line train. Apart from train there are also roads leading to the main junction station, the Sahebs, the wealthy and people with car usually reach there by road.

But Byomkesh did not get down at the station, he signaled to the rickshaw puller to turn around and drive elsewhere. I asked, "What happened, you did not get down?"
Byomkesh said, "You must not have noticed, Doctor Ghatak was standing in front of the ticket-booth buying tickets."
"Is it so? I asked Byomkesh few more questions, but he pretended not having heard me and didn't answer.

As we rode through the bazaar, we saw a car parked out the large convenience store. Byomkesh stopped the rickshaw and got down. I also

stepped down. I asked,"What do you want again? Do you want more essence?
He laughed and said, "Oh no, no."
Then what hair oil or Liquid Alta?"
"Come on, Let's go in."

We entered the shop and saw Deputy Ushanath Babu. He was buying a leather suitcase. After seeing him the following words came out of mouth automatically, "Are you also going to Calcutta?"
Ushanath Babu was startled and said, "Who me? No, I am the Treasury Officer, do I have permission to leave the station? Who told you I was going to Calcutta?" His voice became harsh.

Byomkesh said in a sassy tone, "No one said." Seeing you buying a suitcase, Ajit thought that you are going to Calcutta. Have you got your angel?"
"Yes, I got it." Saying so Ushanath babu turned his face away uncomfortably and started talking to the shopkeeper.

We got back into the rickshaw. I said, "What happened? Why did Ushanath babu suddenly get upset?" Byomkesh said, "I don't know. Maybe he wants to go to Calcutta, but he can't leave the station, so the temper is hot.
 The Rickshaw puller asked, "Now here to go?"
Byomkesh said, "D.S.P. Pandey."

Mr. Pandey's office was located in his house. He welcomed us. Byomkesh asked, "Everything is fine?"
DSP Pandey said, "everything is fine."
"When is the train?"
"At half past ten at night. It will reach the junction station at quarter past eleven."
"When is the train to Calcutta?"
"At quarter to twelve." "
"And the Western Mail?"
"Eleven thirty-five."

Byomkesh said, "Well then, I will reach Mahidhar babu's house around five o'clock and you shall reach there by half past five. If Mahidhar babu

does not accept my request, he cannot ignore the request of the police."
With a serious smile Pandey said, "I also believe so."

I could not decipher their enciphered conversation. But there is no use in asking Byomkesh; I know that if I ask a question, Byomkesh will cheekily say, "Police secrets, cannot be revealed."

We went to the bank from Pandey's office as we had to withdraw some cash. The bank was overcrowded; It will be closed for the next two days due to New Year. Amresh babu saw us and said, "Withdraw all the money you need cause the bank be closed tomorrow and day after."

Byomkesh asked, "When are you coming back?"
"I will return day after evening."
A clerk came and started discussing official matters with him. We were returning after withdrawing the money, we saw Doctor Ghatak entering the bank. He could see us but pretended not to see us and stood in front of a bank counter.
Byomkesh looked at me and blinked his eyes. Then he jumped on the rickshaw and said, "Let's go home."

At five o'clock in the evening, Byomkesh and I arrived at Mahidhar babu's house. He was in the living room. I saw that his health had deteriorated. The smile on his face had vanished and his plump cheeks were drooping. He said, "Please come in Byomkesh babu. You will live long; I was just thinking about you people. It seems Byomkesh babu that your body has quite recovered. Good, very well."

"But your health doesn't look good," said Byomkesh.
Mahidhar Babu said, "I was a little ill but now I have recovered well. But a problem has happened in my life due to which I am a bit worried, Byomkesh Babu."

"What has happened?"
"Rajani left Calcutta last night."
"Has she gone alone? Did she not inform you?"
"No, No nothing like that. I have sent Ramdin, our old servant alongside her."
"But then what to worry about?"

Mahidhar babu has no trickery in his mind. He started to speak directly, "Listen, I will tell you. An aunt of Rajini lives in Kolkata, she raised her! Yesterday afternoon, we received her telegram, she is seriously ill and has requested for Rajani to come to her aid." I sent Rajani to Calcutta by the night train. She travels like this often; it is only a five- or six-hours journey. Rajani reached Calcutta this morning, I received her telegram.

I received two letters this morning; One of them is in Rajini's aunt's handwriting and dated yesterday. She wrote a very simple letter, there is no mention of ill-health." Mahidhar Babu looked at Byomkesh with alarmed eyes. Byomkesh said, "It is also possible that she suddenly fell ill after writing the letter."

Mahidhar babu said, "It is not impossible at all. But I haven't talked about other letters yet. Anonymous letter, read this." He handed an envelope to Byomkesh, looking at the post office imprint on the envelope, it can be understood that it has been posted in this city. Byomkesh took out the letter and read it. A white coarse paper with these few words written on it.

Behind your back a dangerous man in the disguise of a gentleman has indulged in an illicit love affair with your daughter. If they elope, there will be huge scandal. Be careful! Don't believe Doctor Ghatak.

Byomkesh read the letter and returned it. Mahidhar Babu said in a trembling voice, 'I don't know who wrote it. But if this is true then I am doomed.
Byomkesh said calmly, "You know Dr. Ghatak. Do you think that he will do such a thing?"
Mahidhar Babu hesitated and said, "I know of the doctor as a good boy; He comes often to my house. But I am not much aware about his character or past. Well, is he here?"

Byomkesh said, "Yes. I saw him this morning."
Mahidhar babu breathed a sigh of relief and said, "If he is here, then it seems someone has sent a fake anonymous letter."

Byomkesh said, "But the doctor is going to Calcutta tonight."
Mahidhar babu again said anxiously, "what he is going today? But then...

Byomkesh said firmly, "Mahidhar babu, please be calm, there will be no scandal, there is nothing to fear." Mahidhar babu held Byomkesh's hand and said, "Are you are telling the truth? But how did you know that you don't stay here?"

Byomkesh said, "I know many things which you do not know. Trust me, I am not giving you false assurances. Rajani Devi will come back after a couple of days. She will not do anything that will compromise your dignity."

Mahidhar Babu said in a cheerful tone, "That's it. Thank you, Byomkesh babu. I can't tell you how much I was relieved by your words. I am old and already Rajani is a widow. I get afraid of such things easily."

Byomkesh said, "Forget this talk now. I have come to you with a request."
Mahidhar Babu said, "Please tell me, anything for you."
"You have to lend your car to me tonight. I will go to the junction, have some urgent work."
"What's the big deal in that just tell me when you need the car?"
"At nine in the night."
"Well, sharp at nine my car will be waiting in front of your house.
"Anything else?"
"Nothing else."
At this time DSP Pandey entered the room. We all sat together, had tea and snacks and then returned home.

Just at midnight Mahidhar babu's eight-cylinder car stopped in front of our house. I, Byomkesh and DSP Pandey sat in it. The car left. A black colored police van was already parked, it started following us.

After crossing the city limits, our car took the long, deserted road to the junction. Both sides of the road were ornated with huge, tall trees. Our car zoomed through the road creating a tunnel of light towards the junction. We did not have much of a conversation on the way. The three of us sat side by side smoking cigarettes, then Byomkesh said, "Your defendant will buy a first-class ticket."

"Yes. I think so too. No matter what class he travels in, Inspector Dubey will be in the next bogie."

"Who else knows the real story in the police circles?"
"Me and Dubey."

We did not want to leak the information hence we quietly took Mahidhar babu's car for this mission. Even those in the van behind don't know where we are going. The maximum amount of information is leaked from a Police station rather than anywhere else. Then there are corrupt policemen, also there are few policemen who like to boast about their plans. Hence, we decided to keep this mission a tight secret. Purandar Pandey is a man of pure character, so he is loyal to his duties.

We reached the Junction at ten o'clock. The station was lit up with numerous red and green lanterns. Two sub-inspectors and a few constables were in the police van. Pandey placed them in various places inside and outside the station. Then he met the stationmaster and said, "I am expecting a log to arrive, please inform me when it does, we are in the waiting room."

We three sat in the first-class waiting room and DSP Pandey started looking at his watch frequently. At exactly half past ten, the station-master informed, "The log has arrived. All is good First class."

Still forty-five minutes remain for the train to arrive. These forty-five minutes seemed to long for me, I was growing restless waiting for the train.

The bell rang indicating the arrival of the train on the platform. We got up and walked up to the platform. We are all wearing overcoats and fur hats, so it is unlikely that anyone will recognize us easily. Then the much-awaited train came and halted on the platform.

Mr. Pandey had chosen the stage of the drama well. All the arrangements made were perfect.

The train stopped; the first-class cabin was right where we were standing on the platform. The wooden shutters of the windows were closed, so the interior could not be seen. Soon the door opened. A porter rushed in and deboarded with two large leather suitcases.

There was only one passenger in the cabin, he came out now. He was a clean-shaven stranger wearing Coat-pant and pale blue eyeglasses. He was arranging to lift the two leather suitcases on the porter's head. DSP Pandey and Byomkesh stood on either side of this stranger. Byomkesh said in a low tone, "Amresh babu, you can't go. You have to go back with us.

Amresh babu! Amresh Raha, the manager of the bank! I could not recognize him at all from seeing his clean shaved face.

Amresh Raha turned his head once to the left and once to the right, then hurriedly pulled out of his pocket a pistol and pressing it to his forehead, he pulled the trigger.

A loud boom sound was heard. In a moment, people surrounded Amresh Raha's body. Pandey blew his whistle and immediately many policemen came and surrounded the place. Pandey said in a stern tone, "Inspector Dubey, seize the two suitcases."

A man pushed through the crowd and entered. It was Doctor Ghatak. He said, "What happened? Who is this?
Pandey said, "Amresh Raha."
"Please check if he is still alive?"
Doctor Ghatak bent down and examined the body, then he stood up and said, "He is dead."

A horrified voice was heard from the crowd, it was of Nakulesh Sarkar, he asked "Amresh Raha is dead? What has happened? Where is his beard?"

Byomkesh said Pointing at Dr. Ghatak and Nakulesh babu, "Your train has also arrived. Now is not the time to explain, come back and listen to the story."

Byomkesh said, "I have made a fatal mistake. Amresh Raha worked in the bank; I did not realise that he might have a pistol license."
Satyawati said, 'No, say it from the beginning.'

"It was the second of January, and we were returning to Calcutta. DSP Pandey, Mahidhar babu and Rajani came to the station to see us off.

After the train left the station Byomkesh said, "Two things got tangled up, one, the theft of the picture: second, the secret love between the doctor Ghatak and Rajani. Their love, though secret, was nothing scandalous. They went to Calcutta and had a registry marriage. Perhaps Rajini's aunt and uncle know, and no one else; nor even does Mahidhar babu. No one will know as long as he lives. Mahidhar babu is not an old-fashioned man, but he is not willing to abandon the old thoughts on widow-marriage. Hence, they got married secretly."

I asked, "Did you get the news from Doctor Ghatak?"

Byomkesh said, "No. I didn't ask the doctor, as he was stubborn. He would bite me if I had said anything to him regarding this matter." I told Rajani secretly, That I know everything. She asked me, "Byomkesh Babu, are we done anything wrong?" I said, "No. You should be proud that even though you defied the norms of social marriage still you did make sure not to hurt Mahidhar Babu. Violent rebellion does not help much, it only arouses the opposing forces. You will be happy in life."

Satyawati said, "Then what happened next?"

Byomkesh began by saying, "If you take the photo theft lightly, it can have many explanations. But if you take it seriously, there is only one explanation. There is someone in the group who wants to hide his face and identity from the public eye."
But for what purpose? One motive could be that there is a tainted criminal in this group who doesn't want to publicize his picture. But this proposition is not viable. Nobody in this group is hiding, everyone knows them. So, there is no point in stealing the picture.

The possibility of tainted criminal must be left out. But if there is someone in the group who is preparing to commit a crime in the future or is trying to get away with committing a serious crime, then he will try to steal his image. Ajit, you are a writer, by just using few words can you describe a man so accurately that he can be recognized on sight? No, you can't. Especially if his appearance is very ordinary, then you can't at all. But a photograph can help identify the person in one go. Hence the police keep a photo of the accused in their files."

"It was hence understood that one of the group members was plotting to commit a serious crime and get away with it. Now the question is, what is the crime and who is the man?"

"Let's take all the group members into consideration. Mahidhar babu will not abscond; He has a huge property also his appearance is not favorable for absconding. Doctor Ghatak may disappear with Rajini, but Rajini is an adult, running away with her is not a legal offence. They why will they steal the picture?"

You can also exclude Professor Som. Even if had decided to break the chain and fly away, there would be no point in stealing this picture alone. Som had more photos; We have seen his photo hanging in Nakulesh babu's room. Then let's take Nakulesh babu; He was in the picnic group. He had borrowed a lot of money from Mahidhar babu, so it is not unusual for him to abscond. But he clicked the photo, his face was not in the photo. So, it is foolish for him to steal the photo."

Only Deputy Ushanath Babu and Bank-Manager Amresh Raha remain. One is the manager of a government warehouse; the other is a bank manager. Both handle enormous sums of money and it makes sense if they abscond with large sum of money.

Let's talk about Ushanath Babu first. He is married and has a wife and son; His appearance is such that even if there is no photo, he can be easily identified. He wears dark black glasses, and when he removes the glasses, it is visible that one of his eyes is made of stone. It is not possible for him to avoid the searching eyes of the police for a long time. Moreover, his character is also averse to such an adventure.

The only person who remains is Amresh Raha. There was no evidence suggesting that he had stolen the photograph. But then if you look closely at him, you will see that there can be none other than him. His appearance is so ordinary, millions of featureless people like him roam the earth. He has a french beard on his face. The advantage of having such a beard is that the appearance changes after shaving the beard and known people cannot recognise him anymore. So, shaving a real beard is much safer and more reliable as a disguise than wearing a fake beard."

"Amresh babu was unmarried. He was getting a good salary yet in his heart he had an insatiable desire for money. This evil idea was harboring in his mind for a long time. Do you remember seeing Gujarati books in his bookcase? He tried to learn the Gujarati language; Maybe the decision was to go to Bombay region with proceeds of the loot money. Gujaratis have a lot of facial and structural similarity with Bengalis, no one would have doubted him if he would have grasped the language."

"He had everything planned and had covered all bases but when he was prepared to roll the plan in action, some unexpected obstacles suddenly appeared. He had to go to the group picnic and in the group picnic Mahidhar babu and others decided to take a group picture. No doubt he was reluctant but finally had to get the picture clicked so that it does not raise suspicions in other people's minds. He thought that he would steal the picture and handle it."

"Anyway, he stole the picture from Mahidhar babu's house. The next day we were present at the tea party and the topic of the stolen photograph was raised. Amresh babu realized that he had made a mistake, it was unwise of him to steal just the photograph. When he went to steal Ushanath babu's photograph he stole the angel as well. He left the key to the iron chest in the lock itself. He created an illusion, it seemed as if stealing the picture was not the main intention of the thief. There was no need to steal Professor Som's picture. I believe he somehow got to know that Malati Devi had already torn the picture into pieces, or it could be that he went to steal the picture, but the picture was destroyed before that. Maybe all he found was the pieces of the torn pieces of the picture."

"Amresh babu was not alarmed by my appearance. His original crime was still in the womb of the future. After he would have disappeared with the money, everyone would know, then there is no harm in me knowing. But when the drunkard Falguni Pal came and stood in front of everyone he was distressed. His plans were about to collapse. What's the point of stealing group photos when there is an artist like Falguni? Falguni was able to perfectly draw the picture of a person just from his memory."

"But Amresh babu was through a major part of his plan, and he could not back out. After stealing the photographs, he had a strong urge to do illegal things. So, on the day when Falguni came to show him his picture, he decided that Falguni should not live anymore. That night he mixed some opium in a bottle of alcohol and went to Falguni's house. It was not difficult to entice Falguni with intoxicants. Then when he passed out, he picked him up and threw him into the well. The angel he had brought with him from the previous night's adventure also went into the well; So that the police consider Falguni as a thief. This happened probably after eleven o'clock at night, when another clandestine meeting was over in another corner of the garden."

"From the post-mortem report, it appears that Falguni died before falling into the water. But Amresh babu wanted to throw him into the water while he was still alive, to prove that he had drowned in the water due to his drunkenness." Anyway, Amresh babu was calm. The picture he showed us was sure to be burned before he left, and there would be no trace of him."

"When I undoubtedly understood that this was the work of Amresh babu, then I told everything to Mr. Pandey. A very intelligent man, he quickly understood the matter. Since then, Amresh babu was always under police lens."

Byomkesh held a cigarette.

I said, "Well, how did you understand that Amresh Raha will escape on this very day? He could have escaped any day."

Byomkesh said, "There is an advantage of escaping a day before a holiday, two days being available. When the bank opens two days later and the theft is discovered, the thief is far away. Ofcourse, he could have escaped even during the Christmas holidays; but from his side, it was necessary to escape during the New Year holidays. Amresh Raha was the manager of the bank, a branch office of a large bank in Kolkata.

At the end of every month, huge sum of money came from the head office here so that the bank's treasury cane be replenished before the new month. Everyone starts to withdraw money in the beginning of a month, apart from the common people there are some mines here, many workers work in them, they have to be paid salaries from the mine at the beginning of the month. Now this huge sum of money came to the bank after the Christmas holidays. Amresh Raha could not have taken much money if he had escaped before the Christmas holidays.

One lakh and eighty-thousand-rupee notes were found from his two suitcases."

Byomkesh lay tall and said, "Any more questions?"
"When did he shave his beard? In the train?"
"Yes. That's why he bought a first-class ticket. Chances of a fellow passenger in first class is very less probable."
Satyawati said, "Who gave the anonymous letter to Mahidhar babu?"
Byomkesh said, "Professor Som. But don't do injustice to the poor man. The man is educated and refined; his life is about to be ruined by falling into the hands of a horrible woman. Som had a troubled marital life and hence he got attracted to Rajani. But even that didn't matter, he was defeated by Doctor Ghatak's fierce rivalry. Hence his jealousy. The vilest instinct is that of jealousy."

He kept silent for a while and said, "Malati Devi's illness is getting grave. No one wants to wish for her death, but if Malati Devi succumbs to her illness at least I will not be unhappy."

I too agreed to him.

Made in the USA
Columbia, SC
10 March 2023

13578228R00117